GARDEN HEAT

Books by David The Good

General Gardening
Start a Home-Based Plant Nursery

Florida Gardening
Totally Crazy Easy Florida Gardening
Create Your Own Florida Food Forest
Florida Survival Gardening

The Good Guides
Compost Everything
Grow or Die
Push the Zone
Free Plants for Everyone

The Good Ideas
Grocery Row Gardening

Jack Broccoli Novels
Turned Earth
Garden Heat

a Jack Broccoli novel

GARDEN HEAT

DAVID T. GOOD

Garden Heat: A Jack Broccoli Novel
David T. Good

Good Books Publishing
goodbookspub.com

ISBN: 978-1-955289-01-6

CONTENTS

PROLOGUE

"We need to do something now!" Professor Hayworth exclaimed, stabbing a bony finger repeatedly on the old paper map hanging on the wall. "See this mess? It's not like all these glaciers are going to melt themselves!"

"Actually, they are," Dr. Elaine Piknik said, frowning. "Unless you're telling me you no longer believe in established scientific fact." She cocked an eyebrow at Hayworth, awaiting his answer.

"You know what I mean," the professor snapped back. "Of course I believe they're going to melt... eventually. It's just not happening fast enough."

"We are seeing a dynamic pivot which may tangibly be, in a sense, countering our bandwidth," Alan Pickle said. Pickle was the director of social media and marketing outreach for the World Environmental Equality Working Executive Endowment.

"Yes," Hayworth said. "This last winter was a train wreck for WEEWEE. Lots of snow, late frost, record lows. We told everyone that global warming would cause crazy weather but they're not buying it. People don't fear a rise in temperature when they're shoveling two feet of snow off their driveways in April."

"Indeed," Pickle nodded. "People kept calling me and sharing their frustration with the paradigm. It was out of our wheelhouse, and no matter how we energized our empowerment outreach, that underlying vector may have skewed our benchmark."

"Exactly my point!" Hayworth said. "We need results—real results, real, tangible results. Condos going underwater in Miami—not just collapsing, mind you, but collapsing then submerging—children getting sunburns in January, maybe even a year without a winter. The climate is changing but it's not going fast enough or consistently enough to scare people!"

"It's optics!" Pickle said, pushing his thick black-rimmed glasses higher on his thick nose. "The time to be strategic is when you're on the vertical."

Piknik sighed and nodded. "I get your point. We've done all we can but nature isn't cooperating. We've done our best. Right now you can't eat a bowl of cereal without reading about climate change on the back of the box. Every gardening book for the past decade—with the exception of a few reactionary holdouts—has had an obligatory chapter warning about the real and present danger of climate change. All the government television channels are on board, the car companies, the banks—everyone who is anyone is with us."

"Except for the little people," Hayworth said. "The ones shoveling snow."

"Exactly, exactly," Pickle said. "Our targeted community needs aggressive onboarding."

"Well," said Piknik. "What are we supposed to do?"

"We need to get Giles involved," Hayworth said.

"No way," Piknik said, suppressing a shudder. "He created WEE-WEE and handed it off to us with very clear objectives. I wouldn't dare bother him. If he knew we were having second thoughts... he might... he might..."

"I might what?" came a nasal voice from the back of the room. In the doorway stood a gawky man in a sweater.

"Oh!" Piknik said. "Sir! We..."

"Mr. Batson!" Professor Hayworth said. "We didn't expect you! We thought you were—well—we—uh..." he stopped awkwardly, somehow out of words.

"WEEWEE is important to me," Batson said, walking right through Elaine. She gasped.

"You're a hologram!" she exclaimed.

"Maybe you're just projecting," Batson replied, waving a flickering hand in the air. "But that's beside the point. Certainly you don't think your meetings are private?"

Batson smiled and pointed to Alan Pickle's perfect hair. "I have ears everywhere."

Alan frowned, then ran his fingers through his expensive haircut, blinking as he found something unexpected. He plucked it off his head. Between his fingers he held what appeared to be a tiny insect.

"You've been bugged," Batson said.

Alan looked at the little insect and blinked repeatedly, for once out of words.

"So," Batson said, looking into Hayworth's eyes. "You don't think it's happening fast enough?"

"N-n-n-no, sir," the professor said. "No, we need to see some serious climate ch-ch-change quickly, or, or, I think, I mean, people are going to lose the plot. They're already losing it. We need to proceed to the next stage immediately."

"I agree," Batson said.

"But it's so drastic," Piknik said. "I mean, they deserve it, but it's really..."

"It's time," Batson said. "As you said, Hayworth, the glaciers aren't melting themselves fast enough. It's time to give things a little push," he said, then tapped Hayworth on the chest. His hand went right through the old man in an awkward manner. Hayworth looked down at the arm going through his chest and made a face as if he were choking on lime-flavored Cheerios.

Batson pulled his hand out of Hayworth's chest and patted Piknik on the head, his hand ending up in the middle of her face. "I'll send you a new action plan shortly. Be ready for it."

"We'll be ready," Pickle said, finding his voice.

"Yes," Hayworth said. "It's time."

"It's time," Piknik agreed, smoothing back her hair. "I know you're right, Mr. Batson."

"Of course I am," he replied, and in a blink of light, he was gone.

CHAPTER 1

Fourteen months later

*The Mung Fu warrior moves not under adversity, even as the worm
grips the ground with his buttocks when his head is stuck in mouth
of bird.*

—A State of Bean: Principles of Mung Fu

It was an unseasonably warm October. Jack finished shoveling loose
soil into the final trench of a fresh double-dug garden bed and rubbed
his hands together in satisfaction. He wiped the sweat off his face with
his sleeve, then leaned his spade against a young pear tree and grabbed
his landscape rake. He needed to level out his bed and get it ready.

As he raked he wondered if the weather would ever cool off. It had
been a long, hot summer—and fall had brought no relief. He didn't
dare wait longer to plant a fall garden, though he worried about how
well his cool-season vegetables would do in the heat.

Jack enjoyed the chance to work in his garden but inside he was
itching for adventure. Nothing exciting had happened since he
and Pak had helped stop a Chinese invasive seed-importing scheme
back in the spring. Jack had returned to the states but Pak had
remained in China, supposedly working on some sort of business
deal with his family. Before he left, he had left Jack with a small
leatherbound book on the principles of Mung Fu and urged Jack to
study it every day. Though Jack preferred instructional videos, he

had faithfully read the volume and attempted to put it into practice. He glanced over at the potting bench where it sat, title up. *A State of Bean: Principles of Mung Fu.* The book was more philosophy than nitty-gritty fighting tactics, unfortunately, but Jack was doing his best.

He'd chatted with Pak a few times but the man hadn't given him any timeframe on his return. All he'd said was, "Be ready."

Being ready was annoying. Even Penny had been busy. She lived in Texas, which made getting together difficult. They caught each other online at least once a week. In fact, tonight they'd planned a chat date. But it wasn't the same as seeing her in person. Long distance relationships were like corn chips without salsa.

"I'll ask her to marry me," Jack said to himself as he finished raking. "Tonight. I'll ask tonight, she'll say yes, then we'll get married and she can move here. Situation fixed."

Jack had thought about popping the question for months but just hadn't pulled the trigger. He'd considered flying out to Texas in the spring and buying her tickets to The Lady Gaia News Fair, then popping the question there. No. Heck with that. Why wait?

Back in the summer he had received a call from Mrs. Hardin informing him that her husband had left him and his brother Drew a substantial amount of money in his will. If Jack could have cried, he might have. But he never cried, so he didn't. He had thanked Mrs. Hardin, who had warned him that the money would be tied up for a while. Jack told her not to worry about it and thanked her, sharing how much he had appreciated Mr. Hardin's influence in his life.

Since the money was still stuck in probate and Agri-Tweak was no more, Jack was working part time at a plant nursery, but it barely paid the mortgage. He never imagined a spy might go broke in between assignments. At least he was good at growing his own food—that was a big load off the monthly budget.

He'd propose to Penny over videochat. Tonight. No use in waiting—it just had to happen.

Jack walked to his shed and picked out an old hoe with a blade rounded from use. It was perfect for making seed furrows, and that's just what he did, cutting four neat lines down the center of his new garden bed.

This bed would be the continuation of his heirloom turnip-growing experiment. He'd use it for the Kiikala turnips his friend Niklas had sent him from Finland. He'd grown a bed of them in the spring and they'd made large fine-fleshed turnips. He'd let almost all the plants go to seed so he could save the ancient variety, then saved that seed for future gardens. It was time to plant again. He went inside and grabbed a small jar from his fridge and poured a tablespoon's worth of seeds into his hand, then headed back to his garden. "There's nothing like growing your own seed," Jack said to himself as he sprinkled a thin line of seeds down each row.

"Nothing?" said a voice from the fence. His neighbor Lisa, a.k.a. Tattoo Infection Girl, was smiling at him. She wore huge sunglasses and a bikini top. Jack read the words "NO REGERTS" stretching from shoulder to shoulder across her chest. The ink looked new and the skin around it was red.

"I can think of, like, thirty-seven things that would be better than growing seeds or whatever," Lisa said. "Why is your shovel so shiny?"

"What?" Jack said.

"Your shovel is really shiny. Did you paint it?"

"No," Jack said, realizing she was talking about his stainless-steel spade. "It's stainless."

"Oh," she said. "Want to come over to my house and show me how to dig?"

"No," Jack said, his gut tightening as his fight-or-flight reflex kicked in. "I have an important meeting I need to attend." He looked at his wrist as if checking a watch. "It's late—I'll see you later."

"Could you at least put suntan lotion on my shoulders?" she asked, turning around to reveal what appeared to be an iguana scrawled across the puffy flesh of her back. "I don't want my dragon to fade."

"Way busy," Jack said, waving goodbye and half running into the back of his house like he'd left a pot of wax boiling on the stove. He got inside and watched through the blinds as Lisa slumped into the rotting sofa on her back porch and lit a cigarette.

Terrible timing. I was almost done with that bed.

HIT HER WITH A STICK, said a loud voice inside his head.

"Brown Wizard?" Jack said. "Where have you been?"

WAITING FOR YOU, the voice replied.

"Yeah, well, I was in a fistfight last month at The Organic Market and you didn't help."

SORRY ABOUT THAT.

"It's okay, I still won," Jack said, ripping open a bag of *Ocean Octaves!* "Dude was mad at me for perpetuating a culture of violence by buying bacon, so he threw a canister of gluten-free pretzel sticks at me. I popped him and half his teeth fell out... and you know why. Their kind all have weak teeth. But still, I was keyed up on adrenaline—I thought you'd show up."

YOU WERE NOT THE CARETAKER.

"What?" Jack said, his mouth full of crisps. "You told me I was the caretaker, whatever that means. And now I'm not?"

There was no answer.

"Brown Wizard?" Jack said, grabbing a celery stout from the fridge and peeping out the blinds again. There was still no answer—and he noted Lisa was also gone. *I wonder if she's really gone or if she's going to come back to the fence as soon as I start working again.*

He stuffed another fistful of *Ocean Octaves!* into his mouth and washed them down with the tail end of his stout, then looked out the blinds again. She was still gone. *Don't be a wuss, Jack. Your gardens are calling.*

Jack chucked his empty bottle in the recycling bin and went back to his beds. Darned if Tattoo Infection Girl would stop him.

He surveyed the seeded furrows and decided to cover the turnip seeds with sifted compost instead of soil. His compost pile was at the edge of his garden area towards the back of the house, giving him convenient access for both dumping scraps and feeding his garden beds. He grabbed his hardware cloth sifter and put it over his wheelbarrow, then shoveled the top half of the pile aside so he could get at the finished compost deeper down. The crumbly humus was full of worms and insects and smelled rich and fertile as he dumped shovel-loads onto his sifter.

In under a minute Jack had enough fine compost for his turnips. He quit sifting and rolled the wheelbarrow back to his new turnip bed and started spreading handfuls of the good stuff over his seeds.

He finished, then filled up a watering can from his rain barrel to water in the seeds. There had been some rain lately but not enough. A single two-gallon can's worth of water would be plenty. He walked down the bed, wetting the newly planted furrows.

Jack stepped back and admired his handiwork. Not bad at all. Seeing the finished bed gave him a sudden impulse to put another bed into production. Yes—a bed of English peas. That would be great. And it would give the soil some green manure for spring, when he could plant it with something greedy, like sweet corn.

Jack eyed out a weedy 4 x 8 plot he'd lined with reclaimed cin-derblocks the previous year, then planted with cantaloupes. The cantaloupes had looked good but tasted too watery, probably because of how much rain they'd had during the spring. Wilted vines and a few volunteer sprouts still remained amongst the nutgrass and pigweed. Yes—it was a good time to clean it up—why not?

Jack decided to attack the area with his stainless fork, then pick the weeds out by hand. The area had been double-dug before and didn't need a full loosening. Just weeding and loosening the top eight inches or so would be fine. He drove the tines of the fork into the soil and whistled while he worked. The afternoon was cooling off as the sun descended towards the horizon. There was simply nothing better than a late Saturday afternoon's gardening.

A half-hour later he had a cleaned and weeded bed. The light was fading but he had just enough time to plant some peas before it was too dark to work. As he planted, he wondered why the Brown Wizard had failed to show up in his head, then shown up again today. He had somehow been "the caretaker," then not the caretaker, then now was the caretaker again? It was almost worth starting a fight or ingesting some mycotoxin just to have a serious conversation with his internal fight coach.

No. Definitely not. Resorting to violence or taking drugs to talk to voices in your head was not the way to find success.

Jack watered in the peas and stepped into the house. His sweat-soaked shirt felt cold in the air conditioning.

He stripped off his clothes and threw them into the laundry basket in the hall, then turned on the shower and stepped in. He ran it on lukewarm just to cool himself off a bit. As he washed he realized the water was pooling in the bottom of the shower. *The drain is blocked*, Jack thought. He reached out of the shower and grabbed the plunger behind the toilet, then tried it on the drain. *POW POW POW!* He depressed the plunger as hard as he could, trying to force water down the drain. No luck. It wouldn't go down.

Jack finished his shower and toweled off. Two inches of water sat stubbornly in the bottom of the shower.

I'll just buy some of that stuff that eats everything away, Jack thought. *Like in that commercial where a tiny man with a chainsaw cuts clogs into bits. That's the stuff I need.*

Jack got dressed and pulled out his phone, looking up "commercial where tiny man with a chainsaw cuts clogs into bits." There it was. Liquid Psychopath(TM). Jack made a note to pick some up from the hardware store, then decided it was time to wash the mound of dishes on his counter.

He started the water in the sink—then found the kitchen sink was clogged as well. Thinking quickly, he realized the chances of both the kitchen sink and the bathtub acquiring blockages at the same time were very, very low. There was only one way to tell if there was a catastrophic problem with his plumbing. He had to flush the toilet.

It was the only way.

He walked back into the bathroom, hands perspiring as he put his fingers on the toilet handle.

He took a deep breath. His fingers trembled on the cold metal handle.

Here goes nothing.

He shut his eyes, then flushed it.

For a moment, he thought the water was going down—and then it started to rise.

"No!" Jack yelled as it rose faster. He got down on his knees and turned off the valve that fed water into the tank. He twisted it until it was tight, then checked the bowl.

He exhaled in relief. The water flow had ceased a scant fraction of an inch from the top of the bowl.

"Close one," Jack muttered. Then he noticed some water on the floor and looked around the back of the toilet to see the valve he'd turned was now dripping.

"Shoot," Jack said. He was going to have to call a plumber. He ran his tongue over the chipped molar on the bottom right side of his mouth. He'd been ignoring a needed trip to the dentist due to short funds. "Sorry, lower right second molar," Jack said. "You're going to have to wait it out. I promise you I'll avoid pistachios until you're set, okay?"

The molar didn't answer, which Jack took as a good sign.

He sighed and grabbed his phone, then reconsidered. Did he really want to call a plumber on a Saturday night? Wouldn't he charge double or triple or something? He looked back at the valve. The dripping was leaving a pool behind the toilet but it wasn't catastrophic—yet. He could just grab a salad bowl from the kitchen and put it under there for now. Yes, that would do it.

Jack knew he had a septic tank out back. It must be full or perhaps roots had invaded from a neighbor's yard. On Monday he could find a plumber that dealt with septic systems and broken valves. No problem. Monday would be fine.

POP! The handle flew off the valve, clattering across the tile floor. A geyser of water blasted across the room, soaking the vintage print of blooming cherry trees Jack had hung on the wall. Jack jumped to his feet and grabbed his toolbox from the closet, looking for a wrench. He found one and dashed to the street to find the water company box buried in the ground. He yanked off its small concrete lid only to discover it was filled to the brim with swarming fire ants, carrying their little white grub babies as they poured out in the monochromatic yellow light cast by the streetlamp above. Gritting his teeth, Jack reached in rapidly with his wrench and found the valve, hissing and saying unkind words as the ants stung him repeatedly. Finally, the line was off. He smacked at his hand to dislodge the ants gripping onto it and stinging him repeatedly.

Then his legs and bare feet started stinging and he jumped up and started dancing and smacking at the ants while making unmanly noises.

"Wow, you had something to do, huh?" came a woman's voice. He looked up to see the glow of a cigarette and a looming pale shape on the sidewalk. Lisa.

"Something came up," Jack said.

"Dance lessons?" she said, then took a drag from the cigarette.

"Yeah," Jack said. "My instructors live in the water box. Come over here and put your hand in if you want to join me."

"No thanks," she said. "Do you think I'm stupid?"

Jack figured it was a rhetorical question and said nothing. He smacked at his legs a final time, then walked back into his house and grabbed the phone book. "AAAA1234 Aquatic Septic and Plumbing, LLC" was the first listing he found for his area. Great. That would work. He dialed the number—400-1234—expecting to get an answering machine. Instead, a man answered.

"Hello?"

"Hey," Jack said. "My plumbing is all backed up and the valve blew behind the toilet. Do you think..."

"No problem," the guy said. "Address?"

Jack shared his address and the guy said he'd be there in a half hour. *There goes this year's income*, Jack thought as he hung up. *I should have asked what it would cost.*

The plumber arrived 28 minutes later in a large battered septic truck with flowers painted all over it. Plastic plants and butterflies covered his dashboard. The driver was a bearded guy with a broad smile and a slight limp.

"Paul," he said, stepping out of the trunk and shaking Jack's hand. "Paul Garrison."

"Jack. Nice to meet you," Jack said. "Thanks for coming out. Where did you come up with such a weird name for your plumbing company?"

"AAAA1234?" Paul replied. "Old family name."

"Oh," Jack said, as the man pulled tools from his truck. "I was wondering what this is going to cost, see... I..."

"You got any rich relatives?" Paul asked.

"No," Jack said.

"Mining rights?"

"No," Jack repeated.

"A stack of old catalytic converters?"

"Nope," Jack said.

"Bullion buried in mayonnaise jars?"

"Definitely not," Jack said.

"Ah, of course. You should say no on that one," Paul grinned and tapped his nose. "TPTB might confiscate again."

"TPTB?" Jack asked.

"Never mind, they're listening. Look, I'll just put you on the payment plan. You'll be fine. Let's see what's wrong and then I'll give you an estimate."

Jack invited Paul inside to look at the valve.

"Not good," Paul said. "Cheap junky piece, like everything nowadays. But it ain't the big issue. It just blew cause you were trying to stop the toilet from overflowing. That overflowing thing is your big problem, right there. And all that water in the shower. When's the last time you had the septic tank checked?"

"Never," Jack said. "I bought the house a few years ago and it's just me living here, so I figured..."

"Jackpot," Paul said. "Then it's full of the good stuff."

"What?" Jack asked.

"Where's the septic tank?"

"Out back," Jack said, leading Paul into his backyard and flipping on the light by the back door.

"Hey now," Paul said, looking at the backyard in the dim light. "You're a gardener?"

"Yeah," Jack said. "It's my main thing. Other than breaking plumbing."

"Sure, sure, me too!" Paul said, suddenly enthusiastic. "You've got tomatoes here, some beans, looks like you just dug some new beds, too—oh—and some hot peppers over there, nice, nice!"

"So you garden?" Jack asked.

"Do I garden?" Paul replied. "Is the pope Catholic?"

"I'm not sure," Jack said.

Paul laughed. "Yes I garden! I'm actually the greatest gardener you've ever met."

"I doubt that," Jack said. "I'm pretty darned good."

"Ha!" Paul said. "That's what they all say. So, where's this septic tank?"

Jack pointed it out. "Do you have some pictures of your garden?" he asked, sure that there was no way this guy was a better gardener than himself.

"You want to see it?" Paul asked, prying up the access port on the top of the septic tank.

"If you think you're the best, you need to prove it," Jack said.

"I will," Paul laughed. "Tomorrow. You come with me and I'll show you the greatest garden the world has ever seen." Paul looked around at Jack's neat beds. "You're good," he admitted. "But you're working way too hard. Way too hard, buddy."

"It takes work to grow a good garden," Jack said. "It's the way things are."

"That's where you're wrong," Paul said. "And yep—this is good and full. I'll bring the pipe out back and we'll get this empty, then I'll fix the valve while the truck does its thing."

"Great," Jack said.

"Tomorrow, though—you up for a ride?"

"Sure," Jack said, wondering what he was getting himself into. "It's gotta be after church, though."

"Fine," Paul said. "Two good?"

"Sure, 2 p.m."

CHAPTER 2

*The training of the warrior's body is second to the training of the
warrior's mind, which is third to the training of the warrior's gut,
which must judge the nose of the warrior, which cannot be trained as
it is a passive observer, like drifting leaves in fall, it must just be; it
is up to the three trainings to interpret that which cannot be trained.*

—*A State of Bean: Principles of Mung Fu*

Jack rode in the passenger seat of Paul's truck. Paul had charged him
$50 to repair the valve—and nothing to pump his tank. Gardener's
discount, he'd said.

"It's still in there," he'd said when he arrived at Jack's house. "The
good stuff I got from you last night."

They were heading out into the sticks now, an AM radio station
playing country music from the sixties, Paul's old GM trunk clattering
along like it was about to fall to pieces. Jack had to admit he was
intrigued by the idea of seeing an amazing garden, but he wasn't
particularly hopeful that it would be as advertised. Jack was guessing
Paul was a few seeds short of a packet.

"It's an old strip mine," Paul said, turning down the radio.

"Your garden?" Jack said.

"Oh yeah," Paul said. "Environmental disaster area. I'm bringing it
back."

They rolled through the countryside, past recently shorn hayfields
and cows, then off onto a little-used access road. "Just a little farther,"

Paul said. "Just wait. We're going to give everything a good feeding, too. I'll let you help."

"Great," Jack said.

They reached a rusty gate with a chain and Paul brought his truck to a clunking halt. "Just a minute—it's only dummy locked," he said, jumping out.

Jack watched him unhook the chain from the gate and swing it open. He came back to the truck and popped it back into gear. Jack felt the drivetrain knock into place and they were moving again. A little ways down the road a series of rusted old buildings and metal and concrete debris appeared. It looked like a great place to shoot an apocalyptic film. Beyond the crumbling buildings was a large pit.

"We'll just pull up where I can feed everything," Paul said, then drove around behind one of the buildings and backed up to the edge of the pit—and the entire view changed. Instead of rock and sand and debris, Jack saw a verdant forest below.

"Whoa," he said. "It's like the garden of Eden."

"You bet your bazooka," Paul said with a big grin. "And it's all natural. Come on, jump out—I'll show you around."

Jack followed Paul down a set of railroad tie steps and into the middle of a rich forest. There were apple trees and tomato plants, maypops and peppers, sumac and black cherry, blueberries and melons and a vast abundance of wildflowers and weeds.

Off to his left was a wasteland of rock and sand. Farther ahead was more sand—but for at least a solid acre, there was nothing but rich, green growth. Jack reached down and brushed away a layer of fallen leaves, uncovering rich, loamy soil. He took a handful and smelled its earthy aroma.

"Wow," Jack said. "This is incredible. How did you–"

And then he stopped, realizing how Paul had made this place. He dropped the handful of soil and wiped his hand on the leg of his pants.

Paul's grin confirmed his realization. "All natural."

"You did this all by pumping septic tanks and blasting it down into this part of the mine?"

"Yep," Paul said, grinning wider. "I told you you were working too hard."

"Well, I can't exactly spray raw sewage all over my backyard," Jack said. "I'm doing what I can. Besides, this all looks great—but it's totally dangerous."

Paul frowned. "Naw. It's natural."

"Food poisoning, drowning, scorpions and hot dogs are all natural too."

"Hot dogs aren't natural," Paul said sullenly.

"It says so," Jack replied. "Right on the package." Paul looked sad so Jack decided he needed to say something more positive. "But still, Paul—you did a great job. This is impressive."

"Oh yes," Paul said, brightening up again. "I didn't even plant any of this."

"What?" Jack said, looking at the ripe apples hanging on a tree by the path. "You didn't?"

"Nope," Paul said. "I just blasted everything down the hillside and what grows, grows. The birds come and plant some, I'm sure, but a lot of these things just grow themselves, you know, from what... passes through... if you know what I mean?"

Jack made a mental note to disinfect his shoes when he got home.

"Here," Paul said, picking a tomato. "Have a tomato."

"I'm okay," Jack replied, taking the fruit gingerly.

"You like peppers?" Paul said, skipping through the brush and coming back with a perfect red bell pepper.

Jack smiled tightly as Paul pressed the pepper into his hand.

"It's all natural, and all mine," Paul said, picking another tomato and biting into it. "I would love to bring tours through here but someone said I'd get arrested for dumping or sued or something. The government goes after people, they say, you know, people who think different."

"Yeah," Jack said. "That's true." His eyes caught sight of a 3' tall sapling. "Wait," Jack said. "That looks like an avocado tree. Did you plant that one?"

"Nope," Paul said. "I just blast the stuff down the hill and what grows, grows. I think it's gonna die when it gets cold, though. They're like a tropical tree."

"Right, sure, but how in the world did that..."

"Hey!" Paul said. "Let's feed everything, whaddya say?"

"Okay," Jack said, carefully stepping around a puddle.

They went back up to the truck and Paul showed Jack where the release valve was. "We just open all these up and it'll pour right down the hillside and bring a bunch of new nature to the area!"

Paul popped the valve open and sewage shot down the hill. Jack could see how the forest had been established progressively over time. To the right side was a lot of young growth, but all the way to the left were more trees and shrubs. The aroma of the flying sewage almost made Jack wish he hadn't come down here, but he did have a whole new respect for the fertilizing power of human waste.

"Yep," Paul said as the sludge rolled down in rivulets over a sandy patch at the edge of his garden. "We should do this all over the place."

Jack had pulled his T-shirt over his face and was taking short breaths. "Sure," he said back quickly, then covered his face again.

"So," Paul said. "You believe in climate change?"

"Sure," Jack said. "The climate changes all the time."

"Yeah, but not like this year, right?"

"Yeah," Jack said.

"Yep, it's real hot. I wasn't sure, you know, after last winter, but man—this summer just keeps going. It's gotta be global warming."

"Yeah," Jack said.

Paul pulled out some sort of tool and scraped the final bits of muck from inside the tank. "You know, they often have dumping yards for this stuff," Paul said. "It's a total waste."

"Yeah," Jack said again. He stuck to that word because saying more would require him to breathe.

"Hey," Paul said, looking at him. "Breathe deep, brother! That's real natural fertility there! Of course, the heat does make it smell more. In winter you can't smell nothing."

Jack just nodded this time.

"Anyhow, I suppose they were right about global warming cooking us all," Paul said. "It's really feeling like we're gonna roast. Should be in the 60s or 70s right now, not the upper 80s."

Jack nodded again.

"All the good people with great ideas, though, they aren't ever appreciated. They should give me a Ted Talk for this garden. Just point and spray, you know, self-planting natural ecosystem. You know, I used to know a brilliant guy that made robots. Still have his name somewhere. He designed an automated septic truck for me. Self-driving."

Jack mumbled something back.

"What happened?" Paul said, getting back into the truck. Jack followed him. Paul started the truck and pulled away from his garden. "I'll tell you what happened. It drove into a governor's motorcade. Made the national news. Brilliant man, though. I should check in on him sometime. Course, he's not getting any Ted Talk. You just run one truck into a limo and bam—people write you off. Lots of people buried in the Great Wall, you know. Innovators."

"I think they were slaves," Jack said, catching his breath. It was better in the truck.

"Innovative slaves," Paul said. "Wanna go out and get some onion rings?

"No, I'm fine," Jack said. "Thanks."

"Suit yourself. There's a great diner on the way home. I'll buy you a drink."

"Fine," Jack said. And then his phone rang. Penny! He picked it up with a wince—he'd forgotten their date.

"Hello?" he answered.

"Jack—are you okay?"

"Sure," he said. "Checking out a friend's garden."

"Oh yeah?" she said, her voice cool. "Have you been checking it out for the last two days?"

"No, I had a plumbing problem."

"Oh," she said. "A serious one?"

"Terrible," Jack said. "The septic tank backed up and the valve behind the toilet broke."

"And then you decided to go see a garden?"

"Right," Jack said. "It's quite a system."

"Tell her about how I made it!" Paul said.

"What's that?" Penny asked over the phone.

"My friend wants me to tell you about it," Jack said.

"I'm not interested," Penny said.

"It's all natural," Jack said.

"Great," Penny said. "Well..."

"Well what?" Jack said.

"I'll talk to you soon, I guess."

"Human waste!" Paul said.

"What?" Penny said. "Did I just hear what I thought I heard?"

"No," Jack said. "Unless you heard the words 'human waste.'"

"I heard 'huge waste'" Penny said. "But it's human waste? So you threw me under the bus to visit some kind of a sewage garden?"

"No, I threw you under the bus because my toilet valve broke and made me forget our date. The human waste garden was just a continuation of me forgetting."

"Wow," Penny said. "Just wow. Have fun, then. I'm off to... go... visit a hair tie museum or something," She hung up.

"She was impressed?" Paul said with a big grin as Jack put his phone back in his pocket.

"She said 'wow, just wow'," Jack replied. "She was amazed by your innovative system."

Paul grinned. "It's the best system. She should see it."

"She'd love it," Jack said.

CHAPTER 3

The Mung Fu warrior maintains his allegiances just as a scroll is dusted by caring slaves or dried meat is kept wrapped in waxed linen.

—A State of Bean: Principles of Mung Fu

When Jack got home and said goodbye to Paul (who he kept calling "Septic Man" in his head), Jack took a long shower then grabbed a bag of *Ocean Octaves!* and a celery stout. He powered up his laptop and decided to watch a few gardening videos. That didn't last long, though, as he'd already seen every worthwhile gardening video posted to YouTube, so he decided to check the news and see what was going on in the world. It had been a long time since he'd bothered.

"Newport News Firefighter Saves Macaw from Burning Tesla"

"Alton Brown Invents New Variety of Biscuit"

"Summer Continues—But For How Long?"

He clicked on the last link and discovered that meteorologists had no idea how long summer would continue, then followed another link about raging forest fires.

"Hot, Dry Conditions Not Responsible for All Fires—Arson Suspected"

Who would deliberately light forests on fire? Jack went to DuckDuckGo and typed in "forest fires arson," then read the list of results.

"Handbags for Spring"

"Antioxidants Linked to Brain Damage in Marmosets"

"Former Muppet DUI Mugshots Released"

And it just got weirder from there. Nothing about fires. He switched to Bing and tried again. This time, "forest fires arson" brought up Extreme Tire Recycling, Party Themes in Purple, Uses for Toothpicks, Zebra Head Injuries and multiple pages on radioactive pantyhose eggs.

What in the world?

Jack typed in "tomato seeds in septic" and got lots of hits that related to his query. Then he tried "human waste good for gardens" and got plenty more. Just the wildfires seemed to be causing the searches trouble. He went back to his history and clicked on the original article that had tweaked his interest and got a 404 error. Page not found.

Now this was interesting. He tried typing in variations of his search. "Forest fires manmade" gave him hits on how the management of timber land let to fires, plus pages on global warming and increased fires, plus warning pages on smoking and campfires. All that seemed normal. But when he went back to "forest fires arson," he got a random mess in return.

Well. So much for that.

Jack shut his laptop and got his phone. He'd ask Pak. He found him on SayWhaat? and sent him a text. "Hey Pak—try searching for 'forest fires arson' and see what you get. Something weird is going on.' "

Pak didn't write him back right away so he put his phone on the charger and headed to bed with a copy of Dr. Ricardo Paulson's *Soil Bubbles: The Curious Roots of Microbial Crack-Up Booms*. He was asleep in moments.

* * *

Jack's alarm woke him up at seven. He rolled out of bed and got into his work clothes, then headed to the kitchen to fry some bacon and eggs with greens from the garden. He considered microwaving breakfast but was checked by his memories of the last five times he'd tried to work out a proper way to microwave bacon and eggs. It seemed there was no way to pull it off properly. The bacon was never right and the eggs liked to explode.

A perfect red bell pepper sat on the counter. *That would be really good with eggs,* Jack thought. *But its pedigree...*

He tossed it in the compost bucket. No way.

After breakfast, Jack jumped into his Mustang. The tank was running low and he made a mental note to pick up some more vegetable oil to make another batch of biofuel. It was a pain to do and he was starting to wonder if converting the car had been a good idea. But no— of course it was a good idea. The fuel came from plants, after all.

When he got to work it was already hot. "Hey Jack," his boss called out as Jack walked into the main greenhouse. "You feel like propagating today?"

Jack's new boss was Randy Porter, a decent guy with a vast knowledge of landscape plants. Jack kept trying to get him to add fruit trees and perennial vegetables to the business but thus far he'd been unsuccessful.

"No problem," Jack said. "Name the species and the count required."

"We need a hundred more one-gallon variegated hostas. You should also stick a few trays of *Nigra arborvitae.* Get some off the mother trees in the back."

"Great," Jack said. "Then maybe we could get some black walnuts growing?"

"No," Randy said. "I don't think so."

"Perhaps some pears?"

"No, Jack. No fruit trees."

"Mulberries, then? They're just a small fruit."

"You're a small fruit, Jack. No fruit trees!"

"Fine," Jack said, shrugging and walking through the greenhouse. "Just the hostas, arborvitae and Nanking cherries."

"Jack!" Randy said. "I swear, if you mention fruit trees one more time..."

Jack didn't hear what would happen to him if he mentioned fruit trees again, as he'd already left the greenhouse and was headed towards the arborvitae. He'd nabbed a pair of secateurs on the way. He filled a bucket with water and was looking for a good semi-hardwood branch to nab when his phone blooped. He took it out of his pocket. It was Pak.

"Am back in Virginia now. Talk soon. We need to take a trip."

Interesting, Jack thought. He wondered if Pak had tried searching out the fires on his own. He also wondered if he'd be able to take time off to travel. As soon as the inheritance check came in, he'd be much freer and might even be able to start his own business.

But one thing at a time. Right now he had plants to propagate.

✳ ✳ ✳

That evening Jack was forking his compost from one bin to another with his stainless spading fork when he heard a someone whistling from behind him. He stopped and turned to see Pak looking over the fence.

"Copper is better," Pak said. "Conducts energy of the earth."

"What?" Jack asked.

"Your fork," Pak said. "Does not matter with compost as much, but if you insist on digging beds, copper is better."

"Wouldn't copper bend all over the place?" Jack said.

"They add tin. It's a concession for the sake of strength."

"Ah, so it's brass then."

"Bronze," Pak replied.

"Great, good." Jack looked at his fork, suddenly finding it less amazing. *A bronze digging fork. Now there is a novel idea.*

"So?" Pak said. "You are not going to welcome me home? Maybe say 'nice to have my old friend back?' "

"Welcome home," Jack said. "I suppose we need to talk."

"Yes indeed," Pak said. "Very much so. I will come over for tea late this evening."

"Great," Jack said. "I'll hunt down the molasses."

* * *

At 10:08 p.m., there was a knock at Jack's door. He opened it and Pak walked in with a small cloth bag, an aquarium bubbler and a five-gallon bucket 2/3 full of rainwater.

Jack unplugged his modem and drew the blinds on the house, then handed Pak a bottle of molasses. Pak added it to the water, then swished the cloth bag around before leaving it in and starting the bubbler.

"Wow, that bubbler is really noisy," Jack remarked.

"Yes," Pak said. "I picked it deliberately because of bad Amazon reviews. The better to hide conversations with, chief."

"Yes indeed," Jack said. "And 'chief?' Where did you pick that up?"

"It's American language," Pak said. "I used it correctly."

"Sure," Jack said. "So—tell me about the wildfires."

"Things are not good," Pak said. "There are similar fires happening in locations around the world. You must have noticed on the news."

"I don't really pay much attention to the news," Jack admitted. "But I did check it the other day and saw an article on the fires. That was why I got in touch. Actually, I got in touch because of what happened after I read the article on the fires. I tried searching for more on it being arson and got totally bizarre responses to my search. And it wasn't just one search engine. I tried a few. Lots of random responses."

"Interesting," Pak said. "I tried a search as well but failed to receive the same response you did. Searches returned few results."

"Really?" Jack said. "I should have taken screenshots. I got a handful of weird responses, then one big crazy set of the same thing over and over."

"What was that?" Pak asked.

"Radioactive pantyhose eggs," Jack said.

"It was probably just an artifact from your normal internet history."

"Do I look like someone who would search for radioactive pantyhose eggs?" Jack asked.

Pak was silent.

"Well," Jack said, after a few moments. "Anyhow, you said things are not good, plus fires are happening around the world. Arsonists?"

"Yes," Pak said. "We believe so. However, no one has been caught."

"No one? No leads?"

"No. And this is just the latest issue—the story goes deeper. But we may be able to intercept this one in progress. That is why we need to go camping."

"Why camping?" Jack said.

"My people have noticed an interesting thing. The fires are moving in fractal patterns."

"Aliens," Jack said.

"Don't be crazy, Jack," Pak said. "This is happening in forests and prairies. Aliens prefer cornfields. But there is a pattern. And we think the next fires will start in Oklahoma, which will be very dangerous."

"Because the wind comes sweeping down the plain?"

"Yes," Pak nodded.

"So we need to go camp in Oklahoma and see if we can catch these firebugs in action."

"Exactly. We will leave tomorrow. This is the decision from the top tin."

"Top brass."

"Yes, if you include copper."

"Great," Jack said. "Though I do have a job."

"This is more important," Pak said. "I told you to be ready. The boil has been swelling. Master Rice trusts you implicitly after your performance in Korea and in the invasive seed affair—he insisted upon your presence."

"I am honored," Jack said.

"Have you been studying the book I gave you?" Pak said.

"I am the unbreakable seed. I am the bamboo in the storm. I am the roots in the cracks."

"Very good," Pak nodded. "Who needs a job when you have Mung Fu?"

"Money is useful," Jack shrugged. "I'm broke until the inheritance arrives. I haven't bothered picking up my career again since I was waiting on you and The Organization."

"I am sorry," Pak said. "We should have paid more attention to your financial state. I will have a few thousand dollars sent your way."

"Seriously?" Jack said.

"It is nothing for an organization of our reach and antiquity," Pak said. "But sometimes we forget that the little people need to eat."

"Little people?" Jack said. "I'm bigger than you."

"I can beat you senseless," Pak replied.

"I'd like to see you try," Jack laughed. "I know you're better at Mung Fu, but I never stopped my other fight training. Just finished working my way through the Chaos University Death Boxing X series. And I've also got special powers from an ancient creature that lives in my head."

"Okay, fine," Pak said. "I give up. You are much more dangerous than me."

"You're just saying that," Jack said.

Pak slapped him on the face without appearing to move.

"Hey!" Jack said.

"What?" said Pak.

"You slapped me," Jack replied. "Right on the face!"

"Nervous twitch, very embarrassing," Pak apologized. "Now make sure you have good shoes. We will get camping supplies when we get to Oklahoma. Call your boss and take the time off. If you don't, people will die."

Pak stood and walked to the door.

"Wait," Jack said, rubbing his cheek. "What about your tea?"

"Use it on your gardens tomorrow morning," Pak said. "I have another batch at home." He turned the knob and left Jack to himself. Jack checked his watch. It was still before midnight and she was two hours earlier than his time.

Maybe he could still call Penny tonight. Heck, if she were in a good mood, maybe he'd propose.

He plugged his modem back in and saw she was online. He dialed and a moment later, she picked up.

"Jack?" she said. She wore a loose green T-shirt and was brushing her hair.

"Yep," Jack said.

"I'm sorry," she said, wincing as she pulled at a knot. "I shouldn't have been snippy the other day."

"It's okay," Jack said. "I shouldn't have forgotten."

"Why is your cheek red?" Penny said.

"I got fresh with a girl," Jack replied.

"I'll bet," Penny laughed. "Anyhow, let's just forget you forgetting and me being snippy. Will you be around tomorrow?"

"Well," Jack said, not sure if he should say anything. "Not really."

"Not really?" Penny said. "What's up?"

"I've got to travel."

"Spy stuff?" Penny asked.

"Uh," Jack said.

"You're investigating aliens?" Penny asked.

"No," Jack said.

"Are you going alone?" Penny said.

"No," Jack said.

"Animal, vegetable or mineral?" Penny said.

"Penny..."

"Never mind, I'm coming along."

"What?" Jack said.

"I'm coming along. There's no way I'm missing an adventure."

"Don't you have some sort of job to do?"

"It's all paperwork, you know. It was only good luck I ended up in the agricultural expo when the building was rigged to explode."

"If that was your good luck, I don't want to be around when you have bad luck. Pak might not–"

"Pak! I knew it!" Penny said. "I've got his number—I'll call him and say you wanted me to come along. Hugs and kisses—I'm off to sleep."

There was a click and Jack looked at the dead phone in his hand, then laughed. She was irrepressible.

CHAPTER 4

Even as vines creep upwards on a wall, so the heart of the Mung Fu warrior grips a challenge and removes paint like tiny fingers, as well as causing mold, leaks and inexorable structural damage in that which he conquers.

—*A State of Bean: Principles of Mung Fu*

"Let's light a fire," Jack said as he surveyed their campsite.

"So you're the one," Pak said. "I never would have thought it, but all the pieces fit."

"Excuse me?" Penny said, taking off her floppy camouflage hat. "Jack is the one? What do you mean?"

"Can I fill her in?" Jack asked. Pak nodded.

"Great," Jack said. "I wasn't sure about opsec. Though you said she could come, so I guess she's fine."

"Yeah," Penny said. "I'm fine." She did a little half spin like a fashion model in her well-fitting camo pants and olive-drab tank top.

"You're ridiculous," Jack said. "Did you go shopping at the LL Bean Army Surplus?"

She shrugged. "Tell me what's up. I'm dying to know."

"Arson," Pak said.

"Right," Jack said. "Someone has been starting fires all over the place and we think this is the next spot where they're going to break out."

"Cool," Penny said. "I was making some guesses on the flight, but they were all plant related. I thought you might have discovered some new kind of corn or something boring."

"Boring?" Jack said, stricken.

"No offense," Penny said.

"Too late," Jack said. "Why did you want to come if you thought I might be doing something plant related out here?"

"Because you're here," she said with a toss of her hair.

Jack smiled. "That works. I am glad you came. Anyhow, we're going to see if we can catch the arsonists in the act and—wait—what's that in your backpack!?"

Something was moving in Penny's pack. Jack pulled his hunting knife expectantly—then saw the head of a small cat emerge from the bag.

"Dinglebat!" Penny said. "I thought I told you to stay home?"

"Lots of people inviting themselves along," Pak said.

"Meow," Dinglebat said.

"So, about that fire," Jack said. "It doesn't feel like camping without a fire."

"True," Penny said. "We could use some of the dry scrubby stuff to light a campfire. If we clear an area it won't spread."

"No," Pak said. "They'll see our smoke rising."

"You're right," Jack said. "I forgot about that." He looked around at the prairie stretching off into the distance. "This is crazy, though. We're in the middle of nowhere. We drove two hours out and haven't seen a single person in miles and miles. It would take a dedicated arsonist to come all the way out here."

"The models don't lie," Pak said. "They may come in on a helicopter."

Jack and Penny looked up at the blue sky, starting to turn pink and gold around the edges as the sun sank below the horizon. It was completely devoid of helicopters.

"They could also arrive in a balloon," Pak said. Jack and Penny looked up again. No balloons. "Or a rocket," Pak said.

"You're joking," Penny said, after looking up for a third time and failing to detect any rockets.

Pak shrugged.

"If we don't have a fire, I can't cook s'mores," Jack said. "Look," he said, pulling a paper bag out of the bed of their rented Ford Ranger. He reached in and produced bag of marshmallows, a few chocolate bars and a box of Graham crackers. "I picked up everything we need when we hit the grocery in town."

"I saw you buy it," Pak said. "I assumed it was your idea of a balanced meal."

"No," Jack replied. "It's not balanced. It doesn't have *Ocean Octaves* in it. S'mores are just a treat. You know, a 'let's reward ourselves for chasing Oklahoma arsonists' treat. But you need a fire to make them."

"You'll have to wait for the arsonists to start one," Penny said.

Jack looked up at the darkening sky. "I don't see any rockets yet."

"I was joking about rockets," Pak said.

"I know," Jack replied, then walked to the truck and popped the hood.

"What are you doing?" Penny said.

"There's more than one way to skin a cat."

"Meow!" Dinglebat yowled indignantly.

"Have no fear," Pak said to the cat, patting it on the head. "It is simply a statue of talk."

"Do they have mosquitoes out here?" Penny asked Pak.

"Yes," Pak replied. "But it has been very dry, and we are not near any piles of discarded tires where they might breed."

"How did mosquitoes reproduce before we invented car tires?" Penny asked.

"They lived in horse troughs," Jack said from the other side of the truck.

"I was just wondering about mosquitoes because we don't seem to have any tents," Penny said.

"Sleeping outside balances the *qi*," Pak said.

"Oh," Penny said.

"There!" Jack said, returning with the truck's battery, some wires and a few parts. "We'll be able to make s'mores later. I have a plan now."

"Great," Penny said. "But I think I want to eat something less sugary first."

"Of course," Jack said. "It needs to be way dark before you make s'mores. Ideally, your eyes shouldn't be able to tell the difference between carbonized marshmallows and melted chocolate."

Dinglebat disappeared into Penny's bag and then remerged with a tin of sardines in his mouth.

"Ew," Penny said. "Where did you even get those?" Dinglebat pulled the tab without gracing her with a reply, then delicately nipped at a fish—then pulled back as if he'd been bitten.

"What is it?" Penny asked. "Is one of them still alive?"

She picked up the can and read the side.

"Aw shucks. These aren't real. They're made of soy. It says 'Soydeens—the taste of the sea, cruelty free.' Oh Dinglebat, I'm sorry buddy. You picked up the wrong ones." She shook her head. "That's what you get for stuffing sardines in my bag. Not to mention your own silly self."

She sniffed at the open can and looked closer. "Yuck. Look, Pak— they even made little spines out of soy. Gross!"

Pak shook his head. "Misuse of a noble bean. Here, I have some food in my own pack." He lifted a satchel and handed it to Penny.

She opened it and pulled out a few square packages. "Ramen? What is this, college?"

"They are a traditional food of my people," Pak replied. "Long ago, in the Ming Dynasty, Li Ramen invented the first dehydrated–"

"Don't listen to him," Jack said. "Ramen came from Japan."

Pak shrugged. "Stolen from China."

"Do we have any water to boil?" Penny said.

"No," Pak replied. "Adding water dilutes the Ramen's energy. Here," he said, taking a package from Penny and tearing it open. "You simply remove the square of compressed noodles, then open the seasoning packet, like so," he said, ripping open the seasoning packet with his teeth and sprinkling part of it on the compressed block of dry wheat noodles. He rolled up the remaining half of the seasoning packet and put it back in his pack, then took a loud, crunching bite of the ramen noodles.

"Do you use all the seasoning packet?" Penny asked, taking a ramen square of her own and preparing it as Pak had shown them. Jack did the same.

"No," Pak replied. "Some remains behind, like echoes of our provisions, meals tasted and untasted, culinary signposts on the road of life, a dusting of eternity, like stars of flavored salt in the front left pocket of one's khakis."

"Wow, that's beautiful," Penny said.

"Also, you can suck on the packets later," Jack said around a mouthful of crunchy noodles. "When you crave more MSG."

Pak shook his head sadly as he chewed the final bite of his meal. "I will not grace this nonsense with a response. I am going to sleep."

"Now?" Jack said. "It's what—8:30 or something?"

"I have been awake continuously for 27.5 hours," Pak replied, unrolling a sleeping bag. "Please watch for arsonists. I would not like to burn to death in my time of slumber."

"How can you sleep when your bed is burning?" Penny said.

"And how can we dance when the earth is turning?" Jack said.

"Gravity," Pak said, shutting his eyes.

Jack could see Penny's outline in the moonlight a few feet away. He gathered up his s'more cooking supplies and set them up a dozen feet from Pak. Penny followed him over after a moment.

"Here," Jack said, handing her his flashlight-enabled cellphone. "Hold the light for me so I can put this together."

"Sure," Penny said. "That looks complicated."

"Not too much," Jack said, running a pair of leads from the truck battery. "Not compared to rigging up my Mustang to burn vegetable oil. You're supposed to do that with diesel engines, not gas engines."

"I had to do some MacGyver style stuff back when I was little," Penny said.

"Yeah?" Jack said, as he lit a portable acetylene torch and started working on the shaping of a crude cavity magnetron from the scavenged rear right hubcap of the Ranger.

"Yes, at the facility where they created us," Penny said. "You see, it wasn't like I had a normal upbringing, with a mom and a dad, in a place where…"

"Hmm," Jack said, wondering if he was going to be able to properly direct the RF emitter or if he'd need to burn one of the truck tires in order to harvest the wires in the sidewall for a crude Faraday cage. No, that would involve lighting a fire, and if he was going to burn a tire, he might as well just cook the s'mores directly.

"…the intensity of the program would have destroyed normal girls, but we weren't normal…"

"Right," Jack said. Maybe aluminum foil would work, he wondered as he created a control circuit from parts of the truck radio. Though would s'mores even be good cooked with radiation? The burned edges were part of the charm.

"…over a thousand clones living their own lives right now. My sisters, my genetic…"

"Sure," Jack mumbled, engaging the device and directing it towards a marshmallow. To his delight, it lit on fire almost immediately.

"So that's the real story," she said with a sigh, then looked at what Jack was doing. "And wow—you made a laser!"

"A laser?" Jack said, hoisting his first finished s'more proudly, then passing it to Penny. "You weren't paying any attention. I made a microwave."

"Same, same," Penny said, taking the s'more and tasting it. "Ew."

"Ew?" Jack asked.

"Yeah. The graham cracker is kind of stale or something. It's like cardboard." She licked her fingers. "I like the chocolate, though. It tastes kinda different."

"What?" Jack said. "I bought a good brand!" He looked at the Graham cracker box, taking back his phone and shining the light at the small print. "No way," he said. "I got the gluten-free ones. Ruined by trendy allergies!"

"Oh well," said Penny. "We can just eat the marshmallows and chocolate."

Jack sighed and looked at his crude and now worthless microwave. "Yeah, I guess so. If I knew the prairie plants better, I'd hunt for a Graham cracker substitute. On the east coast we have *Buccellatum grahamii*, with its wafer-like nutmeats. Out in Oregon there's *Panem meltuberculum*. You have to roast the roots, but they're great. Here, though, I've got nothing. Lost in the woods, so to speak. Or grasslands, as the case may be."

"It's okay," Penny said. "I think it's romantic that you tried to use a laser to cook me a s'more."

"Thanks," Jack said. "I'd better throw these bits and pieces back in the truck so the dew doesn't mess them up."

"Did you break anything reusing the bits like that?"

"Nothing serious," Jack said. "I'll put everything back together tomorrow."

"Great," Penny said.

Jack loaded his microwave into the back seat of the truck, then sat down next to her. She leaned her head onto his shoulder and he slipped his arm around her waist. This could be the moment, he thought. Would it be weird to propose to her in an Oklahoma prairie? What if she said no? Maybe I should sing that "I'm just a girl who can't say no," song to her to kind of prime the pump.

Like when a salesman asks a bunch of questions which all have yes answers, so you're in a yes mood, then he asks "would you like to buy this 3,000 dollar vacuum with a built-in lounge chair on payments with 26.4% annualized interest" and you automatically say "yes," then ruin your entire future. But it wouldn't ruin Penny's future if she said yes. In fact, it would give her the best future possible.

Jack imagined the two of them raising a crop of little Broccolis. Maybe I'll buy a station wagon. A station wagon would be cool. One of those huge ones from the 70s with the fake wood on the sides. I could refurbish the entire thing, he thought. A total restoration, and it would be awesome because everyone usually does that with muscle cars. And then–

"Well," Penny yawned, standing up and patting him on the shoulder. "I'm off to sleep. See you on the flip side."

She walked over to where Pak was and pulled out a sleeping bag, leaving Jack alone with his failed s'mores.

"Should've just asked her," Jack muttered to himself. He looked at the box of pseudo Graham crackers, picked it up and hurled it off into the night. Nature could eat them. If they were even biodegradable.

* * *

The next morning dawned bright and windy. Something was tickling Jack's nose. He swatted at it, eyes shut. It started again almost immediately, causing him to snap awake and try again. It was Penny with a long stalk of *Sorghastrum nutans*. Jack sneezed and snatched it from her.

"Good morning, sleepyhead," Penny said.

Jack checked his phone. It was eight, local time. He grunted. "You make coffee yet?"

"Tea," Penny replied.

"Then I'm going back to bed," Jack replied, rolling over. Then he remembered something he needed to do. What was it? Something important? Propose to Penny? No, that wasn't it. It was something else.

"Jack," Pak said, kicking him gently in the ribs. "What happened to back hubcap?"

"Magnetron," Jack replied, deciding he might as well get up.

"You are claiming a comic book villain stole the hubcap?"

"No," Jack replied. "I'm claiming I turned it into a magnetron. For the microwave. Which I used to make s'mores. Which ended up lousy, even after all that work, because someone decided to take a very important wheat protein out of their popular brand of Graham crackers. You'd know these things if you didn't go to bed so early."

"Early to bed and–"

"Yes, I know," Jack said, getting up and sniffing at the pot of green tea Pak had made over a small alcohol stove. "It's easier with coffee, though." He looked at the little stove. "Hey, wait a minute—I could have just used this thing last night. Didn't know you brought a stove."

"I liked your laser," Penny said.

Jack sighed and looked up at the chalky blue sky above. "I don't see any helicopters or anything."

"If it's going to happen, it will happen today," Pak said. "We must keep our eyes open."

"Good," Jack said, digging into his bag of groceries and taking out a misshapen chocolate bar. "I'll get the truck back in shape." He took a bite of the chocolate and frowned. "What the heck?" He looked at the side and made a rude noise. "Carob and soy!?"

"Hey," Penny said, pointing off into the distance. "Do you see smoke?"

"Where!?" Pak said, dropping the sleeping bag he was rolling.

"Over there," Penny said.

Jack and Pak strained to see—and there it was! A small wisp of smoke rising in the air. As they watched, another plume appeared, this time half-way between them and the smoke Penny had spotted.

"Someone is lighting fires!" Penny said.

"Yeah," Jack replied, pulling the truck's battery from the back seat of the truck. "And they're coming this way."

"Jack," Pak said. "Why did you take the battery out of the truck?"

"S'mores," Jack replied, popping the hood. "Don't worry, we'll be running in no time."

Pak pulled out a pocket camera and took photos of the rising plumes. He zoomed in, sweeping his view back and forth across the strangely empty prairie. "I don't see anyone," he said in frustration.

"Cloaking technology?" Penny said.

"Naw," Jack replied, pulling his ill-fated microwave cannon from the back seat of the truck and carrying it towards the hood. "Bending light is a pain—no one has a good cloak built yet. They're probably staying low." He popped the hood open and set the cannon down.

Something whizzed past Jack's ear as he prepared to pull apart his microwave, startling him into dropping his wrench. It had been something about the size of a hand and similarly quicker than the eye. The mysterious thing zipped back through the campsite again, revealing itself at last. A dragonfly. It stopped and circled around Penny, then settled in a patch of dry grass.

"Thing made me jump," Jack said, looking at the insect, then picking up his wrench from the dirt. "Just a dragonfly."

"Hurry up," Pak said. "I see more smoke rising, this time about a half-mile to the east."

"Jack!" Penny said with a shriek.

Jack banged his head on the hood of the truck, then looked at his girlfriend. "What is it?"

"Fire!" Penny said, pointing to a small patch of burning grass where the dragonfly had landed. "I think it lit the grass on fire!"

Jack walked over and stamped out the grass before the little fire could spread. "That's weird. It just lit on fire where the dragonfly was sitting?"

"Yeah," Penny said. "I wasn't watching, but if I didn't know better, I'd say the dragonfly lit the fire."

Jack looked around, then saw the dragonfly flying in a circle a few dozen feet from them. "Look," he said. "It's landing."

Pak, Penny and Jack watched as the little insect settled on a blade of grass. They stepped closer, then were shocked to see a small tongue of flame emerge from the creature's mouth, jetting right into a clump of dry thatch.

"It's a literal firebug," Jack exclaimed.

"A real dragonfly!" Penny said.

"A hot commodity," Pak yelled.

"That doesn't work," Penny said.

"We need to catch that bug," Jack said, then snapped his fingers and ran back to the truck. He quickly pulled the truck battery back out and hooked it to his portable microwave cannon. He pointed it towards the flame-spitting insect and pulled the trigger. POP! The little creature fell to the ground at the edge of a now spreading patch of burning grass. Pak pulled his t-shirt over his face and scooped up the insect, then tried to kick out the fire. As he did, the wind picked up and the flames jumped another five feet towards the campsite. Pak ran out of its way as the flames licked at his jeans.

"Jack!" he said. "Is the truck running?"

"Not yet," Jack said as he jammed the battery back into its place under the hood. "In a minute."

"We don't have a minute," Penny said. "Look! The flames are coming from over there, too!"

"Meow!" Dinglebat exclaimed, jumping into Penny's arms.

"He can sense danger, Jack," Penny said. "If he thinks it's dangerous, it's definitely dangerous."

"I know it's dangerous," Jack said, reattaching the fan belt to the alternator. "Just a minute!"

Then the wind gusted and the flames spun and danced towards them.

"Jack!" Pak yelled. "We need to run—now!"

"No," Penny said, coughing. "We need to just get in the truck."

They piled in and slammed the doors shut, coughing as the flames raced around the vehicle. The heat grew rapidly and the inside was stifling in moments.

Sweat dripped down their faces. Pak closed his eyes in meditation. The smell of burning rubber and plastic was almost unbearable.

EVERYTHING IS A WEAPON!

"Against fire?" Jack replied.

I'M JUST GETTING HERE, the voice replied. *IT'S A FIRE?*

"Yes!" Jack replied.

"Yes what?" Penny gasped.

"Shh!" Jack said. "It's the Brown Wizard!"

THAT'S NOT ACTUALLY MY NAME.

Jack's head swam as the heat increased and the air thickened. His heart pounded like a tomato stake being driven into hard clay. He struggled to stay conscious.

"We need... help!" Jack said. "We're... going to... die..."

THE CARETAKER MUST NOT BE HARMED!

"Any... ideas... would be good," Jack croaked.

HOLD UP YOUR HANDS AND CALL THE FINNISH WIND IN THE NAME OF AKRAS

"Whaa?" Jack said.

DO WHAT I SAY

"Okay," Jack said, lifting his hands with what was left of his strength. "Acrid wind... I need you to finish this!"

The windshield cracked suddenly and sagged inwards as he said it.

NO THAT IS WRONG. CALL THE WIND FROM FINLAND. YOU MUST SAY THE WORDS OR I CANNOT HELP.

"Wind... from... Finland?" Jack said weakly. He looked over at Penny. Her face was pink and her eyes were closed as she panted shallowly.

YES—HANDS UP, CALL THE FINNISH WIND IN THE NAME OF AKRAS

"Finnish wind, come in the name of... Akras!" Jack said, holding up his hands.

The sky darkened suddenly and the fire whipped around violently. Huge gusts rattled the truck, then the windows turned white—then Jack fell into darkness.

He woke up on the ground, shivering under a blanket. He blinked and looked around. The world was black and white with ash, the skies above hazy with smoke. He sniffed the barbecue-scented air.

"You are alive," came Pak's voice. Jack sat up dizzily and saw Pak and Penny huddled together, sharing another blanket.

"I'm passed out for a minute and you snuggle up to Pak?" Jack mumbled at Penny.

She shrugged weakly. "You looked dead."

"What happened?" Jack asked, turning to look at their destroyed vehicle, covered in soot and melting ice.

"A freak wind," Pak said. "It covered the truck in ice and stopped the flames."

"Akras," Jack murmured. "I wonder if that's his name or if it's his boss or something."

"What?" Pak replied.

"Meow," Dinglebat said, emerging from beneath Pak and Penny's blanket.

"It doesn't matter," Jack said. "We're alive. We need to take our firebug and figure out who made it, then track down this felonious fire-starter."

CHAPTER 5

Sunshine grows the bamboo even as it sweats the forehead.

—A State of Bean: Principles of Mung Fu

After a long hike through the smoldering ruins of the prairie, Jack, Penny and Pak finally made it to a road and flagged down a passing 18-wheeler. Penny and Pak sat in the cab but Jack rode in the trailer, surrounded by crates of turnips, redolent with the scent of earth. He was exhausted but a million thoughts raced through his head. What did "Akras" mean? Who had released the robotic dragonflies? Why would anyone remove gluten from Graham crackers?

Jack leaned back into a pile of loose turnips and felt his aches and pains wash away as the energy from the turnips entered his weary form. They were disconnected from the earth now, unable to replenish their vital forces, but they had saved up for the winter and for the next year's seed production so they had plenty to give. Jack felt the benevolence of the turnips and accepted their gift, finally falling into a peaceful sleep. He awakened at a small town truck stop in the middle of nowhere, pulled from his rest by the truck's cessation of motion. He stretched and jumped down from the bed, meeting Penny and Pak as they exited the cab.

"Thanks for the ride," Jack said as the driver joined them.

"You were lucky, boss," the driver said. "Fires are still spreading something fierce. I almost didn't make it through myself, though it had cleared some by the time I picked you up."

"It was a close call," Jack said.

"Yep, heard all about it from your friends. Good luck."

"You too," Jack said, waving goodbye.

"Running Buffalo Truck Stop and Sausage Emporium," Penny read out loud, looking up at the sign over the door. "Sounds nice."

"It is a cage for visitors," Pak said.

"Tourist trap?" Jack offered.

"Oh! Look at that!" Penny said, pointing to one side of the building where a giant pink prairie dog lay on top of a crushed station wagon, grinning a bucktoothed grin while holding a string of sausages. "You never sausage a place!" she read, looking at the big plywood word bubble next to the massive rodent's mouth. "That's so cute! Take my picture!"

"She is falling into the cage," Pak warned. "Better get her inside."

"Come on, Penny," Jack said, pulling on her arm. "There are other giant groundhogs in the sea."

"No there aren't!" Penny said as he pulled her indoors. "Look at all those sausages!" she gasped as they entered. Strings and strings of sausages hung from the ceiling like an infestation of *Cassytha filiformis*. "I have to buy some to take home."

"Okay," Jack said. "Sausages are good."

"And look at the Indian feather circle things!" Penny exclaimed.

"Nighttime vision procurers," Pak explained.

"Wow—that looks so real!" Penny said, looking at a huge photorealistic painting of an endless field of grass.

"That's the back window," Jack said.

"Amazing," Penny said. "I love this place."

"Let's eat some food at their diner," Pak said. "I am hungry. Then we can get a taxi to somewhere and rent a car."

"I want to ride in one of those," Penny said, pointing to a small replica of a covered wagon.

"You can't fit inside," Pak said.

"Okay, enough," Jack said. "Let's just eat lunch. Penny, you can wander around all you like, but I'm with Pak. I'm starving."

"Me too," Penny said. "I suddenly want sausages. Jack—do you think they're made of real buffalo?"

"Groundhog," he replied. "You saw the statue."

"Oh."

They picked a small table and sat down to discuss their plans in between sampling spicy sausage, sweet sausage, butter sausage, prairie delight sausage, old time sausage, and a variety of other sausages. Jack was quite hungry, but after his eighth sausage he realized his gallbladder was not optimized for this level of processed meat consumption.

"...I will take the dragonfly to our people," Pak continued as Jack pushed his plate away and decided to order a dish of lemon wedges to cut the grease in his gut. That would help.

"I'll be back in a bit," Penny said, taking her purse. Dinglebat stuck his head out and snagged one of Jack's sausages as she stood. "I wanna go look at the authentic arrowhead display."

When she was gone, Jack leaned closer to Pak.

"What's going on here, man?"

Pak sipped his water and remained silent.

"Come on, Pak," Jack said. "Spill what you know. Who would be lighting fires on purpose—with robots?"

Pak looked around, then leaned in. "It's dangerous to talk about it."

"How will they find out? We're in a noisy tourist trap."

Pak mimed holding a phone to his ear, then pointed to Jack, making a "gimme" gesture.

Jack nodded and pulled his phone from his front pocket and handed it to Pak. Pak took it and his phone, then pulled some aluminum foil from his pack, turned off both phones, wrapped them in it, then stuck them both in the bag.

"There is plenty going on," Pak said. "We have our suspicions and are pursuing one front at a time. I only pulled you in on the arson because you had figured something out already. They did not wish to activate you unless they had to."

"Why not?" Jack said. "After giant mushrooms and the invasive seed attack, you'd think I'd be on speed-dial."

"You are at the top of the list, Jack," Pak said, helping himself to a Swiss-Cheese-stuffed sausage. "The top bronze know your passion, your talent. They knew of your father. But there is something holding them back."

"They didn't like me spending so much time in and out of the hospital?"

"No," Pak shook his head. "They are somewhat afraid of you."

"I admit that my brilliance scares me now and again," Jack replied, "but wouldn't they want someone brilliant?" He took a sip of his water, glanced around the room, then back at Pak. "Wait. Is it my powers?"

Pak nodded, then reached into his pocket and removed a small metallic cylinder. "Do you mind?" he said.

"Mind what?" Jack said.

"Just lean closer."

Jack did, then Pak moved the metal device around Jack's torso and head, muttering to himself. A dim light came from the device. Pak looked at the small cylinder and shook his head. "It is as I feared."

"What?" Jack said. "What did you fear?"

"Your chlorophyll count is off the scale," Pak said.

"Lemme see," Jack said, snatching the cylinder from him. He looked at it, realizing it was a cheap LED flashlight. "Dang it, Pak! This is a flashlight."

"Chlorophyll responds to light."

"Enough of this nonsense," Jack said. "I am all in. I don't want anyone holding me back. I'm ready to rock—you tell them that. And so far, the voice in my head has been useful."

"Your incantation was good timing," Pak admitted.

"Incantation sounds scary," Jack says.

"You called on a deity of some sort," Pak said. "And it answered. This is somewhat concerning, though it has been benevolent so far. It is an unpredictable element."

"Yeah, it is," Jack admitted.

"No," Pak said. "I misspeak. It was not entirely unpredictable."

" 'Not entirely?' " Jack frowned. "I swear, if you say something about an ancient prophecy, I'm going to beat you with a string of sausages."

Pak sat silently, looking across the table at him.

Jack stared at him, but Pak said nothing. "Come on, Pak! Tell me the whole truth."

"You will hit me with meat products," Pak said.

"What?" Jack exclaimed. "There is seriously an ancient prophecy?" Pak nodded slightly.

"And they're afraid I'm some sort of important figure?" Jack pressed. "Dangerous, somehow?"

Pak nodded again.

"You're killing me, Pak," Jack said. "I don't believe it."

Pak shrugged. "Our taxi should be here soon."

"Don't change the subject," Jack said. "You're supposed to give me reasons to believe it."

"Will you promise not to hit me with string of meat?"

"Sure," Jack said. "If you promise you're telling the truth." His gut flipped inside him as if a sausage was punching his liver, but he suppressed the feeling. He looked for their waitress so he could get some lemon wedges but she was missing in action.

"I always tell the truth," Pak said, taking back his flashlight. "They are concerned about your strange abilities, though I don't believe the prophecy fits you."

"You don't?" Jack said.

"No," Pak replied. "But I do think you are special in your own way."

"Thanks, Mr. Rogers," Jack said.

Pak shrugged. "Even Mr. Rogers could have fulfilled the prophecy. That is the problem with many of these archaic writings. Many outcomes and many individuals could be made to fit."

"The land of make believe," Jack said. His stomach jumped again. Now the sausages were having a cage match.

"Perhaps," Pak said. "I told them that your particular situation matches nothing in our history. It is as if some warrior spirit has taken you as his own and granted you his energy in a very non-Chinese way."

"Because Chinese people don't sound like professional wrestlers."

"Correct," Pak said. "And your description of this entity from the vision you had does not fit any sinomythological pattern."

"Waitress!" Jack said, spotting her at last. "Would you get me some lemon wedges?"

"You bet your britches, honey," she replied with a wink, then disappeared into the kitchen. She returned a moment later with two bowls of sliced lemons and a fudge sundae. "Here you go, sugarplum," she said, putting them in front of Jack. Jack looked up and realized the waitress had changed outfits, done her hair and put on makeup—and perfumed herself with *Jasminum officinale*, though it might also have been *Jasminum humile*. She sat down next to Jack. "I got you a sundae."

Pak raised an eyebrow at Jack, who shrugged back at him. "Thanks," Jack said to the waitress as he took a slice of lemon. She wasn't getting up.

"Did you know I am almost certainly the culmination of an ancient prophecy?" Jack said as she smiled at him.

Pak cleared his throat but Jack ignored him.

"I knew it as soon as I saw you," the girl said with a sigh.

"Yep," Jack said, wondering how weird he could get before she left. "I also have a pro wrestler living in my brain."

"That's so fascinating," the waitress said adoringly, curling a lock of hair around her index finger.

"He's Finnish," Jack continued. "Likes to yell at me. Gave me the power to whip a cop with his own pants." He popped a second lemon wedge into his mouth and chewed it up. It felt like the sausage coliseum in his stomach was starting to clear.

"Wow," the girl sighed. She was sitting very close.

"I also threw a love seat leg through a man's chest. Knocked him right out a second story window."

"A loooove seat," the girl purred.

"Hey!" Penny said, showing up at the table with two bags full of goods. "What's going on?"

"The waitress brought Jack some lemons," Pak said. "Then sat next to him."

"And I got you a sundae," Jack added.

The waitress's mouth opened and shut in surprise and she stood, eyes suddenly brimming with tears. She looked at Jack reproachfully, then dashed back to the kitchen without a word.

"Hmph," Penny said, sitting next to Jack.

Jack looked in the top of one of her bags. "Is that a dead possum?"

"It's a coonskin cap," Penny said.

"Taxi?" said a man, walking up to their table.

"Yes," Pak said. "We are ready to go."

Jack chewed up a few lemon wedges and washed them down with ice water, then tossed a ten on the table for the waitress.

Though she later married a successful accountant and raised four children, she kept the crumpled bill for the rest of her life.

CHAPTER 6

The sprouting bean may become a warrior, yet never trust fortune to have the best in mind for the sprouting bean. It is blind like the worm.

—*A State of Bean: Principles of Mung Fu*

Before saying goodbye to Penny and Pak at the airport, Jack took multiple pictures of the fire-breathing dragonfly drone. Pak was headed to China to meet with the Secret Chinese Organization while he was stuck heading back to his barely affordable mortgage and a landscape nursery job. Pak assured him that he would consult with his superiors and get back to Jack, but that wasn't enough. Even without Pak, Jack was determined to chase this mystery. But right now, he felt uncharacteristically down.

Count your blessings, Jack, he told himself as he sat in his seat looking down the wing of the aircraft at fluffy cumulus clouds. *Name them one by one.*

One, I'm thankful for my gardens.

Two, for my sweet ride and free vegetable oil to run it on.

Three, I'm thankful for Penny. And good soil. And always having enough to eat. His stomach grumbled and he suddenly had a burning craving for *Ocean Octaves!*. It was so strong he almost doubled over, then got himself under control. Wow—how long had it been since his last bag? The craving was intense.

It was hard to be thankful without *Ocean Octaves!*. And when you didn't have enough money to—wait a minute, Pak had said they were giving him some cash.

Okay, good, Jack told himself. I can be thankful with no hangups. Except for the *Ocean Octaves!*.

He looked down out of the plane window, wondering how many bags of *Ocean Octaves!* they might be flying over at the moment. It wasn't the most common snack, but they had certainly flown over at at least a dozen bags so far. Maybe even hundreds if they went over a few organic groceries.

Don't think about it, Jack, he told himself. You can get some when you get home. It's only a few hours.

But right down below there could be someone opening a bag right now.

Wait—maybe the flight attendants had a bag? Would they? The chances were really low. Most people hadn't heard of *Ocean Octaves!*, let alone thought to offer them on domestic flights. No, they wouldn't have them. Still...

Jack's finger stabbed the button to call a flight attendant before he thought any further. He had to know for sure.

"Yes?" said the middle-aged flight attendant once she reached his row. "Oh, it's you," she said, looking closer and batting her eyelashes. "How are you, darling?"

"Hungry," Jack said. "For something quite specific."

"Oh really?" she said, leaning in.

"*Ocean Octaves!*," he said.

"What?" she said, pursing her lips. "Never heard of them."

"Never mind," Jack said. "I thought that might be the case."

She made a sad face and patted him on the shoulder. "I'm sorry, darling—but if there's anything else I can do for you, please let me know. I'm just a pushbutton away."

As she left she put significantly more swing into her hips than could properly be explained by turbulence. Jack was used to this sort of behavior from the fairer sex.

I wonder who would have the tech to create a tiny dragonfly capable of lighting fires? Jack wondered, sinking back in his seat and trying to push *Ocean Octaves!* out of his head. Maybe a government, or a big corporation.

Wait a minute—Septic Man said something about a guy that made robots. Maybe he might have a lead? Maybe I can check with him after searching online. If I can't flush something out, I'll call a plumber.

When Jack got home, he checked his gardens. He noted with satisfaction that his turnips had sprouted. After a few minutes of watering and weeding, he went inside and logged on to his laptop in search of fire-breathing dragonfly drones. An image search revealed lots of cartoon dragons, dragonflies and a few drones, some of which appeared to shoot fire—but no fire-breathing dragonfly drone. He also got pictures of glowing pantyhose eggs. He switched to a text search and got more of the same. No dice. Time to call Septic Man and see if he could get in touch with that robotics expert.

He dialed the number for AAAA1234 Aquatic Septic and Plumbing, LLC. Paul picked up on the second ring.

"Yello, this is Paul."

"Paul, it's Broccoli. Jack Broccoli."

"Jack!" Paul said. "How's your gardens?"

"Fine," Jack replied. "And it should be 'how are,' but that's not important right now. Remember your friend—the guy you said should be recognized for his robotics work?"

"Oh yeah," Paul said. "Jonny."

"Can you put me in touch with him?"

"Well," Paul said, sounding hesitant. "You know, we aren't so friendly anymore."

"I can call him if you give me his number," Jack said. "What's his full name?"

"Jonny Layton," Paul said. "But I should probably help you get in touch."

"You said you weren't friendly with him," Jack said, walking to the kitchen and looking in the cabinets in case he forgot some *Ocean Octaves!* somewhere.

"Right," Paul said. "But he's less friendly with other folks. He's a brilliant guy, you know, and you know how the world rejects the geniuses."

"I wouldn't know," Jack said, standing on his tip-toes to see if there might be a forgotten bag on the high shelf in the pantry. "But I need to talk with him right away."

"You gonna make one of those robot garden things that does the planting, watering and weeding and all that?" Paul said.

"No. Robot farming doesn't connect you to the plants. It's unnatural. But I need to talk to him about something similar."

"I'll take you tomorrow—three o'clock. I can pick you up and we'll go to his vineyard," Paul said.

"Vineyard?" Jack said. "That's cool, but why we can't just call him?"

"No phone," Paul said. "He's been burned too many times."

"By the phone company?" Jack asked, giving up on his search for lost seaweed crisps.

The sound of gurgling water came from the other end of the line. "Whoop," Paul broke in. "I gotta go."

"No problem," Jack said, scooping up his keys. "See you tomorrow."

He hung up and headed out the door for the organic market. The ocean was calling.

* * *

Paul arrived ten minutes early and handed Jack a bag of tomatoes, peppers and apples as he walked around to the backyard to look at the gardens. Jack set it gingerly on the porch with what he hoped was a believable 'thanks.'

"Homegrown!" Paul said. "All natural. And hey, I see you got some radishes comin' up here!"

"Close," Jack said. "They're turnips."

"Those never show up in my gardens," Paul said.

"No, I'd imagine not," Jack replied.

"Alright, let's go," Paul said after another moment of looking at the garden. He spun on his heels and headed to the truck.

"Just a minute," Jack said. "Let me put the produce inside and grab my stuff."

He went inside, then came back with a pen and notebook, a bag of *Ocean Octaves!*, and a packet of yeast.

"Yeast?" Paul said, looking at the packet as he started the truck.

"You never know," Jack said.

"That's true," Paul said. "But there should be plenty of yeast where we're going. Jonny makes wine, you know."

"Right, you said something about vineyards," Jack replied, ripping open his bag of *Ocean Octaves!*. "Should have remembered."

"He's been working on them for a long time," Paul said. "But nothin' is selling. His labor is cheap, though."

"Is he hiring under the table?" Jack asked.

"You'll see."

Fifty minutes later, or about 18.51 1960s country tunes later, they arrived at a tall razorwire fence surrounding rows of grapevines. The gate was flanked by a half-dozen threatening signs.

BEWARE OF DOG

HIGH VOLTAGE

MAMMALS NOT WELCOME

PREMISES UNDER SURVEILLANCE

NO SOLICITORS

TRESPASSERS WILL BE ELECTROCUTED AND MANGLED

To the left of the gate a battered plywood sign featured a faded silhouette of a robot hoisting a wineglass. Beneath the image, it read "Welcome to AutoWine Vineyards."

"Lots of warnings," Jack said.

"He's not a people person," Paul shrugged.

"How do we get in?"

"There's a little talkbox thing by the gate," Paul replied. "I'll call him." He put the truck in park and stepped out, walking slowly to the gate. "You don't wanna go too fast," Paul yelled back to Jack. "It looks like a threat."

"I don't see anyone." Jack said.

"You won't," Paul said. "Until they electrocute and mangle you. Shh. I'm calling him!"

He pushed the button and spoke into the box. Jack couldn't hear what he said, but the conversation was quite animated. After a minute or so of back and forth, the gate clicked, then opened by itself.

Paul walked very slowly back to the truck with his arms at his sides, then stepped in carefully.

"Why did you walk like that?" Jack asked as Paul started the truck and drove slowly through the open gate. The truck was lit with blue light for a moment and Jack smelled ozone as they drove through.

"Electrocuting and mangling," Paul explained unhelpfully.

Jack looked in the rear-view and saw the gate close behind them. This felt like a very bad idea. His heart thumped as the gate clanged closed and there was a crackle of electrical discharge.

YOU RANG? came a voice in his head.

"No," Jack replied.

"What?" Paul said.

"Not you," Jack explained. "Talking to the voice in my head."

"Gotcha," Paul said.

WHY IS THE DRUG IN YOUR VEINS?

"We're driving through a crazy guy's vineyard," Jack replied quietly. "My friend here is giving me vague warnings about being electrocuted and all that. It's probably adrenaline. You see any danger?"

THERE IS NOTHING I CAN SEE.

"Nothing?" Jack asked.

"There's danger all right," Paul said. "They're watching us."

"Who?" Jack said.

"The dogs," Paul said, as if Jack should know.

"Brown Wizard—you see any dogs?" Jack asked.

THERE ARE NO DOGS—AND THAT ISN'T MY NAME.

"What is it?" Jack said.

AKRAS.

"Akras," Jack said. "You brought the wind."

YOU ARE SLOW.

"I guess," Jack said. "Are you sure there are no dogs? My friend says there are dogs."

THERE CANNOT BE DOGS—DOGS ARE PART OF EVERY-THING.

"Good," Jack said, relaxing a little. "Thanks."

The grape vines came to an end in front of a large metal building and a small cabin. Paul stopped the truck and Jack grabbed the handle to get out.

"Wait!" Paul yelled, and Jack froze.

"What is wrong with you?" Jack said. "The voice in my head said that there were no–"

And then he stopped, as a half-dozen silver-grey metal hounds with glowing eyes shimmered into view in front of them. They walked slowly towards the truck with a strangely fluid motion. One moment there had been nothing but the two buildings—and the next, terrifying robot dogs.

"How did they do that?" Jack asked.

"Cloaking devices," Paul replied. "We gotta wait for Jonny to call 'em off. We'll stay in the truck, okay?"

Staying in the truck seemed like a really good idea. They sat and waited, watching the robot hounds walk around the truck. Every few moments, one of them would stop, emit an 8-bit howling noise, then its body would light up with a crackle of electricity before returning to its pacing.

"Mangled and electrocuted," Jack said. The sign now made sense.

"Down, boys," came a gruff voice from the porch of the cabin. Jack looked to see a man in black with a bristling brown and gray beard and thick glasses. He stepped off the porch and walked towards them with a scowl.

The dogs backed away from the truck, then shimmered away into invisibility.

"Whoa," Jack said.

"Nope," Paul replied. "Down boy! is what you say to a dog. You say 'whoa' to a horse."

"Get out of that hunk of junk," the man growled to Jack and Paul. "Come on, they won't kill you now."

Jack took a deep breath and opened his door. Paul did the same. They walked towards the man in black. Jack shivered involuntarily, imagining an invisible robot dog biting into the back of his neck.

"Paul," Jonny said, frowning at the plumber. "You have some guts to come back here."

"I know," said Paul, extending his hand to shake. He grinned a gap-toothed smile. "I missed you."

"Sure you did," Jonny said, his voice gruff. After a moment, he took Paul's extended hand with a sigh. "You don't know when you aren't wanted, do you?"

"Naw," Paul said. "Friends are friends."

"You're too good for this world," Jonny said, shaking his head.

He turned his attention to Jack. "You CIA?"

"No," Jack replied. "Though if I were, I would also say no."

Jonny smiled slightly. "You aren't as dumb as you look."

Jack shrugged.

"You know, I'm still not happy with Paul here," Jonny said. "I almost didn't let you boys in. Dunno why I did."

"Aw, Jonny—you don't mean it," Paul said with a big grin, patting the man on the shoulder.

"You made me look like a fool," Jonny said. "You misused my technology and ran it into the governor's motorcade."

"It worked great, though," Paul said. "I trusted it, then kind of fell asleep."

"I told you it still had bugs," Jonny replied. "You put it on the road before I was done."

"Aw, I just had faith in you," Paul said. "I figured bugs for you would be nothing. You know, little things. Besides, the governor was no good anyhow."

Jonny nodded. "Yes, but it got around that it was my truck. And with the situation I'm in from back in the old days, that sort of thing is very, very suspicious. I was already on the outs—and you turned me into a pariah."

"I don't know what that is," Paul said. "You're great, man."

"I was once," Jonny said. He looked off into the distance, then shook his head. "So, Paul—your friend here a wine critic or something?"

"No," Jack answered. "A gardener. I am impressed with the vineyard."

"Put a lot of work into it," Jonny said. "Not like it's worth much now."

"It's always worth planting fruit," Jack said.

"Planting, sure. Growing, yeah. It's the marketing that kills."

"People don't like the logo?" Jack said.

"For starters," Jonny said. "You saw the one on the gate? It isn't working."

"I like it," Paul said. "What do you mean it isn't working?"

"No one buys the wine," Jonny said. "I got it into multiple outlets, then almost no sales."

"Because of your logo?" Jack asked.

"Because people are idiots," Jonny said, spitting on the ground. "They say the name reminds them of cars, and the robot with the glass..."

"What about the robot with the glass?" Jack asked.

"They think he's drinking oil!" Jonny said. "Who would think that? Can you imagine?"

"No," Jack said, even though he could. "That's terrible."

"Terrible?" Jonny said. "Of course it's terrible. I tried to get away from my past, from that awful man with his ugly sweaters and his ugly accent. And I completely automated the creation of wine. I could take you in that building over there and show you the vats and the robots and even the AI that keeps everything running smoothly. I named him Edgar Vintner. Brilliant. He's not doing much now, though. Can't get sales worth keeping him online. Do people appreciate all of that? Do they? No. They say it looked like I was selling motor oil. Robots don't drink oil."

"Yeah," Jack said. "I'm no expert, but I don't think they have to drink at all, right?"

"Darn right," Jonny said. "What's your name again?"

"Broccoli," Jack replied. "Jack Broccoli."

"And you're a gardener?"

"Right, but that's not why I came," Jack said. "Right now I'm interested in something else. Can I show you a photo?"

"You're not gonna show me your kids or a blue watermelon or anything sappy like that?" Jonny said.

"No," Jack said, pulling up a picture of the dragonfly drone on his phone. "Not sappy. Look at this."

Jonny squinted through his thick glasses, then gasped. The color drained from his face. "Where did you find this thing? Do you have it?"

"No," Jack said. "A friend has it. We found it on a camping trip and I took a photo. It spit fire and almost killed us by igniting the grass. I tried hunting it down online, but—"

"You searched for this thing online?" Jonny said, eyes widening.

"Sure," Jack said. "That's the world's library."

"It's not a secure library," Jonny replied, shaking his head. "You put yourself at risk. If he finds out..."

"Who?" Jack asked.

"His ex-boss," Paul chimed in. "He's a big, powerful robot guy."

"He's a robot?" Jack asked.

"Of course not," Jonny said. "He's in robotics. He owns robotics. And his people are the only ones that could have made this thing," he said, looking again at the image on Jack's phone.

"Do you have a lead where we can find these people?" Jack asked. "They're lighting fires everywhere. Did you know that?"

Jonny's shoulders slumped. "Of course I know. You see this?" he said, waving his arm around. "All this. This is my prison. I don't even have a phone now, as I'm sure Paul told you. So long as I don't mess with him, he leaves me alone. This is my island of Elba. My Patmos. My Siberia. My Sado island. My midnight 7/11 with a burned out alternator off I-95. But I'm SICK OF YOU!" he shouted at the sky, shaking his fist. "YOU TOOK MY LIFE'S WORK!"

"We need to know who made these things," Jack pressed. "It will save lives."

"Not unless you work for God himself. You can't save anything. It's too big."

"I have to try," Jack said.

Jonny shut his eyes and took a deep breath. He clenched and unclenched his fists, then abruptly turned around and walked into his house, slamming the door behind him.

They watched him go, and Paul shrugged. Jack looked away from the door and over the rows of vines, wondering if Jonny was going to come back with a 12-gauge. As he surveyed the vineyard, there was a buzzing sound from between the rows. Jack's heart thumped—then he saw the source of the noise. It was a drone, spraying something on the grape leaves. It went around the end of the row and continued away from them down the next. Jack took a deep breath and let it out.

"Something else, eh?" Paul said, pointing towards the retreating drone. "Man is a genius."

The door creaked open on the porch and Jonny walked back towards them, obviously agitated. He held out his hand to Jack. "Here, hang on to this. For luck."

He dropped a small token into Jack's hand. On one side was the image of a robot pouring wine, on the other, the head of a handsome dog.

"One for you too, Paul," he said, and pressed one into Paul's hand. "Just something to remember me by."

"You aren't going anywhere," Paul said.

"They're gonna kill me eventually," Jonny said. "And if I tell you what you want to know, they'll kill you too."

"We need to know," Jack said.

"And I'm tired of keeping it to myself. But I mean it—you will end up dead. I have to warn you about that."

"Then so be it," Jack said. "There are other lives than my own."

"I wish I had your guts when I was young," Jonny said, looking off into the distance. "They have a huge plan," he said quietly. "The robots are part of it, but it's bigger than that. They have their fingers in research around the globe. Climate change research you would not believe."

"What's wrong with researching climate change?" Paul said.

"They're not researching why it's changing," Jonny spat. "They're researching how to change it. And they've got multiple fronts. When it goes down, I won't be safe here. No one will be safe anywhere, unless you're with them. Getting inside to see what they're doing is almost impossible. This one place, they've got—out in the desert—back when they were planning that thing, I was still on the team. It's an abomination. If you saw it, you would fall on your knees in terror. I don't know if they ever built it, this doomsday thing, but if they ever launch them..."

"So the fires aren't the only thing?" Jack asked.

"Of course not," Jonny said. "They're masters of chaos. But if you destroyed that thing—or better, destroy the madmen at the top. But no, it's impossible..."

"Where do we go?" Jack pressed.

Jonny shook his head. "It's your head," he said. "The main facility is in—no—look!"

"Nolook?" Jack said. "Is that in Canada?"

"No—look over there!" Jonny said, pointing over the vines. A cloud of black was approaching. "NO!" he yelled. "How did they get through the field? Defend! Defend!"

At the command, his dogs reappeared, encircling the three men and facing towards the incoming cloud. The cloud's movement reminded Jack of a swarm of bees—but the movement was more fluttery, some-how. The black cloud came closer and the dogs lit up with crackles of electricity, howling and snatching at the cloud. Then Jack could see the little pieces of it, like dancing pixels. It appeared to be a large swarm of insects.

"They're some sort of bugs!" Paul said as it moved closer. Jack could hear them—like the sound of crumpling paper.

EVERYTHING IS A WEAPON! came the voice of Akras.

"Can you see the swarm?" Jack asked.

I SEE YOU AND TWO MEN. AND SOME GRAPE VINES.

"They aren't part of everything," Jack said. "Non-organic! If they're not organic, they're not everything!"

"Of course they aren't organic," Jonny yelled. "Get in your truck. You and Paul get out of there—they're after me!"

The swarm reached the dogs and they snapped and jumped at the swirling cloud but it flew upwards and evaded them easily, finally hovering about ten feet over Layton's head.

"Come on!" Jack yelled to the man. "You come with us!"

"I can't," Layton replied, staring upwards at the swirl of what appeared to be tiny moths as if mesmerized. "I can't leave."

"Come on, Jack," Paul urged, pulling on Jack's arm. "We gotta go."

"At least tell me where the location is—you were about to say!" Jack said to Layton.

"The location!" Layton said. "That's why they're here! They heard us! They'll kill you too!"

The buzz of the swarm intensified, like the sound of amaranth greens hitting a pan of hot oil. It swirled faster above their heads.

"Come on!" Paul said, dragging Jack away through the circle of dogs and towards the truck. He was surprisingly strong.

"Layton—where is it! Where are they making these things? And who is making them?" Jack yelled back at the roboticist.

"Giles Batson! And he's making them in AAAAAAAAAAAR-RRRRRRRRRRRRRRRRRRRGGGGGGGGGGGGGGGGGHHHH-HHHHHHHHgarglebarglegargleGARGLE!!"

Layton screamed as a cone of tiny creatures dove down from the swarm and flew directly down his throat, choking off his words.

Two more cones appeared, pointing towards Paul and Jack.

"Get in the truck!" Paul yelled at Jack.

Jack jumped in, glancing back at Layton's fallen form. It felt wrong to run—but he had to admit, the man looked as dead as a malnourished Blue Hubbard vine with a *Melitta curcurbitae* infestation.

They slammed the doors shut and Paul started the truck—just as the forked swarm started their way.

"Windows up!" Jack yelled, cranking up the passenger side window as Paul did the same on the driver's side, while simultaneously backing up.

The tiny creatures in the swarm pipped against the sides of the truck and covered the windshield. Jack could see the individual creatures now.

"Some kind of moth!" Paul said.

"They look just like *Paralobesia viteana*," Jack said in wonder. "But those don't normally dive down people's throats."

"Evil robot versions of things do," Paul said, jerking the truck around and speeding back towards the gate. It was hard to see because of the sheer quantity of tiny moths on the windshield, but they made it. Paul gunned his truck right through the gate, scattering warning signs in his wake. As they broke through the property's perimeter and encountered the same blue flash they had on the way in, the moths suddenly quit moving and fell from the truck.

"They died!" Paul said.

"Looks like it," Jack agreed, then noticing multiple dead robot moths just inside the AC vent. It was pointed towards his face. "Good timing, too," he added. "They were about to come through and get us."

"Man oh man," Paul said. "That was awful. We were lucky bunnies, I'll tell you what. But they killed him! They killed Jonny!"

"Yeah," Jack said. "They must have gotten the moths in somehow, past his forcefield. It must be some kind of EMF shield or something. We need to call the police."

"Don't do it from your phone," Paul said. "They'll track you and think we did it or something. Or maybe Giles will come get us. Or send more evil robot insects!"

"Good point," Jack said.

"We could use a payphone," Paul said.

"Are there even payphones any more?" Jack asked.

"I dunno," Paul admitted.

"Maybe we could just kind of borrow someone's phone."

"I guess that's a good idea," Paul said. "But then the police might get on their cases, right?"

"We'll borrow a phone from someone who looks suspicious," Jack said. "Then maybe the police will nail them for something at the same time they go and investigate Jonny's place."

"How do you know if someone looks suspicious?" Jonny asked.

"Physiognomy," Jack said. "They did studies on it. You can tell if someone is a thief or a liar or a used car salesman, just by looking at their face. People are better at judging than a computer. Just by looking at a face."

"I guess that makes sense," Paul said. "I once saw this guy wearing a clown mask and carrying a knife—knew right away he was up to something, even before he slashed up the inflatable pool display at Walmart."

"I don't think that counts as physiognomy," Jack said. "Though if we found someone like that, we could totally borrow his cellphone."

"If he were a hardened criminal, he would tell us to shove off if we asked to borrow his phone. We'd have to tie him up."

"True," Jack said. "We might have to. Just pull into the next town and we'll wing it. We'll see if we can borrow a cell phone and make a report. We can look for a payphone first, then just borrow a phone if that doesn't pan out."

"I don't want to get in big trouble," Paul said, starting to look nervous about the plan.

Jack nodded. "I used to be like you, before I became a super secret spy. Now, my name is trouble."

"On your mom's side?" Paul asked.

"No, I was speaking dramatically," Jack said.

"Oh, okay," Paul said. He thought for a moment, then nodded to himself. "You're right. Trouble is okay. Trouble is what it takes to do the right thing, sometimes. I can play the spy game too." He started to get more enthusiastic as he drove, speeding up perceptibly. He shook his head with more vigor. "Yeah! Yeah, that's right. They killed my friend. Killer bugs, man. It's like a movie, but it's real. And you're in the middle of it, too. No one is gonna stop us, Jack! We're going to make sure we get justice. We'll fight back, even if it puts us in danger." He thumped Jack in the shoulder with his fist. "We'll get a phone, man. We'll make the call. I'll be your sidekick."

"Thank you," Jack said, touched. "Just don't drive too fast. That's another way to get in trouble."

"Right!" Paul said, stamping the brake and causing the truck to rattle and lurch as it slowed. "Of course. Still working on the spy thing."

"Hey, looks like a good bet here," Jack said as they approached a gas station. "Let's stop. I'll do the call—you can stay in the truck and keep the engine running."

As they rolled up, there was no evidence of a pay phone. The place was a combination taco restaurant and service station, with bright beer signs in the windows. In the absence of a payphone, Jack decided on plan B. He got out of the truck, eyeing the parking lot for anyone suspicious.

Two girls walked past in tight tops. Both looked Jack up and down as they passed, then one whispered into the other's ear as they entered the shop. They giggled and one of them winked at him.

Not suspicious.

An older trucker with a gut and an eye patch limped past him, giving Jack a nod before spitting tobacco juice into the drain.

Not suspicious.

A trio of tattooed El Salvadorians dragged a decapitated boar through a side door into the restaurant.

Not suspicious. This wasn't working out well.

Then Jack found a target. A lean man with a mustache in a sweatshirt and jeans was stepping out of his parked Camaro. He was headed to the front door.

He nodded slightly to Jack, who quickly intercepted him.

"Excuse me, sir," Jack said, noting how the man looked suspiciously normal. "May I borrow your cell phone?"

The man frowned. "You don't look particularly underprivileged. Where's your phone?"

Jack shook his head. "It's not with me." This was technically true, because it was in the truck. He glanced over involuntarily and saw Paul give him a thumbs up. The mustachioed man followed his glance and frowned at the ugly truck. "Friend of yours?"

"Yeah," Jack said. "Listen—I need to call the police."

"Really?" The man said. "Looks like you're in luck." He reached into his pocket and pulled out his wallet, flashing his police ID. "Off-duty."

No wonder he looked suspicious, Jack thought. *What bad luck!*

"Ah," Jack said, thinking fast. "Did you see that show where that guy accidentally called the police?"

"No," the policeman responded, hand going to a bulge at his waist. "Why do you need to call the police?

EVERYTHING IS A WEAPON! came the voice in Jack's head.

"Not now, Akras!" Jack said under his breath.

"Did you just call an officer a bad word?" the cop said, eyes narrowing. "You got a little problem with authority, bud?"

"Sorry," Jack said, suddenly deciding to simply tell the entire truth. "I respect the law and your authority. I wanted to call the police on someone else's phone because I didn't want the bad guys to track me down. There's been a terrible accident and I think the guys that did it can tap our phones."

The cop frowned. "Are you off your meds?"

"No," Jack said. "I'm not on any meds. I'm telling you the truth. There's an old guy that runs a robot vineyard. We were visiting and a bunch of bugs jumped down his throat and killed him, so we came to get help."

The cop shook his head. "Well, alright then. I think we need to go in to the station for a little talk. Now, you can go easy or you can go—"

The cop fell to the ground hard, his legs inexplicably wrapped up in a piece of flexible tubing.

"Get in the truck!" Paul yelled, as he quickly rolled up the struggling officer in a blue tarp.

"Holy cow," Jack said, jumping in. "I'm not sure that was the best..."

Paul jumped in as the one-eyed trucker yelled at the two of them to stop.

Paul gunned the engine, tearing out of the parking lot and onto the main road.

"Sweet corn, Paul!" Jack said. "They're gonna send every cop in town after us in five minutes!"

"This is bigger than the police," Paul said. The truck careened down the highway, shaking and rattling. There was no sign of pursuit—yet.

"Listen, Jack," Paul said. "He was going to arrest you. And then you'd die, man. Like Jonny! The police are just people—but swarms of robot bugs are swarms of robot bugs!"

He stamped the brake, slowing down.

"Get ready to jump out when I tell you, okay? No one is around us now—we should be able to make a clean break!"

"Jump out?" Jack replied.

"Yeah! Now!" Paul said, taking the truck off the road into the tall grass. Jack threw the door open and sprawled into the weeds. He rolled to his feet and watched Paul accelerate farther on through the grass another hundred yards—directly into a retention pond! Jack watched in horror as the truck disappeared beneath the water.

Then he heard the sound of an approaching siren. He pressed himself flat on his belly in the grass. It neared, then mercifully passed. With any luck, they were headed out of town. The siren was followed by another—and a minute later, yet another. They came from town, then they left. They must have thought the truck was still heading off on down the highway. Paul's plan was insane, but it appeared to have worked. As the sirens faded in the distance, Jack cautiously raised his head. A small flash of blue on his left caught his eye. There was a beautiful *Mertensia virginica* in full bloom. He looked at it for a long moment. The sight gave him hope. Cautiously, he got up and looked across to the lake. A few bubbles marked the spot were the truck had vanished, but there was no sign of Paul. Had that crazy plumber sacrificed himself just to throw off the police? *What an insane waste!* The *Mertensia* nodded with the wind, as if in agreement.

"Jack!" came a voice to his right. He dropped back down into the grass, started—then realized who it was.

"Paul!" he said, getting back up and taking in the sight of his dripping wet partner in crime. "I thought you'd drowned yourself in the lake!"

"Naw," Paul said. "I've been submerged in way worse, believe you me. I had to ditch the truck. Powerful forces are after us and all that. If that cop had got you, the next thing would be some mechanical centipede coming into your holding cell in the night and ZAP—killing you with some gamma rays or something."

Jack remembered the swarm of tiny moths diving down Layton's throat. "Thanks, man. Of course, now we're stuck in the middle of nowhere without a truck, plus–"

Another siren wailed in the distance and they dropped to the ground.

"–I was gonna say the cops are looking for us, but I suppose I don't need to say it."

Paul shrugged. "Probably not."

The siren whipped past them on the highway, then faded into the distance.

"I still think we should call in Layton's death, but man," Jack said, the reality of the situation hitting him. "If they can make flying insect drones and target a genius, plus make internet searches go awry, they can pretty much do anything."

"Yep," said Paul. "They'll get us. And you ain't gonna bring back Jonny by making a phone call. He's gone."

"Yeah," Jack said, the image of Layton's corpse flashing into his mind. "He sure is."

A sudden ring interrupted his morbid thoughts. "My phone!" Jack said, feeling his pocket and coming up empty.

"Right here," Paul said, handing him his phone. It was in a sandwich bag.

"How did you manage to–"

"Wait," Paul said as Jack prepared to answer. "Remember they're listening!"

"Right," Jack said, swiping to answer. "Penny? Yes. No. Don't worry. I'll be home soon. We can talk then. No—no problems. Just sightseeing."

After a few hours of hiking and not hearing any more sirens, Jack and Paul hitchhiked home with an out of work machinist. He had long hair and repeatedly told them they shouldn't be hitchhiking, then shared what seemed like dozens of stories about hitchhikers who had been killed in awful ways. When he was half-way through a particularly lurid tale about two unwary hitchhikers who had their spleens removed with a plastic fork by an out-of-work machinist, Jack and Paul thanked him for the ride and got out. Paul had just enough cash to take a taxi back to his shop. After he and Jack talked for a bit about the day's madness, Jack borrowed Paul's bike and rode home.

The cool evening air felt good. The bike was an old three-gear Peugeot, well-kept and a good city ride. When Jack got home and checked the mail, he found two seed catalogs and a brown padded envelope with no return address. He opened it to find three hundred-dollar bills inside.

Probably from Pak's people, he thought. Though he thought Pak had said they'd send him a few thousand. He stuffed two of the bills in his pocket, then unlocked his Mustang and stuck the third under the passenger side mat, just in case he got stuck somewhere without cash.

He went inside, grabbed a celery stout, looked unsuccessfully for a bag of *Ocean Octaves!*, then powered up his laptop and did a little research on how to protect his IP address. After a few minutes of reading, he decided that a VPN was a good idea, so he googled "top VPN software," and picked the third one on a list of ten.

Never trust the first couple of options, he thought.

He installed the software after paying a $19.99 license fee, then started browsing for information on Giles Batson, robot moths and radioactive pantyhose eggs.

The latter search took him to a single sentence on an anonymous message board: "the sixth seal will blacken the ice." It was signed "radioactivepantyhoseeggs42."

Jack shook his head and shut his computer down. That made no sense and he needed sleep.

CHAPTER 7

The response of a warrior to his nose must not be influenced by the forgotten dry meat.

—A State of Bean: Principles of Mung Fu

After a good night's sleep, much enhanced by the previous day's hiking, rolling out of cars, watching people get strangled by robot moths and being chased by cops, not to mention an evening bike ride across town, Jack knew what he needed to do next. As the morning light shone in the windows and Jack finished his bowl of Haughty Farmer Tastee-Os, he called in to work and took the day off. His boss was not happy, but the world hung in the balance. He needed to think, and the best way to think was to disconnect and work on a project— and the Mustang needed a new batch of fuel. Two birds with one stone.

He got in the car and cranked it up. Nothing felt like a 429 Super Cobra Jet Mach 1 burning discarded oil from a Chinese restaurant. Nothing.

As he pulled out of the driveway and got on the road, feeling the purr of the vehicle and smelling the slight General Tso's Chicken aroma of the exhaust, he laughed for the thousandth time at those who said a gasoline engine couldn't burn biodiesel. His could. He had changed the rules.

Jack took the car down the interstate towards Emporia. There was a strip mall there with a place that had hooked him up with 40 gallons of oil once. The Golden Wok, if he remembered correctly. This time he had six 5-gallon gas tanks crammed into the trunk and back seat. It wouldn't be much oil, but it was a start. And the fuel-making was just an excuse to think, he reasoned. A couple of times he'd had a friend with a truck drop off a few 55-gallon drums of used oil from another shop nearer to home, but that place had closed down. He needed a steady supply. Maybe if he filled all his tanks he could buy a few more at Walmart and cram them into the back of his car. Somewhere.

Though it was only 10 a.m. when he arrived at the plaza, his stomach growled as he passed the Taco Bell at one end. The Tasteeos he'd had for breakfast weren't really sticking. He'd also forgotten to pick up more *Ocean Octaves!* on the way out of town. He had already driven beyond the Taco Bell so he parked at the corner of an Arby's lot next door and walked back. A few extra steps would be good for him before he went inside. He set his mind on getting a few cheap bean burritos and a cup of that nasty nacho cheese substitute to coat them with. The flavor of the fake cheese had a slight resemblance to *Ocean Octaves!* It would take the edge off his cravings until picked up a few more bags.

Inside, he ordered two burritos, a cup of nacho cheese and a Mountain Dew, then reached into his pocket and took out his wallet, only to find he'd left his two hundreds at home. He paid with his debit card instead, wondering if he would be tracked by the transaction.

At least he still had a hundred under the mat in the Mustang in case he needed to hit Walmart. He didn't dare spend much on his card.

Jack sat and ate his lunch in silence, wondering what he should do next. If every phone call could be monitored and every search tracked, he was in big trouble. *Who knows?* he thought. *Perhaps even the VPN is controlled by the bad guys.*

Bad guys could even be tracking him now. A few tables over, a thin and balding man was carrying on an animated conversation with a tired-looking woman, though he kept looking down at the table during the conversation as if talking to his food as well. An old guy in a John Deere cap was looking at the man as if he were nuts, which he probably was. Jack tried to think, but having other people around was distracting. Fortunately, the weird guy with the tired girlfriend left a few minutes after Jack sat down, followed by the guy in the John Deere cap.

The phrase "the sixth seal will blacken the ice," popped up in Jack's mind. For a second, he wondered where he'd heard that, then remembered his search the night before.

The internet was full of nonsense—though still, it might mean something. He pulled his phone from his pocket and typed in the phrase. A site pulled up, covering a prophecy in the Book of Revelation about a sixth seal darkening the sun. Jack frowned. The sun was most definitely not made of ice.

Then he realized that he'd just done a search on his phone, which was most likely being tracked.

"Stupid," Jack said out loud. The chubby teenage girl behind the counter looked at him and he smiled at her. "It's nothing," he said.

He needed to keep moving in case they were tracking him. He turned his phone off, then wondered if they could still track a phone that was turned off. *Probably.* He opened the back of the phone and removed the battery.

Something flicked across the outside window next to his booth and he looked up. Outside was a *Harmonia axyridis* in the common 19-spot form. Jack looked at the little ladybug and frowned. It was an invasive species, introduced to control aphids and now causing harm to native ladybug populations. It sat outside the glass, as if looking back at him.

There was a soft "plink" as a second invasive ladybug impacted the glass outside.

Jack wondered if the insects enjoyed seven-layer burritos as much as he did, then realized that, like him, the small insects certainly couldn't afford to upgrade past the basic burrito options.

Two more ladybugs landed on the glass outside and walked to the portion of the window just outside where Jack sat.

Then another.

And then Jack had a horrible thought. *What if...*

As he had the thought, three more ladybugs landed on the glass. They were now moving into a roughly circular pattern outside, perhaps a foot across. A few more landed, and moved to the center of the circle.

It looked like—wait—was it a BULLSEYE!?

Just as Jack saw it, a flash of white appeared from across the lot. Jack realized his danger and hit the floor—just as a cattle egret hurtled through the window across Jack's table!

The impact showered him with broken glass and the remaining contents of his medium Mountain Dew. The girl behind the counter yelled something very unladylike as the bird skidded across the floor in a tumbling heap, twitching and jerking.

Jack army-crawled across the floor towards the fallen bird, his grafting knife in his teeth.

YOU RANG? Akras said.

"No," Jack whispered back. "Egret rang."

The damaged creature turned to look at Jack as he approached, then began to smoke. Its eyes flashed once, then it burst into blinding flames. The egret incinerated in seconds, leaving nothing but white ash and metal filaments behind. *Another drone!*

As Jack got up from the floor and put his pocketknife back into his jeans pocket, he made a mental note to carefully consider his future internet searches.

"What was that!?" the girl behind the counter asked as she was joined by two other employees from the back.

"Bird came through the window, then lit on fire," Jack said, putting his grafting knife back into his pocket and returning to his table to observe the damage. The impact point was exactly where his head had been moments earlier. These roboticist psychos weren't messing around. He saw no sign of the ladybugs.

The sixth seal will blacken the ice, he thought. *What did that mean— and why would it make a robotic egret want to murder him?*

It was time to call Pak.

He picked up his phone and its battery from the floor and stuffed it in his pocket, then headed for his car. The girl behind the counter said something about calling the police but he ignored her. When he reached his car, he had a thought and looked around at the surrounding area. Patchy grass, a Peebles, a car lot, and some unhealthy looking forest in the distance. Plenty of places for killer robots to hide. He pulled his phone out and reinserted its battery, intending to dial Pak, then thought better of it. Maybe a mechanical mockingbird would crash through his roof and kill him while he was talking. Or a robotic rat snake would slither in the door and strangle him. Or a bionic botfly would inject him with Ebola. Or a second electronic egret would successfully remove his head. He took his phone and hurled it far into the grass beyond the parking lot.

He could always get a new phone. Getting a new head would be difficult.

Jack unlocked his car and sat down inside. *I can get another phone at Walmart*, he thought. He pulled up the mat on the passenger's side—and there was nothing beneath it. No $100 bill. *How in the world?* he wondered. *Could they have sent a drone to take his money? And would they have re-locked the door after doing so? They must have.*

Whatever happened, he was $100 poorer, and he was angry. Far from clearing his head, this trip had only deepened Jack's confusion. He suddenly realized that the only place he had Pak's number was in the phone he'd just chucked far out into the grass.

He got out of his car and went to retrieve his phone, looking in every direction for threats.

It took him a good ten minutes to find it, but there were no more ladybugs—and no egrets. Maybe they thought they'd gotten him. Maybe the attack had been initiated before he pulled the battery from his phone.

Maybe he could drive home without further incident.

He hoped so. If the day continued along these lines, he'd definitely need to calm his nerves with some more *Ocean Octaves!*

No, he needed *Ocean Octaves!* no matter what the day decided to do.

Jack started his car and jumped back on I-95, his sights set on Lynn's Organic Market. Once he had his seaweed crisps, he'd figure this thing out.

CHAPTER 8

The vine grows tall only when there is that which may be gripped.

—*A State of Bean: Principles of Mung Fu*

Lynn's was busier than usual as the working men and women of the world stopped in to buy overpriced lunch options. Jack walked past the produce display and noticed they had white pomegranates on sale for a startling $8 per fruit. He was tempted to buy one so he could start the seeds, then remembered he was too short on funds. *Punica granatum* also came second to *Oceanum octava*.

He found the snack aisle and sighed with relief when he saw it was well-stocked with *Ocean Octaves!* He picked up four bags and turned to go when a voice came from near his feet.

"Jack!"

Jack looked up and down the row, then ducked down to peer between the shelves. Packed in behind the Fresh Valley Organic Wasabi and the Fruitful Life Parmesan Cashews was Pak.

"Pak!?" Jack exclaimed.

"Shh," Pak said. "Very dangerous to talk."

He must have been laying horizontally along the shelf, behind a variety of snack items, Jack noted. His feet had to be somewhere between the Green Elf Kale Nuggets and the Sustainable SoyShark Nibbles. Jack only saw Pak's head, facing sideways.

"How did you know I would be here?" Jack asked, wondering if Pak was also tracking his phone.

"You are predictable," Pak said.

"Still," Jack said, "how long have you been crammed on that shelf, waiting for me to appear?"

A skeletal white woman in dreads walked behind Jack and looked at him quizzically as she passed.

He quickly pretended to be interested in the Gourmet Artisanal Vegan Goldfish Fun-Sized Snack Biscuits and she walked on.

"Stop talking to me, Jack," Pak said, then held up a note reading, "Meet at the Golden Wok in twenty minutes. Do NOT bring phone."

"I was actually headed there already," Jack said.

"I know," Pak replied.

"Man alive, I really am predictable," Jack said. "Not a good trait for a spy."

"Shh!" Pak said, then pointed again to the words, "Do NOT bring phone."

"Right," Jack whispered. "I actually threw it away once, then got it again. I was afraid–"

Pak pulled a bag of Uncle Timmy's Original Licorice Locusts in front of his face, ending the conversation.

Jack nodded and gave Pak a thumbs up—which he almost certainly couldn't see—then stood and headed to the checkout with his *Ocean Octaves!* He'd already opened one of the bags without thinking by the time he reached the checkout girl. She cocked an eyebrow at him as he paid.

"You're not supposed to eat in the store," she said.

"The ocean beckoned," he said around a mouthful of seaweed and natural flavors.

She rang him up without further complaint, writing something on the receipt she stuffed in his bag. He glanced at it in the parking lot. It was her phone number along with an invitation to "break more rules." He tossed it. Before getting in his Mustang he hid his phone in the branches of the *Ilex x attenuata* growing in the parking lot island next to the car. He could always retrieve it later. He looked up and saw a mass of dark clouds to the East and wondered if rain was coming. The air was hot and still. Perhaps it wouldn't make it this way, and he had to put the phone somewhere. He'd already dinged the thing up chucking it across a field, so it wasn't like he was in love with it or anything. Especially not when people were using it to target his life.

He opened his car, stowed three and a half bags of *Ocean Octaves!* in the back seat, then locked the door and walked across the lot to the Golden Wok.

The Golden Wok was wedged into the other side of the strip mall between a check cashing store and a tattoo parlor. As Jack smelled the aroma of cheap Chinese food, he wished he hadn't already eaten two bean burritos. Pak would probably offer to pay and then he could have really loaded up. Though he was sure he could at least find some room for sweet and sour chicken nuggets. He left his gas cans in the car— he'd ask them about oil after talking with Pak—and headed into the restaurant.

The girl at the front smiled widely at Jack and almost tripped in her rush to greet him.

"Welcome, sir, are you alone?" she said, as if she wished for him to be.

"No," Jack replied. "I'm meeting a friend. May I look around?"

She pursed her lips in disappointment. "A lady friend?" she ventured.

"No," Jack said.

She smiled again and said, "Oh good, good. Yes, you may look for your friend."

Jack found Pak seated beside a fish tank filled with what appeared to be eels.

"Are those eels?" Jack asked.

"Yes," Pak replied.

"Excellent," Jack said, reassured in his taxonomic abilities. He'd never sat so close to an eel before, let alone a tank of them. They looked like they were watching him—could they be? No, that was insane. There's no way someone would have snuck robotic eels into the tank just in case someone showed up that they needed to randomly kill.

He watched one writhe, snake-like, across the glass.

Then again, killer egrets were insane too.

"We can talk here," Pak said. "It is safe."

"Are the eels safe?" Jack said.

"I am sure they were carefully vetted," Pak replied.

The waitress brought the two men plates and silverware, winking at Jack before returning to the front.

Jack looked at Pak. "I'm broke."

Pak nodded. "Perhaps the money has not arrived in your mail."

"It did," Jack said. "I accidentally left $200 at home and the third hundred was stolen from my car."

"I will cover the meal," Pak said.

"I'm actually not that hungry," Jack said, "but I could fit in a few things."

"Do so," Pak said. "We will fill our plates, then return and have conversation."

Jack stood and went to the buffet, first taking some of the sweet and sour chicken nugget things, then adding a little tapioca pudding to the side, then a few shrimp with cocktail sauce, along with a few mussels, a cube of rubbery orange jello, some stir-fried mushrooms—and the next thing he knew, he'd overloaded his plate.

He got back to their table. Pak followed him a moment later, setting down three plates of various shellfish.

Jack looked at the eels, wondering if they also ate shellfish.

"Jack," Pak said, picking up a shrimp with his fingers and deftly removing its carapace. "We have a serious problem."

"I know," Jack said, quickly recounting the Taco Bell assassination attempt that had almost removed his head.

Pak's eyes widened. He nervously dismembered a crab as he talked. "Jack, this is very bad. They are definitely on to you. We must catch them before they kill us."

"They're already lighting fires. What else could they be doing?"

Pak shook his head. "Trying to kill my friend with robot birds," he said.

"Oh, actually," Jack said, remembering the previous day's murder, "they also killed a roboticist."

"How do you know?" Pak asked.

"I was there," Jack replied, sharing the story of Jonny's death and how he and Paul had narrowly escaped being murdered by mechanical moths.

"Giles Batson," Pak said. "He has done a lot of charity work in Africa, for many decades. Your father may even have met him at some point."

"My father?" Jack said. Jack's father had disappeared in Africa when Jack was 12, while working for F.O.R.E.S.T., the top-secret Forestry Operations Reserve Espionage Strike Troops. "How would he have met Giles Batson?"

"We found a photo of a well dedication ceremony," Pak said. "Both Mr. Batson and your father were there."

"Do you think..." Jack said, letting the question trail off.

"No one knows what happened to your father," Pak said. "We researched you and your past extensively after deciding to add you as an asset. He simply vanished."

"If I ever find out who did it, they're going down," Jack said, taking an angry bite from his jello cube. "It's one thing having Batson try to kill me. It's another knowing he may have been involved in the disappearance of my father."

"Understandable," Pak said.

"One day I will dig deeper," Jack replied. "If your people don't know, there must be someone who does."

"I hope so," Pak said.

"But enough of this," Jack said. "We need to get the people trying to kill us now."

"Yes," Pak said. "I have been authorized to pull you in completely. Though Master Rice is still concerned about the loyalties of the entity in your mind."

"Akras," Jack said.

"Akras," Pak replied, with a nod. "Did you look up his name?"

"No," Jack replied. "Is it important?"

"Perhaps," Pak said. "He appears to be a minor Finnish deity."

"A god?" Jack said. "A Finnish god? Do all Finns sound like wrestlers?"

"No," Pak replied. "Not that you would know. Most Finns don't bother speaking to Americans as they consider them all borderline retarded."

"I guess I should be honored, then," Jack said. "Akras said I was the 'caretaker'."

"This is a clue," Pak replied. "As he is an agricultural god, we are guessing that he sees your gardening as somehow important and has decided to help you."

"Why the heck would a Finnish god choose to help a gardener in Virginia?" Jack said. "I mean, I am the best gardener in Virginia, but still—it makes no sense. He just randomly showed up across the Atlantic because he want to help me kick tail?"

"Not kick tail," Pak said. "Kiikala."

"Kiikala?" Jack replied. "The heirloom turnip seeds Niklas sent me last year?"

"It makes sense," Pak said. "You told me about the variety. Smuggled inside a small wooden statue."

"A little carved wood bear, yeah," Jack said. "If you ship seeds internationally, they're likely to get confiscated unless you have a phytosanitary certificate, which is a pain. Niklas just got that wood bear and filled it with seeds. Do you think this god came along?"

"Not in the bear," Pak said. "But the seeds you are growing are a very old variety. Likely hundreds of years before the crusade of Birger Jarl, back when Finland followed the old gods."

"Great," Jack said. "My pastor will love this."

"You can assure him that Akras is not really an evil god," Pak said.

"We only get to have one," Jack replied. "You can't just start running around with other gods. Entire nations get sold as slaves for that sort of thing."

"You will have to work this out in your own head," Pak shrugged.

"He may not even be a 'god', as you think of it. More like a bodiless entity that blesses turnips and protects fields."

"And helps me beat up cops."

"That too," Pak said. "He is protecting the caretaker, which is you."

"I rather like him," Jack admitted. "He was gone for a while, you know."

"When?" Pak asked.

"During the winter. Oh—wait—that was after I–"

"–dug up your turnips!?" Pak completed his sentence.

"Exactly!" Jack said. "And before I planted my spring turnip bed! I put the seeds in the ground and—bam—he was back!"

Pak broke the tail off a crayfish and squeezed the meat into his mouth, chewing thoughtfully. "If you are concerned with his appearances, then, you know what to do."

"Stop growing Kiikala?" Jack said, considering it, then realizing it was a complete impossibility. "No, absolutely not. I have to preserve the variety. And there's no way I'm plowing under a garden bed of anything, let alone my rare turnips."

Pak shrugged. "He has been helpful so far. You would be dead without him."

"Quite possibly," Jack said, then frowned. "Have you heard from Penny?"

"I do not know," Pak replied. "I have not contacted her—and now that I know you were almost killed because of your phone, I will certainly not call her unless we can do so over a very secure line."

"It's tough," Jack mused, eating a spoonful of sweet and sour sauce. His fried chicken nuggets were gone and he'd already eaten the crumbs. "Tech is a two-edged sword. If you hadn't been waiting for me at Lynn's, I would have had to stake out your house. I wouldn't dare call after this morning. They can control everything."

"Not quite everything," Pak said. "This location is secure. The Chinese do not trust your big tech companies due to American spying and manipulation of data. Back door entries and such."

"Don't the Chinese companies do the same thing?" Jack asked.

"Yes," Pak replied. "But they are run by Chinese. It is different."

"Okay," Jack said, not seeing why. He thought back on the egret attack. "Pak, does 'the sixth seal will blacken the ice'" mean anything to you?"

"No," Pak admitted. "Is this a prophecy?"

"I don't know," Jack said. "It's similar to something in the book of Revelations but it's not the exact same. It was the last thing I looked up before the egret tried to remove my head. I found it during a search for radioactive pantyhose eggs."

"You have weird hobbies," Pak said, pulling a vein from the back of a shrimp. "Why did you look for this?"

"Because when I looked up the fires, I found that phrase—'radioactive pantyhose eggs'—and when I looked it up, I found the message 'the sixth seal will blacken the ice.'"

Pak pulled his phone from his pocket and did a search. "I see nothing," he said after a moment. "No results."

"They probably erased it," Jack said.

Pak typed in another search, then spoke to Jack as he looked at the screen. "If all this does go back to Mr. Batson, it's a very big deal. He is perceived as a man of great generosity. We know he is not exactly what he presents to the public, of course, because no man is. Yet he has done much to help poor nations. He worked on robotics projects in India among the Dalits. He also commissioned the design of an ultralight wheelbarrow which is being used to transport crops in Uganda. In addition, he is fighting climate change."

"How so?" Jack asked.

"He established WEEWEE," Pak said.

"Yes," Jack said. "I read about them. They're the ones who were setting up monitoring satellites for the weather. And tracking polar bears and watching the melting ice caps or something. And spraying stuff out of airplanes. Cloud seeding or something."

Jack scooped up the final bite of his tapioca as Pak pulled a mussel from its shell with his teeth.

Then Jack dropped his spoon—and at the same time, Pak dropped the mussel shell.

"Melting ice..." they said in unison.

"The sixth seal will blacken the ice!?" Jack said. "Do you think that could mean the ice caps? What would blacken the ice caps?"

Pak shook his head. "In the 70s, scientists talked about painting the ice caps black to stop global cooling."

"I heard about that," Jack said. "Did it work?"

"No, they never did it," Pak said. "But now we have global warming. Who in the world would want to paint the ice caps black right now?"

"Or light wildfires!" Jack said. "Pak—we need to go to the North Pole!"

Pak pushed his plate away and motioned to the waitress to bring the check.

"Perhaps," he said. "It is a far aiming distance for a target, however."

"A long shot," Jack said.

"Yes," Pak said.

"But the 'sixth seal'—what could that be?"

"It could just be spammy nonsense on the internet," Pak said.

"You're probably right," Jack said. "Okay—let's start with what we know. So far we know they've killed a vineyard owner and lit some wildfires. They also tried to kill me with a robot egret. Is there anything else they've done?"

"Most certainly," Pak replied. "Yet we have no motive. What is the motive?"

"Motivation is the first thing we should look for after discovering a crime," Jack said.

"Mr. Layton knew something they wanted covered up," Pak said.

"He was basically a prisoner on his vineyard, the way he told it," Jack said. "He freaked out when he saw the pic I took of the dragonfly drone. Maybe Batson doesn't want the world to know he's creating killer insect drones."

"Possibly," Pak said. "Though lots of people are trying to do the same thing. There must be more to the story."

There was a low rumble outside and the faux Chinese lantern above their table dimmed for a moment.

"A storm is coming," Pak said.

"Sounds like it," Jack said. "We should grab more food in case the lights go out and it's too dangerous to visit the buffet."

Pak nodded. "This is wisdom," he said, and the two got up to get fresh plates of food. They were half-way to the buffet when the lights went off and there was a loud bang from the front of the restaurant. Then the howling began. It sounded like a train was hurtling past the front of the Golden Wok—and CRASH! The front windows exploded inwards and there was a scream from the front counter!

Without thinking, Jack moved towards the scream. The howling sound was now accompanied by whistling and moaning as wind tore through the building.

"Tornado!" Pak yelled. "Get to safe place—find plumbing!"

Plumbing, Jack thought, continuing towards where he'd heard the scream. *The very thing that started this whole mess.*

"Help!" a woman screamed. Jack found the hostess in the weird green light coming through the whipping curtains of the broken window. She was pinned under part of the fallen counter.

EVERYTHING IS A WEAPON! Akras said, as Jack tore the counter away from the girl and scooped her up. "Thank you," she sobbed into his shoulder as he carried her deeper into the restaurant.

"Get to the washroom!" Pak yelled over the howling wind. "Jack—quickly!"

A bicycle crashed through the open front window, knocking over the gumball machine in front and scattering 25-cent gumballs across the floor, almost tripping Jack up. The bicycle was followed by a motor scooter.

Pak stood in the door to the ladies room, LED flashlight in hand. "Come on!"

"I can't go in there, Pak," Jack yelled back, almost deaf. He felt like his eardrums were going to explode. He looked down at the woman in his arms. "And she can't go into the men's room."

Pak grabbed him and pulled him in.

CARETAKER, WITHOUT YOU THEY ARE IN DANGER.

"Who are?" Jack said, putting the girl down beside the sink.

"Thank you," she said.

"Are you okay?" Jack yelled.

THE CROPS ARE IN DANGER, Akras broke in.

"I'm fine," the girl said, feeling herself. "I think I bruised my legs but they are not broken."

"Good," Jack said.

IT IS NOT GOOD FOR YOU TO GET KILLED, Akras replied.

"I agree," Jack said.

YOU SEEM PRONE TO BEING IN DANGER, Akras continued.

"Hang onto the pipes," Pak said.

"Where did you learn that trick?" Jack said.

"From watching television," Pak replied.

YOU MUST NOT DIE OR THEY WILL DIE, Akras said. *YOU MUST CHECK ON THEM REGULARLY!*

"I know, I don't want to die," Jack replied. "But I cannot get to the turnips right now—we'll have to hope this storm ends soon."

"Are you married?" the hostess said, hugging onto Jack's arm.

"Almost," Jack replied, wondering if the eels had escaped from their tank and were even now slipping across the wet floor towards them.

The winds dropped off outside, then there was silence.

"Let me go out first," Jack said to the woman. "Stay here."

He got up and went out. No eels in the immediate vicinity, but the restaurant was a mess. Part of the roof had torn off and light shone through from above. The eel tank had broken and multiple eels were struggling across the floor. Worst of all—the buffet was destroyed! Jack was horrified at how much food was scattered across the tile floor. It was enough to feed him for a month—all destroyed, thanks to a freak weather event.

Two women and a man emerged from the kitchen, speaking rapidly in what Jack assumed was Chinese. The older woman was very upset as she surveyed the damage.

"It's safe," Jack yelled back into the ladies room, convinced that nothing else was going to fly through the front window. Pak emerged and helped the bruised hostess to a chair.

The man from the kitchen found a battery powered radio and set it on a table, then flipped it on.

"...severe weather event in the Holly Branch Shopping Center, where we have reports of a freak tornado. We will keep you updated on the situation, and urge everyone to stay indoors at this point as..."

"It *was* a tornado," Jack said, shaking his head and trying to clear the ringing from his ears. "That thing hit fast."

"It did indeed," Pak replied. "It is good we are safe."

"Yeah," Jack replied, then had a thought. "Pak! My car!"

He ran to the front of the restaurant, almost slamming into the wall as he skidded on a gumball, then opened the front door. His car was eight parking spaces from where it had been parked—and it was upside-down.

"No!" Jack yelled, racing out into the lot. "No, no, no!"

As he neared his car, his heart almost stopped. It was not only upside-down, the top was smashed in as if it had been dropped from a height.

"My *Ocean Octaves!* are in there," he muttered in complete shock.

"I'm sorry, mister," an old guy said from behind Jack. "That your car?"

"Yeah," Jack said. "It was."

"It was just about the epicenter," the man said. "I was right over there eating an ice cream in front of Pepe's, waiting on my wife. Saw the funnel come right down next to it. Landed right on top of the holly tree that was there." The man pointed to the parking lot island that had been next to the parking space formerly occupied by Jack's Mustang. "Tore the tree right out of the ground."

"My phone," Jack said, the color draining from his face. "The tornado landed right on my phone."

CHAPTER 9

Planting corn in winter leads to hungriness; planting daikon in summer is madness.

—*A State of Bean: Principles of Mung Fu*

"First it was the fires," Pak said. "And now we know, assuming that the tornado was not an improbable coincidence, that they can also control the weather."

"Which is also something they say about global warming. That the weather will get worse."

"Yes," Pak nodded. "Extreme weather events."

They sat in Pak's Honda, which was parked in a wide-open field that had recently been plowed. It seemed like a good idea to get into an open spot, far from microphones and cameras, which also had good visibility.

Jack put his hand on his pocket, thinking he would check the time on his phone, then remembered he no longer had a phone. There was a small lump in his pocket, however. He pulled it out and realized it was a crushed fortune cookie. The fortune inside read "You will meet new experiences today" on one side. On the other side was a handwritten note reading, "Jenny Lin, 675-2324."

"You have too many girlfriends," Pak said, looking at the note in Jack's hand.

Jack shrugged. "Speaking of girlfriends, we need to get in contact with Penny."

"I would say it is too dangerous," Pak said. "It is obvious that they decided to kill you just for having been at Mr. Layton's place. If you call her, they may very well send a storm on top of her head."

"Or an egret," Jack said. "This is not good at all. We're completely disconnected."

"No," Pak said. "We are not completely disconnected."

He reached into the glovebox in front of Jack and pulled out what looked like a chunky black walkie talkie. "We have a satellite phone."

"Pak," Jack said with a sudden thought. "Penny may be okay, because she wasn't really tied up in all this—but what about Paul? He was there at Jonny's! Can I call him?"

"You can try," Pak said. "But I would be cryptic."

"Cryptic?" Jack said.

"Yes. It means like a puzzle. Don't say anything that might draw down fire on him. If he is alive, that is."

"If," Jack said, shaking his head. "This is insane. It's hard to think that way."

"But it is the way we must think," Pak said, extending the phone's antenna and pushing the red "on" button. After a few seconds, it loaded up. "Do you know his number?" he asked.

Jack thought for a moment. "I think so. It was an easy one. 444-1234, I think."

"Dial 001, then the area code and number," Pak said, handing Jack the satphone.

Jack did. The phone rang and a woman answered in Spanish.

"Hi," Jack said. "Is Paul there?"

There was a silence on the other end of the line, then the woman hung up. Jack looked at the phone. "Maybe I remembered wrong. Too bad we don't have a phone book. I know the last four numbers were 1234. Maybe..."

Jack took the phone and dialed again. It rang twice, then he heard Paul's voice. "It was 400-1234!" he said to Pak, then spoke into the phone. "Paul—listen—don't say anything about who you're talking to or whatever. This needs to sound like it isn't suspicious."

"That sounds suspicious," Pak said to Jack. "And you just called him by his name."

Jack nodded his head and put his hand over the mouthpiece. "You're right. I got it."

"Hi Jack," Paul replied. "You'll never guess where I am. I'm standing in front of a warehouse here, and I think it's important."

"It is spring in the city and the goose is made of cheese," Jack said.

"The cats fly south when the bats get the yarn," Paul replied, then gave him an address in the industrial district.

"We're on our way," Jack said, forgetting himself.

"Tell him to ditch his phone as fast as possible," Pak whispered. "But don't be obvious about it."

Jack thought fast. "Itch-day or-yay ellphon-say, SAP-Ah!"

"Okeyday!" came the answer.

"Earious-Say," Jack said. "Or-yeah oo-yeah ill-way eye-day!"

"Oppy-cay!" Paul said. "Et-gay ver-o-ay ear-hay ow-nah!"

"Oo-yeah ott-it-gay," Jack replied, then hung up.

"Well handled," Pak said.

"Thanks," Jack replied. "It sounds harder to do than it really is. You just kind of mix up the syllables and add the 'ay' sound. Now let's get going before they come after him."

Pak nodded and gunned his Honda up the dusty road and back towards town.

Jack flipped on the radio and found the news station. "...multiple injuries and thousands of dollars in damages. Some environmentalists blame the freak tornado strike on global warming. The World Environmental Equality Working Executive Endowment has issued a statement urging state and federal governments to work together to promote awareness of the very real dangers caused by climate change..."

"WEEWEE!" Jack exclaimed. "They had a statement ready. Pak—we were talking about wildfires, and now we've got tornados. What if they really are going to paint the ice caps black. But why? Why would they do that?"

Pak shrugged. "Perhaps Mr. Batson is being held hostage by anti-eco-terrorists of some sort."

"I doubt it," Jack said. "Jonny was convinced he was evil."

"If he is, he controls too much of the world to be allowed to continue."

"And he wrecked my car," Jack said grimly. "Trapping my *Ocean Octaves!* inside. That's more than enough reason to compost him."

After some searching, they found the address Paul had given them. It was after five and the district was dead. The building had multiple loading docks and was surrounded by a tall fence topped with razor-wire.

Out front was a small doorless jeep with a plastic snake on the dashboard. In the driver's side sat Paul, munching on a tomato. He saw Jack and Pak and jumped out. "Hey, what was all that about taking out a loan or something?" he asked Jack.

"Ditching your phone!" Jack said. "You were supposed to ditch your phone!"

"Aw, I was just joshing you," Paul said, punching Jack in the arm. "I wrapped it in tin foil and threw it into the back of a passing gravel truck. I didn't learn my Pig Latin yesterday, you know."

"Good," Jack said, with a sigh of relief. "A tornado came down and destroyed my phone—and that was after a robot egret almost took my head off."

"Whoa," Paul said. "I ended up losing that coin Jonny gave me when we went in the pond. Kinda feel sad. I loved that guy."

"I stuck mine in my wallet," Jack said. "Managed to keep it so far. You can have it."

He fished it out and handed it to Paul.

"You guys were close. I barely knew him."

"Aww, man," Paul said. "That's really nice of you. I'd just lose it though. You keep it for me."

Jack shrugged and put the coin back in his wallet.

"You Japanese?" Paul said, turning to Pak.

"Chinese," Pak said with a slight twitch. "I am Pak Choi."

"I'm Paul Garrison," Paul said, shaking his hand. "I figured you were either Chinese, Japanese or Micronesian. I'm usually pretty good at pickin' people out."

"Pak knows a bunch about international spy stuff," Jack said. "We're putting together some ideas on what might be going on." He gestured towards the building. "So—what the heck are we doing here?"

"Like I said, I got a clue," Paul said. "I've already made a way in. I found the address in an old supplier list I got when Jonny gave me my old robotruck. There was a listing in there that said something so weird I had to check it out."

"Really?" Pak said. "A drone company, or perhaps a note on weather control equipment?"

"Nope," Paul said. "Weirder."

"Weirder?" Jack said.

"Yep. There was this address, then Jonny had scrawled three words."

"What words?" Pak said.

"Radioactive pantyhose eggs. Don't that strike you as weird? Sounds like a code to me."

"Whoa," Jack said. "I found that phrase before. Good work, Paul. You gotta have a crazy bit of wiring in your brain to follow that up, but I'm glad you did."

"Let's get inside before something kills us," Pak said. "Does this place have security?"

"There ain't no security," Paul said, pointing to the back seat of his jeep. Jack and Pak looked in to see the prone body of a security guard.

"You killed him?" Jack said. "That's hardcore."

"Naw," Paul said. "Sleeping. I gave him a shot of a special brew I whipped up. You wouldn't believe what goes down the drain in a pharmacy."

"Good work," Pak said. "But risky if you are just following a hunch."

"I didn't get to be the CEO of my own company by playin' it safe," Paul said with a grin. He picked up a large backpack off the passenger side seat and hoisted it over his shoulder. "Come on around the back— that's where we can get in."

There was a muffled thump of something exploding far away, followed by the shriek of brakes, a crunch of metal and what sounded like falling gravel.

"You hear that?" Jack asked.

"Probably kids joy-riding," Paul said. "Kids are crazy."

Jack and Pak followed Paul along the edge of the fence to a neatly cut gap.

"Bolt-cutters," Paul said. "I buy the good ones. Very handy."

"Indeed," Pak said, then they crawled through the gap.

Around the back of the building was an entry door. Paul had already removed the door knob. He pushed the door open.

"Bad security," Pak said.

"Looks like a normal construction supply company," Jack said, his eyes adjusting to the dim light.

"Perhaps," Pak said, looking around at shelves containing boxes of hardware, engine parts and various adhesives. "It does not look promising."

"Oh, it gets promising," Paul said, pointing towards a second door. Jack and Pak looked closer, then saw it. The universal symbol for radioactivity was stenciled on the door. "I got a suit," Paul said, pulling a coverall from his backpack.

"You have a radioactivity suit?" Jack said in amazement.

"Sure," Paul said. "You know what I do for a living."

"I'll go in," said Pak, taking the suit.

"No," Jack said. "I'll go in. I'm closer to Paul's size than you. Plus, you have all the connections."

Pak nodded. "Be careful."

Jack slipped into the suit and Paul helped him seal it up. Pak handed him his flashlight.

He took a deep breath and opened the door.

CHAPTER 10

*A Mung Fu warrior survives drought with watchful meditation,
in time harvesting enemies like papery pods of beans plucked by a
handsome woman slave in garden.*

—A State of Bean: Principles of Mung Fu

The door opened into another room. Cool blue lit the space. Jack
entered, gave Paul and Pak a thumbs up, flipped on the flashlight, then
shut the door behind him.

Jack's palms were sweating inside his suit. His heart thumped in his
chest. Radioactivity was the stuff of nightmares. He hoped Paul's suit
had been maintained better than his old truck. Or his doorless jeep.

where are you? came a small voice.

"Who is that?" Jack asked, turning around.

it is me, caretaker, came the voice, sounding even smaller.

"The Brown... turnip god?" Jack said, looking at a second door.
This one was a heavy metal one with a large latch. It looked like a vault
from an old sci-fi film.

*i am... trying to help you. i felt the call from your veins. it is hard to
stay. bad energy.*

"It's okay," Jack said. "I'm not in a fight. I'm in a radioactive room
in a warehouse, standing in front of a really heavy door." Jack turned
the heavy wheel latch and the door opened. "Just show up when I get
in my next fight," Jack said, breathing hard.

There was no answer.

"Akras?" Jack said.

Still no answer.

Jack stepped into the vault, taking care not to let the door close behind him. Mist swirled around his boots, licking at his ankles. It was a large space and very dim. The walls looked wet and strangely organic. Steps led down to the middle of the space. Jack walked down, slow and careful, reaching the edge of a dim circle of swirling mist.

Then he saw them. The eggs.

He shone his light across the space.

There were hundreds of them.

If they were pantyhose eggs, they were huge. The radioactive part had been correct, though. Unless that was just an elaborate ruse. Lacking a geiger counter, it was hard to say for sure. "Bad energy," Akras had said. So yeah, radioactivity. He would go with that.

Jack knelt down next to a cluster of the eggs to take a closer look. They looked harmless enough. Large plastic eggs. He picked one up and looked it over. It was lighter than he expected. There were no markings on the plastic except for a seam around the middle.

He gently pressed the sides in and there was a pop as the egg opened, spilling out the largest pair of pantyhose he had ever seen. They glowed faintly blue—except for a little white square near the waist. A tag!

It read "Frú. Jólasveinn Nærföt Kvenna Búningur, Norðurpóll."

Jack ripped it off and tried to put it in his pocket, then realized he had no accessible pockets.

Suddenly, the blue lights went out. The room was dark except for Jack's flashlight. There was a muffled yell from somewhere outside—and a crash! Jack dropped the pantyhose and raced back up towards the vault door, almost tripping on the stairs in his hurry.

He got through the vault door and stopped. There was the sound of scuffling on the other side of the second door, which was still shut. The suit he wore was bulky and would hamper him in a fight. He made a decision and slammed the vault door shut, then quickly stripped off his suit, hoping he wasn't radiating his guts by doing so. Jack stuffed the pantyhose tag into his shirt pocket, then found his grafting knife in his jeans pocket. He wouldn't even have to open the blade, as The

Brown Wizard could use the wood handle in his fist more effectively than he could use the blade. Jack's heart was in his throat as he put his hand on the door handle.

"Brown wizard?" he whispered. "You there?"

No answer.

That wasn't good. He had sounded weak before—but now he was gone? Jack shrugged and opened his knife.

Jack heard someone bark a command outside the door. There was more than one person out there. The fighting seemed to have ceased.

Then the doorknob was torn from his hand and he was knocked backwards as someone kicked the door open.

Jack slashed at the man in an attempt to execute a tongue-and-groove graft. The man dodged the knife, rolling fluidly and came up with a gun, which he pointed at Jack's head, stopping him faster than you can say "parafilm."

"Drop the knife," the man ordered. He was dressed in black, face obscured by a balaclava and a pair of reflective sunglasses. Two more men with raised weapons came through the door, faces also invisible.

Jack slowly let the blade fall to the floor. He was outnumbered and outgunned.

The man with the gun nodded to the two behind him and they moved forward, restraining Jack and searching him for weapons. Satisfied that he had nothing else, they tied his wrists and ankles, then dragged him into the next room and tossed him roughly on the floor in front of a pallet of engine parts. Pak was already there. He had been treated the same way and one of his eyes was blackened.

"Pak—you all right?" Jack whispered.

"I tried to fight them," Pak said. "They are surprisingly strong."

Jack looked around. The room was very dim, lit only by the sunlight leaking in around the doors. The men in black were ignoring the two of them, and appeared to simply be standing in place and waiting for something. There were four Jack could see. *And where was Paul?*

He looked at Pak.

"Four," Pak whispered.

"What are they doing?" Jack said, looking at their motionless captors.

"Not currently hitting me in the face," Pak said. "Which is an improvement."

For a full minute, the room was silent. No one moved. Pak and Jack looked at each other in suspicion. Pak said it first.

"Robots."

"Yeah," Jack replied. "Some sort of super warrior android bots or something. They seem to be ignoring us now."

"Maybe like T-Rex from movie," Pak said.

"Can't see movement?" Jack said. "Let's see."

He rolled onto his side and tried to worm his way towards a shelf filled with coils of electrical wire.

The closest man in black moved quickly to intercept him, grabbing Jack by the collar of his shirt and dragging him backwards to his previous location next to Pak.

"Stay still," the man ordered. "Don't try to escape."

"Let me go," Jack said.

The man laughed. The laugh was too chipper and Jack could have sworn it looped at least twice.

"Stay still," it ordered again. "Or I will kill you."

"I thought that no robot can harm a human?" Jack replied, trying another tack.

"Or through inaction cause a human to come to harm," the man replied.

"Right!" Jack said. "So you are a robot, then?"

The man said nothing.

"Fine," Jack said. "You don't want to say. That's okay. I understand. You probably got teased in school."

Still the man said nothing.

"Here's the thing," Jack said. "I've got to use the little boy's room. If you don't untie me, you will cause my kidneys to be destroyed, and that is definitely causing a human harm."

"Your kidneys?" the man said.

He walked over and kicked Jack in the left kidney, hard. Jack grunted in pain, crumpling to the floor in white-hot agony.

"Stay still," the robot ordered.

"But..." Jack said, teeth gritted against the pain. "But... you caused me harm..."

The robot laughed its weird laugh. *Definitely a few loops in there*, Jack thought.

Then it kicked him again, this time in the other kidney.

"Stay still *and* be quiet," it said.

There was a slight scraping sound from overhead, off in the corner of the room. Jack, Pak and the four men in black looked up at the drop ceiling with its yellow-tinted panels. It was hard to see in the gloom but Jack's eyes were adjusting, despite the tears of pain in them. An air conditioning vent fell to the floor in a crash of metal and dust.

Then Jack saw it. Something was emerged from the shadowy ceiling, above where the vent had fallen. Something snakelike. Perhaps a tentacle?

No, more like a snake, Jack thought. Or an EEL? A very thick eel??

There was a hissing POP and the giant eelsnake exploded into the room, whipping around wildly and ejecting hundreds of gallons of cold fluid.

Their captors raced towards the creature—and then slipped, jerked and fell in the rapidly spreading puddle on the floor.

"Water!" Pak said. "It's a firehose!"

Jack looked in amazement as the hose shot around the room, disabling their captors.

"They're shorting out!" Pak said, as one of the men's arms lit up with a spray of sparks. In a moment, all four were down for the count.

The door burst open from the other side, flooding the room with light. "Come on!" said a familiar voice. "Gotta get out!"

It was Paul!

He carried a huge pipewrench, ready to fight their guards, but they were already sprawled on the floor. The hose had whipped itself into a corner and gotten wedged behind a shelf but it was still going strong. Jack was already laying in an inch of water.

"You're tied up," Paul said. "And you already killed those guys?"

"Just get us out," Pak said. "Talk later."

Paul nodded and dragged Pak outside, then came back for Jack.

"Thank you," Jack said as Paul cut through his bonds.

"Don't mention it," Paul said. "I had gone back to the jeep to see if I had a geiger counter, then these guys in black zipped in past me and went inside. That's their SUV over there," he said, pointing at a black SUV with tinted windows. "When I heard Pak yell from inside, I decided to use the fire hose as a distraction. It's easy to do when you got the right tools." He grinned and held up his wrench. "'Course, the building isn't up to fire codes now. I wouldn't have done it if I knew you guys had already taken them out..." He frowned, a confused look on his broad face. "...though I didn't know you could take them out while still tied up."

"You took them out," Jack said. "Or more precisely, the water did."

"They appear to have been humanoid robots," Pak said.

"Wow," Paul said. "Could have fooled me. So they shorted out!"

He frowned. "Hey, wait a minute... what about the guy in my jeep? Was he also a–"

Multiple shots rang out and Paul staggered forward, then fell to the ground. Pak spun as he caught a round in his side that tumbled him. The two men were between Jack and the source of the shots. Jack hit the ground fast, noting the security guard approaching with a long pistol in his hand.

EVERYTHING IS A WEAPON! Akras roared.

"Glad you're back," Jack hissed as he scrambled behind the corner of the building, cursing himself for never getting his concealed carry permit. What kind of a spy was he?

He looked at the gap in the fence. He'd have to run away from the building and across the lot to make it—too open!

He ducked behind a dumpster full of drywall and rusty bracing and heard the PLINK of a round hitting the other side. His pursuer had rounded the edge of the building.

He needed something organic, fast. He stayed low and ran along the back end of the building into a roofed storage area filled with tall shelving, loaded with construction supplies.

Another PLINK hit a galvanized panel to his right and he ducked lower, weaving his way through towards the back of the yard. It was only a matter of time before the robot got him.

Heck, even without a permit I should be carrying, Jack thought. Better to be tried by twelve than carried by six. Would killing an AI even count as a crime?

Then he saw the oak tree hanging over the fence behind some shipping containers.

Please, let there be a dropped branch or something! Jack thought. He skittered across the gravel between a rusting dump truck and an old cement mixer, then around the container, looking frantically for something he could throw at his pursuer.

Then he saw them. Acorns!

He scooped them up from the gritty ground as fast as he could.

I CAN WORK WITH THESE, Akras said.

"Good," Jack said. "Because we don't get second chances." He took one from his palm and readied himself to throw as hard as he could.

USE THEM ALL.

"I won't get any aim that way," Jack said, but he filled his hand anyhow—and then his pursuer appeared at the other end of the shipping container!

He threw the entire handful of acorns. There was a crack as they broke the sound barrier and tore through the air towards the robot. Jack was almost deafened as they ripped half the metal off the far end of the shipping container—and smashed his pursuer into smoking pieces, scattering limbs across the yard.

"Holy tree nuts, Akras," Jack said, heading towards his fallen foe. "He exploded!"

ACORNS IGNITE AT HIGH SPEED. FULL OF OIL.

"I need to remember this trick for next time the squirrels steal my peaches," Jack replied.

He looked down at the body of the psuedo security guard. It was a mess of silicone, wires and spilled fluids. Beside the robot lay the pistol, broken in half. It was a CO_2 powered model of a type unfamiliar to Jack.

CO_2 is linked to global warming, Jack thought grimly. Of course it was a CO_2 pistol! The pieces were coming together.

Paul and Pak! he thought, remembering his friends. He ran back through the shelving and along the side of the building, then around to the front. Paul lay face-down where he'd fallen. Pak lay against the wall, holding his side as a red stain spread across his shirt.

"Pak!" Jack yelled.

"Check... on... Paul..." Pak said, gritting his teeth against the pain.

Jack raced to the fallen man's side and carefully turned him over. He had been hit multiple times in the chest.

"No!" Jack said, feeling for a pulse. It was there, but it was weak.

Paul's eyelids fluttered open and his eyes focused slowly on Jack. "Jack..." he said, then coughed.

"Don't talk," Jack said. "I'll get you help."

"I can already see the other side," Paul said, his eyes losing focus.

"No!" Jack said. "Stay with me!"

"It's a garden, Jack," Paul whispered. "It's a beautiful garden."

"No!" Jack said. "You've got your own garden!"

"Isss okay," Paul mumbled. "This... is a better garden."

He shut his eyes.

"I will avenge you," Jack swore. "Whoever is behind this, I will make them pay!"

"No," Paul sighed. "Don't... waste life... on vengeance..."

"It's not a waste," Jack said. "It's worth it. And I WILL avenge you!"

"Isss... not.. what I... wan..."

"Shh," Jack said. "Don't worry. I'm going to kill them all!"

"I... would... prefer it... if you didn't ki..."

"None of that defeatist talk!" Jack said. "I can and will do it!"

"But..." Paul said, then he drew in a final rattling breath... and was gone.

"NOOOOOO!!!" Jack yelled, frantically feeling for a pulse that had stopped. "NOOOOOOOOOO!!!"

"Don't... yell..." Pak said. "Need to get... out of here."

"Sorry," Jack said, carefully laying Paul's body on the gravel. "I swear it, Paul. I will avenge you," he whispered into the corpse's ear, then turned to Pak.

"Pak—can we get you into the jeep? Anything vital hit?"

"I don't think," Pak whispered. "I think I can grip onto outside."

"You mean you think you can hold out?" Jack offered.

"Yes," Pak said. "Round went through body... I think... wide of important pieces... hurts bad... maybe bleeding inside..."

"Hang on to me," Jack said, and scooped Pak up. Pak gasped in pain when Jack had to pull him through the gap in the fence, but they made it to the jeep.

"I'll get you to the hospital," Jack said, then realized he didn't have the keys to the vehicle. "Rats," he said. "Paul has them. I'll be right back."

Pak nodded weakly. "Cover me with blanket," he said, trying to point to an old flannel in the back of the jeep. "Less... suspicious... if someone... comes... can't see blood."

"Good idea," Jack said, quickly putting it over Pak's middle. "Stay put—I'll be right back."

He cut back through the hole in the fence to where Paul lay.

Jack felt anger burning in his heart as he searched through the man's pockets and found the keys to the jeep.

It felt wrong to leave him here. Still, carrying the body with them would probably get them nailed by the cops. He thought back to when Hardin died. They had left Hardin in the dugout of a baseball diamond, which seemed better than how he was leaving Paul. Still, there was really no good way to haul around a body unless you were driving a hearse or something. A doorless jeep was not a good option. If someone called the police they would all be killed in some horrible way.

He had to be left here, Jack decided. Paul was gone now. All that was left was to avenge him.

Mind made up, Jack raced back to the jeep.

"Took you... a while," Pak said.

"I couldn't figure out what to do with Paul's body," Jack said, starting the jeep and pulling out. "I just decided to leave him."

"It's... what.... he would have wanted," Pak said.

"Seriously?" Jack said. "I doubt he would have wanted to lay dead in the gravel of an industrial building. Probably would have prefered to be laid to rest in a septic tank."

"I was just... being comforting..." Pak said.

* * *

The sun was setting as Jack pulled up to the Emergency Room drop off at Piedmont Baptist Hospital.

"Take... satphone... from my pocket..." Pak said. "Then... you run... don't take jeep..."

"And just leave you?" Jack said, taking the phone and wiping the blood off it before putting it in his own pocket.

"You... already left Paul..." Pak said.

"Hey!" Jack said. "You said–"

"Also take... my wallet..." Pak said. "You... are always... broke..."

Jack took his wallet.

"Now go!" Pak said as he waved weakly to a nurse emerging from the sliding glass doors. "They will... kill you if you don't go."

So Jack did, walking away from the jeep and off through the hospital lot.

Now he was alone.

CHAPTER 11

Daikon seeds left on woven bamboo couch may be forgotten in cushions; the warrior's honor is never thus, even when sat upon by concubines.

—A State of Bean: Principles of Mung Fu

Jack was washing up in the restroom of Karl's Koffee when he heard an unfamiliar ring. He'd cut through a park and a few backyards, then come out on 24th. He had blood on his shirt, though the cloth was navy blue and didn't show much unless he was in the light.

Ring! Ring!

The satphone!

Jack pulled it from his pocket with wet hands and found the button to answer.

"Hello?"

"Hello," came a high-pitched voice from far away.

"Who is this?" Jack asked, tucking the phone into the crook of his neck so he could get back to washing his hands.

"I ask the questions," the voice replied. It sounded like a woman.

"Okay," Jack said, putting his hands to the bottom of the paper towel dispenser, then realizing it was empty. "Darn it," he muttered, then punched the button on the hot air dryer. "If you're looking for Pak, he's stepped away from the phone for a minute."

"We know," the voice said.

"What?" Jack said. The hot air dryer was quite noisy and something inside it was rattling.

"We know," the voice repeated.

"Great," Jack said. "Well, this is probably expensive to call on, so I should probably hang up."

"We have Penny," the woman said.

"What?" Jack asked, gripping the phone tightly as ice ran through his veins. "Did you say you have Penny?"

"Yes," she replied. "Do I have your attention now, Jack?"

Jack's heart stopped for a moment and the world spun. He put his hand against the wall to steady himself, then spoke.

"What do you want me to do?"

"Turn yourself in to us," the voice replied.

"If I surrender, you'll let her go?" Jack asked.

"That is the deal," the voice said.

"And if I don't?"

There was silence for a moment, then a woman's scream of pain.

"Stop it!" Jack yelled. "If you hurt her...!"

"Do we have a deal?" the woman's voice said again.

"Where and how?" Jack asked.

"Go to FiveGees Internet Cafe. Log in under the name Wimpy-LoserMan. We will find you."

Jack gritted his teeth. "Fine," he said after a moment. "But how will I know you've set Penny free?"

"You won't," the woman replied. "But you have no choice."

Jack had another thought.

"How do I even know you have her now?" he said.

There was silence on the phone, then a "hello?"

Penny's voice.

"Penny," Jack said. "Are you okay?"

"No," she said. "I'm trapped somewhere. I was out with Jessie at Tommy Tomatoes what seems like forever ago. They had a little robot waiter, really cute—he brought us some free drinks. Then I woke up in a green room, it's all tiles—no windows—and there is a huge pile of pantyhose outside my room—no one is telling me what's going on—

she zapped me with this thing around my neck—this mean old lady is the first person I've seen since..."

The cold woman's voice broke in again. "That's enough you nasty little–"

Then there was another scream of pain and the line was dead.

Blood thumped in Jack's ears. They had connected him to Penny— she had been kidnapped because of him. Of course they knew about her, he thought bitterly. All they had to do was read his email or find his SayWhaaat logs and they'd find her. He had a picture of the two of them on his profile, for goodness' sake.

Or maybe the dragonfly had filmed her in Oklahoma with them. Maybe it had been transmitting video?

They were torturing her! His Penny!!!

He pulled himself together and walked out of the bathroom into the coffee shop. His options were down to zero. He had to turn himself over.

Jack walked to the front and ordered a triple espresso. His head was foggy and his thinking was frayed. The barista was an overweight young guy with an unkempt beard and dark-rimmed glasses.

"Cream or sugar?" he asked Jack.

"Sugar," Jack said. "Two sugars."

His stomach rumbled.

"And two macadamia nut cookies," Jack added.

"They're vegan," the guy said, as if this was good.

"Then throw in some bacon," Jack snarled.

"We don't have any," the guy sniffed.

"Just give me the cookies," Jack said.

"Whatever," the guy said. "That will be $10.56."

Jack paid from Pak's wallet, mind in a fog.

He took a table towards the middle of the seating, remembering the incident with the ladybugs and the egret. Jack took a sip of his espresso. It was piping hot and quite good. Then he took a bite of his first cookie. It was also good.

Jack wondered if it were possible to push the growing zone of macadamia nuts as far north as Virginia. He reached for his phone to check the extent of their growing range, then realized he had Pak's satphone in his pocket, not his smartphone. *No, Jack! This isn't the time to be looking up plants! How could I forget Penny, even for a second? I have to rescue her.*

He took a slug of his espresso, savoring the burn in his throat.

How?

By turning myself over to the bad guys, he thought.

That really made him angry. They had Penny. Then he remembered Paul as well. Though he'd only known the man for a short time, he already felt like they had been best friends.

He took another slug of his coffee. It was strong and good. Just as he was strong and good. He could get through this. Even in surrender.

One of the principles of Mung Fu from *A State of Bean* popped into his mind.

A bean, though flicked by a finger, impacts the unprotected eye with damaging force.

They had flicked him, that was for sure. He had to follow the trajectory upon which he was sent—and direct himself towards their unprotected eye.

Jack cracked his neck and drummed his fingers on the table. The caffeine buzzed in his head. It had been a long time since his last cup of coffee.

Or *Ocean Octaves!*, he thought, as a craving hit him. *Why did I leave them in my car?*

Because you were headed into a Chinese buffet.

He remember his smashed car and how he'd attempted to reach the *Ocean Octaves!* within. They had been just out of reach.

They kidnapped Penny. They wounded Pak. They killed Paul.

Rage filled him as he recounted the crimes against him.

...and they took my Ocean Octaves!

Jack picked up his paper espresso cup and took another swig. His heart was pumping now.

EVERYTHING IS A WEAPON! Akras yelled, causing Jack to jump and crush his coffee cup, shooting a geyser of espresso into the air.

"Holy hickory king, Akras," Jack spat as coffee dripped down on him. He looked up at the splatter of coffee on the white ceiling. "You really did not need to give me super strength at this particular moment in time."

THE DRUG IS IN YOUR VEINS.

"It's coffee," Jack replied, looking around. A gal was looking at him wide-eyed over the top of her laptop. He waved to her. She blushed and hid behind her computer.

OH, said Akras after an awkward silence.

"I'm in trouble though," Jack said, wiping down his table with a napkin. "The bad guys took Penny."

SHE IS THE CONSORT OF THE CARETAKER.

"Yeah," Jack said. "And they're going to kill her if I don't let them capture me. And if they capture me, they might kill me. They're tying up loose ends."

YOU CANNOT DIE.

"I wish that were true," Jack said. "But I don't seem to have a choice. I have to turn myself in or they say they'll kill her."

WE CAN RESCUE HER.

"That's the goal. I must walk into the trap and then see if I can find a way out. I must do this."

YOU MUST NOT SEEK DANGER—YOU ARE THE CARE-TAKER.

"Danger sought me, buddy," Jack said. "I must... wait a minute." Jack put his hand into his shirt pocket and pulled out the tag he'd ripped from the huge pair of pantyhose in the warehouse vault. "I almost forgot—she mentioned a pile of pantyhose. This is the tag off a pair I found in the warehouse. Can you read this?"

LOOK AT IT WITH YOUR EYES AND I WILL TRANSLATE.

Jack looked at the tag.

Frú. Jólasveinn Nærföt Kvenna Búningur, Norðurpóll

THIS IS THE LANGUAGE OF THE ENEMY.

"It is?" Jack said.

WE BROUGHT THE WIND YET HE ESCAPED!

"Okay," Jack said. "I'm not sure what that means. So what language is it?"

THE TONGUE OF OLAF.

"You can't read it?"

WITH PAIN—IT SAYS SOMETHING LIKE: MRS. SAINT NIKLAS UNDERWEAR PANTRY, NORTH POLE.

"The North Pole," Jack said. "Called it."

Jack looked out the window at the moths circling the lights outside. "We're not headed there tonight, though. We need to get to FiveGees. Any idea where that's located?"

Akras said nothing, perhaps offended to be mistaken for a search engine.

"Hey," Jack said, calling to the barrista. "Do you know where FiveGees is?"

"Yeah," the guy said. "Their coffee stinks."

"Don't care. I need to meet someone there," Jack said.

"Don't you have Google maps?" the guy said petulantly, picking through a bin of sugar packets.

"Don't make me kill you," Jack said.

The guy looked up, intending to say something snarky, then saw Jack's face.

"Geez, man. It's on Norfolk and 37th, behind the Walgreens."

Jack reached in his pocket for his keys as he pushed through the exit door, then realized he didn't have a car. He couldn't even call an Uber.

Good thing he was fit. It might be a long walk. Outside, he caught his bearings. The town was based on a grid system so it shouldn't be hard to find where he was going. If this was 24th, he could just find the next intersection and start figuring out his way from there. He started walking towards the red light he saw a few blocks ahead. If things got too hairy, he could navigate by the stars. Jack looked up at the sky. It was half cloudy and the stars were dim from all the light pollution of the city. Okay, back to the street idea. Or—wait—he could build a compass with a piece of magnetized wire and a small container of water. Another option might be to–

"Hey," someone said. "You look lost."

Jack turned around to see a homeless man on a bench.

"I'm looking for FiveGees," Jack said.

"Down to the intersection, go right. About 12 blocks, I'd say, you go left on Norfolk. You won't miss it. Right by the Walgreens."

"Thanks," Jack said, somewhat disappointed he hadn't figured that out himself.

A half-hour later, Jack walked in to FiveGees and sat down at a table. He reached for his phone—then again remembered it was gone. *What was he supposed to log in with?* he thought. He looked around and saw a girl with an expensive-looking Apple laptop. *She'll let me borrow her computer if I ask*, Jack thought.

"Excuse me, miss?" Jack said, and the girl looked up. She was a mousy brunette, slightly overweight.

"Yes?" she said.

"May I borrow your computer for a moment?"

"What?" she said, flustered. "I, I don't know, I mean..."

"Just for a moment," Jack said. "It would mean a lot to me."

"Uh... okay," she half mumbled, clicking out of a few windows and pushing the computer towards him.

"You are beautiful," Jack said. "Don't ever let anyone tell you otherwise."

"They don't," the girl said.

Jack nodded distractedly, pulling up her wifi settings and logging out of the network. He had the computer rescan for networks and it found the cafe page and asked for his name. Gritting his teeth, he typed in "wimpyloserman" and joined the network. Then he logged out again and pushed the computer back to the girl. That should alert the bad guys.

"Julie," the girl said, extending her hand.

"Jack," Jack replied, giving her hand a squeeze. "Thanks. Sorry to bug you."

"No bother," the girl said with a blush, then shut her laptop and scurried out of the cafe.

Jack considered ordering a coffee then decided against it. He was already too keyed up. Maybe a brownie.

"Jack?" came a soft voice from behind him.

Jack turned around to see an older man at the next table. The guy did not look like a psychopathic robot—but neither did cattle egrets. Yet some of them were.

The man sat alone. Thin-framed glasses, thinning hair, a checkered blue and white shirt.

"I am he," Jack said, standing and moving to the man's table. He grabbed the man's hand as he sat down. It felt warm and he could feel a pulse. "Do you bleed red, old man?" Jack said, pulling out his grafting knife and holding it low so other patrons couldn't see what he was doing.

"Whoa, whoa," the guy said. "Now let's take it easy... we're here to meet and greet, not–"

"You took Penny," Jack hissed under his breath, squeezing the man's hand tighter. The old guy winced. If he were a robot, he was a convincing one. "Meeting and greeting is not high on my to-do list," Jack said. "Getting my girl back from you scumbags is. You messed with the wrong Broccoli."

"Please let go of my hand," the man said. "I do bleed red and I also bruise easily because of certain medications I must take."

"Don't care," Jack said, squeezing tighter. "Tell your boss to let Penny go."

"Ow!" the guy said. "Look, he'll kill her—I'm not the enemy here. I'm trying to help."

Jack looked into the old man's watery brown eyes. The edges were a cloudy blue with age, lids rimmed in red. He didn't look like a robot. Jack let go of his hand.

"Talk," Jack said.

"That is why I am here," the man said, taking back his hand and rubbing it. "I am indeed quite human. I suppose I could cut myself to prove I bleed but that's not even a very good test anymore, not since the new models."

"Enough talk," Jack said. "Where's Penny?"

"Someplace safe," the man said. "I do apologize for..."

"Someplace cold?" Jack asked.

The man blinked quickly, confirming Jack's guess.

"Someplace safe," the man repeated.

"Someplace safe where Santa lives?" Jack hissed.

The man blinked again. "I'm not here to talk about Santa," he sputtered. "I'm here to talk about you."

She was at the North Pole.

"Talk," Jack said.

The old man nodded and took a sip of water from the paper cup in front of him.

"You've been a hobby of mine for a while," the man said. "I've been keeping an eye on you for my boss, ever since you first appeared on the radar."

"Glad to be appreciated," Jack said. "Who are you?"

"Professor Hayworth. You can call me Spence."

"Fine, Hayworth. Tell me what you want and how I can get Penny."

The professor took off his glasses and cleaned the lenses with the tail of his shirt.

"Well, we don't really want Penny, you know," he said.

"Then why did you kidnap her?"

"We want you," the Professor shrugged.

"Your robots tried to kill me," Jack said. "Multiple times. But now you want me? Alive?"

"It was an unfortunate accident," the professor said.

"Tornadoes, choking swarms of *Paralobesia viteana* and death egrets? There were at least three accidents, then. And that doesn't count the dragonfly."

"You walked into that one," Hayworth said. "As for the others, it's one of the perils of AI," Hayworth shrugged. "All part of the defense system. You never should have visited Jonny. He was a bad man. You got tagged as also being a bad man. They learn, then they deal with issues so we don't have to. It's moving all of us towards a better world where we can follow our dreams in peace, painting and singing and living without money or clothing, engaging in large numbers of no-strings relationships with attractive women, no scarcity, no war..."

"That's enough commie talk," Jack said. "So now you're meeting me here to apologize? Makes zero sense," Jack said. "You've kidnapped my girl."

"Obviously," the man replied. "We didn't mean to kill you. That was just a normal reaction by the matrix, as I said. My boss figured it would make more sense to change tacks and have a nice little chat with you instead."

"By kidnapping my girl," Jack said.

The professor shrugged. "He can be a little unorthodox in his methods. He's used to getting his way. Fortunately, he has a soft spot for Broccolis."

"I prefer turnips," Jack said.

The professor chuckled. "See, that's why we didn't approach you directly. Any man that likes turnips can be quickly sorted into the 'difficult' category."

"Nothing wrong with turnips," Jack said.

"Studies disagree," Hayworth replied. "The turnip is the most hated vegetable in America."

"Preposterous," Jack said. "What studies?"

"Scientific ones," Hayworth shrugged. "It's scientifically proven that Americans hate turnips more than any other vegetable."

EVERYTHING IS A WEAPON! Akras shouted inside Jack's head.

"Shh," Jack said out loud.

"You asked me to talk," the professor said with a shrug. "I am talking."

"Let me recap, then," Jack said. "You think I'm difficult so you kidnapped my girlfriend. You also want some hippy-dippy world run by machines. You think the best vegetable on earth is terrible. This isn't telling me where Penny is and I am rapidly running out of patience."

"Americans think they're terrible," Hayworth corrected. "I am just reporting the facts."

"Whatever," Jack said.

"You must learn patience," the professor said, taking another sip of his water. "Or your girl will be dead. Or worse."

Ice ran down Jack's spine.

"Worse how?" Jack said.

The professor shrugged. "I shouldn't be so negative. I'm sorry. We've really started out on the wrong foot, haven't we?"

He smiled thinly. "Trust me, Jack. You'll want to work with us. Despite us having a rough start to our working relationship, what we are doing is for the greater good. You'll see it too."

"I doubt it," Jack said. "Just tell me what I need to do to get Penny."

The professor chuckled dryly. "You remind me of your father."

"My... what?" Jack said.

"Your father. Giles speaks fondly of him. Unfortunate, really."

"Keep my family out of this," Jack said. "Tell me what I need to do next. Or I swear, I'll graft your nose onto your elbow."

"You need to come with me," Professor Hayworth said, grabbing Jack's arm and squeezing tightly. "I've been trying to be conciliatory, but I can see you just aren't that smart."

Jack was shocked at the man's grip. It felt like the bone in his forearm was about to snap. The professor noticed Jack's face and smiled. Jack made a grasp for his grafting knife but Hayworth moved his other arm in a flash, snatching the blade from the table. Jack tried to jerk from the man's grasp but it was impossible—the grip was like a vise and despite the old man's apparently frailty, he was anchored to the ground like a steel beam in concrete.

The man clicked the knife open and pointed the tip at Jack's throat for a moment, then lowered it towards Jack's arm.

"You guessed correctly the first time," Hayworth said, lowering the blade further, then jabbing it into the flesh of his own arm. Nothing leaked out. Instead, it looked like the flesh was some sort of rubber foam. The professor cut deeper, revealing a glimpse of wires and tubing.

"It's better this way," he said. "My biological body is dead, yet I live on."

HE IS NOT PART OF EVERYTHING, Akras said.

"Thanks, you could have keyed me in sooner," Jack muttered back.

"You were right about the bleeding," Hayworth said with a smile. "You could have known quicker if you'd been more ruthless. I am an older model. Before the boss did his hostile takeover of 'I Can't Believe It's Not Meat, LLC and got their RealBlood(TM) formula.' Now— let's go," Hayworth said, pulling Jack along beside him. "There's no time left to talk."

Jack let himself be pulled along, planning to put up a serious fight in the parking lot, provided he could find a stick or something to beat down the mad robot.

As the professor pulled him out the door, he saw the mousy girl with the laptop standing outside.

"Hey," she said as she saw him, "I just came back to–"

Then she noticed he was being pulled away by the professor.

"Sorry," Jack said. "Can't talk. I'm being dragged away by a psycopathic robot."

"Why do I even bother! Every time I meet a nice boy..." the girl sobbed, fleeing to her scooter.

NOW? Akras yelled.

"Now," Jack said, jerking his arm free with a mighty tug, unbalancing the professor. He looked around for a weapon as the robot regained his balance but found nothing but some patches of dying grass at the edges of the sidewalk. He yanked up a handful and threw them as Hayworth closed in. They burst into flame, doing nothing but leaving black marks on the metal man's blue and white shirt. The robot swung a fist at Jack's face which Jack blocked, barely protecting his nose. The impact almost broke Jack's forearm and knocked him down onto the sidewalk. He scrambled back, desperately searching for a weapon—and then Hayworth charged him, slamming him brutally into the wall. Jack gasped for air as the surprisingly heavy Hayworth drove into him. He grabbed the robot's head and tried to choke him but it was useless. Then he drove his knee up into the professor's crotch. No effect. Jack drove the flat of his palm into the robot's neck. Still no effect. It was like fighting with an industrial metal coatrack. Every move Jack knew for hand-to-hand combat was predicated on the antagonist having human weaknesses. He grappled to free himself as Hayworth held him tight but the robot pinned him like a butterfly, locking him to the wall.

"Now you'll come with me, Jack," Hayworth said calmly, doing something with his right hand, then bringing it down on Jack's bicep. "We can continue our conversation later."

Jack felt a burning sting, then the streetlights started to spin around in a nauseating dance—and all went black.

CHAPTER 12

Spring and fall, winter and summer. They pass the young tree, yet even in time without leaves, it holds nests of birds like headless worm still holds ground with buttocks.

—A State of Bean: Principles of Mung Fu

Jack awoke in a green room. He felt woozy, like he'd downed too much Benadryl on an empty stomach.

The tiles on the wall kept drifting sideways in his vision, flowing up towards two o'clock, moving faster as he tried to focus. He clenched his eyes shut and his stomach flipped for a moment, the inside of his head a spinning blackness.

A green room. Penny had been in a green room, he remembered.

He opened his eyes again and stared at the ceiling until the room quit spinning. He felt strangely compressed and tried to move his arms. They refused to move and he realized he was restrained by something. He lifted his head slightly and saw that his body was under a blanket. It felt like his limbs were tied. He felt his adrenaline rising.

For a mad second he thought perhaps his head had been transplanted onto a robotic body.

Then he felt an itch on his left foot and let out the sharp breath he'd been holding. "If I was a robot, I wouldn't itch," Jack whispered to himself.

YOU COULD STILL BE. IT MIGHT BE A PHANTOM PAIN.

"Like when people lose limbs," Jack said, his heart skipping a beat. His foot itched more and he tried to move it. He could turn it slightly but not enough to help with the itch, then realized he had another need.

"My kidneys are telling me I'm human," Jack said. "Please don't tell me there is such a thing as a phantom bladder..."

I ALREADY KNEW YOU WERE ALL HUMAN, Akras replied. *YOU ARE PART OF EVERYTHING.*

"Sheesh. You had me going there for a moment."

"How are we?" came a chipper digital voice, as what appeared to be a four foot tall robot waiter rolled into the room with a tray containing a glass of orange juice and a bagel. "Is sir ready for a little lunch?"

"I'm ready to be untied," Jack said. "Is there a bathroom around here?"

"Oh yes, sir, no problem at all," the robot said. "There is a facility in this room, but for your safety the door to the hall will be locked to ensure your complete comfort."

"I'd be comfortable if you left it open," Jack said as a metal lattice dropped over the doorway. It hit with the floor with a clang and Jack heard a clank of bolts engaging.

"Sir will also be fitted with this convenient collar," the robot said happily, fixing a band around Jack's neck.

"Hey," Jack said, "I'm cool without it."

"We have adjusted the temperature of this room for your complete safety and happiness, as well as provided this collar especially for you," the robot said as the collar locked into place. Jack could hear the collar hum slightly, as if electrified.

"Great," Jack said. "Now can I get up?"

"Oh yes sir," the robot said, pushing an invisible button on the hospital bed. The straps clicked loose and Jack carefully moved his arms and legs. The robot beamed at him with the digital LED display that served as his face.

"Sir is now free. But may I please request that you do not attempt to damage this servile unit or anything in your quarters as that would require us to extend additional layers of hospitality."

"Sure," Jack said, looking around for a weapon. "No problem."

The room was irritatingly prisoner-proofed. No curtainrods, no chairs, no carpeting hiding oh-so-sharp tack strips—nothing. Jack decided to simply use the bathroom, then return to his bed. When he did, he noticed the orange juice and bagel and his stomach growled.

Could they be poisoned? Jack thought.

His stomach growled again and he decided to risk it.

The servant robot was bumping from wall to wall in what appered to be a random pattern, vacuuming the floor while humming tunelessly. It noticed Jack watching. "Sir may please enjoy your meal," it said. "We must apologize for the inconvenience of vacuuming time but it is the time for vacuuming."

"No problem," Jack said, wolfing down the bagel and chasing it with orange juice. Too late, he realized he could have used the bagel as a weapon. Maybe he could regurgitate it and... no. No, that was just nasty.

"When are you going to let me out?" he asked.

"If sir is not completely satisfied he may speak with the management," the robot replied as it scooted to the door, apparently finished with the vacuuming.

Jack thought for a moment he would follow it through—but the bolted security grill came up and the inside door closed so quickly after the retreating bot that it was too late before he'd even left the bed.

"Speak with the management," Jack mumbled to himself, then collapsed on the bed, weak and woozy. He was asleep in moments.

"We want you to be happy," Hayworth said, opening a semi-translucent door that glowed with what appeared to be sunlight. It swished open and Jack looked out at a beautiful garden. It stretched out for what looked like a mile in all directions. A garden was the last thing he'd expected to see at the North Pole, but here it was— lush, verdant, and filled with a huge variety of tropical foliage. Was I mistaken? Jack wondered at the sight—it was stunning. It was paradise!

He blinked up at the bright light of the sky and saw a clear dome far above, its seams dusted with snow.

Gotta be the pole.

Jack looked over at Hayworth. The man—robot, Jack corrected himself—had woken him up and escorted him through a series of hallways, saying little on the way. They had encountered no other people on their walk. The professor smiled at him when he saw Jack's glance.

"We thought you'd like it. Let's walk down and through, shall we?"

Jack followed Hayworth. The air was rich with the aroma of fungi and dew. Butterflies from dozens of nations flitted through the air as a slight breeze stirred the leaves of heliconias, colocasias and some jungle plants even Jack couldn't name.

"Are you a hundred percent robot?" Jack asked Hayworth.

Hayworth chuckled. "I'm not even sure, actually. Transhumanism is a heckuva thing, you know."

"Where you leave your bodies behind," Jack said. "Stupid scientist dreams about immortality."

"Perhaps," Hayworth said mildly. "Giles has poured billions into it. He decided to test it on me first, as I am one of his closest associates."

"Not on himself?" Jack said.

"No, no. Giles is too important. When we know for sure it all works, then he'll do it, I'm sure."

"I'm sure," Jack said. "So what did they do to you?"

"It was quite a process," Hayworth said, plucking an orchid flower and peering into it as he spoke. "He uploaded my mind into this forever body. It was terrifying but worked out in the end."

"Uploaded your mind—or transplanted your brain?" Jack said.

"I don't actually know," Hayworth admitted. "It's very difficult, you know."

"What is? To transplant a brain?"

"Yes. It's not actually my field, of course, but there are lots of nerves and vessels and such."

"Right," Jack said. "So, tell me about this collar I'm wearing and why the heck I am walking through a greenhouse with an android. And where Penny is. And who I can kill to avenge Paul."

"So many questions," Hayworth said. "So many–"

"Nevermind, you'll do for starters." Jack wheeled and punched him in the face as hard as he could, knocking the robot backward into a beautiful *Ficus auriculata*.

"Could you feel that in your brain?" Jack said, holding his hand in pain. That had hurt like heck. Though the man's face had been weirdly squishy, with what felt like a metal casing inside.

Hayworth rose smoothly to his feet, ignoring Jack's question.
THERE ARE WEAPONS EVERYWHERE!

"That's a new phrasing," Jack replied, snapping off the branch of a convenient *Ficus religiosa*.

"You shouldn't have attacked me," the professor said, dusting off his shirt. It was the same blue and white checkered shirt he'd been wearing

the night he kidnapped Jack. "I will answer your questions eventually. I just think we should enjoy this space for a while and be harmonious."

"I'll show you harmonious," Jack said, then swung the branch, the leaves whistling as it broke the sound barrier before slamming into the robot's chest. The explosive blow drove Hayworth backward into the trunk of a towering *Ficus benjamina*, cracking its trunk. The robot jerked spastically and tried to pull itself free.

"Wait," it said, voice garbled. "I wanted to talk more about your future with us."

"You have no future," Jack said. He yanked a handful of fruit off a *Ficus palmata* and winged them explosively through the robot, punching juice-spattered holes through Hayworth before he could free himself. Jack grabbed another branch from a gently weeping *Ficus lyrata*, and swung it in a perfect arc, knocking the metal professor's head clean off his shoulders. Jack watched it sail into a faraway stand of *Bambusa chungii*.

"Fore!" Jack called as an afterthought.

MAYBE YOU SHOULD HAVE ASKED MORE QUESTIONS BEFORE SMACKING OFF HIS HEAD, Akras said.

"I don't give a fig about that creepy robot professor," Jack said, sitting down on a little Japanese bench by a running stream and splashing some water on his face. "I told Paul I was going to avenge him. There's my first payment on the debt."

"And your last," came the voice of professor Hayworth.

Jack wheeled back to where the broken robot lay—and then saw another Hayworth standing just to his right. Jack jumped up, cocking his fist back—and froze as a jolt of electricity pulsed through his body, radiating from the collar on his neck. He yelled in pain, grasping at the collar.

"That body was expensive," Hayworth II said calmly as Jack twitched and jerked. The robot walked up to the paralyzed man, pulled back his arm, then punched Jack in the face, knocking him onto the slate cobblestones of the path. Jack quit jerking as the collar quit its pulsing.

He could barely move. Every muscle felt overtightened and sore, as if he'd just run a marathon while carrying a sleeper sofa on his back.

"You..." Jack managed to say. Blood dripped from one of his nostrils and a bruise was already forming under his eye. "You..."

"Yes," Hayworth II said. "Me. You didn't think I was locked in just one body, did you? Of course not. Now you've cost us, though. We'll have to arrange some sort of payment plan. It cost over ten million, you know."

"Don't... care." Jack growled as he forced his way up from the ground. "Bill it to the digital devil when I send you to silicon hell." He snatched at a *Ficus psuedopalma* branch, intending to knock the head off Hayworth II—then was stopped again by a jolt from the collar that made him gasp in pain, clutching at his throat. He was helpless.

"Please stop this nonsense," Hayworth II said. "It's all so tiresome. Just have a seat here and relax. We can talk later."

Jack gave in and collapsed to a sitting position.

"That's better," Hayworth said, crouching next to him and balancing perfectly on his haunches. "You know, if you won't be swayed by science, I'll bet you'll be swayed by marketing. Most people respond better to rhetoric, you know." He nodded to himself, looking up into the sky thoughtfully. "Yes, that might be what you need. I'll set up a teleconference with Alan and you can talk later. He's much better at that sort of thing. I'll also have to talk with accounting about my other body. Awful waste. Awful."

The robot professor shook his head at Jack and wagged a finger at him. "No more violence for you. That's not the way we're going to make our brave new world! Not until we've exhausted all other options, I mean."

He turned and strode away. In front of him, the ground opened in a black circle. Hayworth stepped down into the hole and dissappeared.

"So that's where he came from," Jack mumbled painfully. "I wonder how many of this guy I'll have to kill?"

CHAPTER 13

Many words falling, even as sacks of rice overflow, is not equal to the swift kick in the liver.

—A State of Bean: Principles of Mung Fu

"So you are at least tangentially familiar with the concept of brand ambassadors? It's a great op, top shelf disruption," Pickle said.

"Sure, if selling your soul along with bathing suits and plastic sunglasses on Instagram can be called great," Jack muttered. He was slumped in a plastic chair in a gray carpeted room, talking to some idiot named Alan Pickle via teleconferencing software. Jack held a wad of Spanish moss to his still-bleeding nose as Hayworth II sat next to him, apparently asleep.

"It really is, if you're approaching the brand holistically," Pickle said. "We're skating to where the puck will be. The ultimate wow factor requires getting people to assimilate the narrative that experts agree their world will burn up in a decade unless awareness goes viral."

"People need to buy that idea?" Jack said. "What about this last winter? It was terribly cold."

"See, that's the nub," Pickle said. "Our experts all agree that it makes strategic sense to give the world a little push so people really feel the heat and find alignment with our vision before the window of opportunity slams shut. That's why we facilitated the manufacture of our little greenhouse ark, you know. Where we have truly organic AC, a cool place, right? Very cool, very agile. And in case the community isn't keyed in before the tipping point, this is our antifragile backup. Which is also a high-level place to escape the runaway plagues, dust storms, starvation, fires and all around bad weather part of the overall enterprise. If you're not onboard, literally, you won't be able to afford the minimum viable product."

Jack's nose was numb and his eye was partly swollen shut. And now his brain was tired. Pickle apparently wanted him to join WEEWEE or die. That seemed to be the gist.

"You simply need to consider brand mobility as well as saturation and natural convexities," Pickle continued.

"Sure," Jack said. "Or you'll kill me."

"That's a crude way to put our advanced client conversion techniques," Pickle said, shaking his head. "You must know we decided to invest in the Broccoli brand primarily because the boss was sentimental. You saw some things you shouldn't have, sure, but he knew your dad and wanted to give you a chance. Your dad understood plants, and of course, you do as well. Plants are a piece of the puzzle, as you can see in our little dome of wonders here."

"I'll consider it if you bring me Penny first."

"You have what we in sales call 'a weak hand,' " Pickle said. "Not a good bargaining position. However, I want you to immerse yourself in this video and tell me honestly that you're not stirred by our vision. The boys in marketing really outdid themselves on this one—just check it out."

Pickle clicked around with a mouse for a moment, then the screen went black. Ominous music began, followed by a rich African baritone.

"The world... is on fire."

A scene of wildfires. Then a riot with burning buildings. Then a volcanic explosion.

"Mother Earth has a fever..."

A shot of bubbling mud. Ocean waves slamming against rocks under a blood red sunset. Then streams of lava running down a blackened hillside and hissing into the sea.

"You can help."

A young Caucasian woman with a tattoo and thick glasses looks up from her computer. Hopeful music begins.

"And you."

A young Asian man on a treadmill looks to the camera and smiles.

"And you."

A half-naked Papuan man spits a gob of betel on the ground and grins a red-toothed grin at the camera.

"And you?"

A question mark appears on the screen.

"Will you help?"

"The Earth Recovery Initiative needs you to make real changes."

Image of a group of children holding hands around a gigantic tree trunk.

"To lend a hand."

A blonde woman reaches out her hand and grasps the hand of an orangutan.

"To make a difference."

A young mixed-race couple hold hands while watching a sunrise over a mountain.

"ERI. It's time for a change."

An aurora swirls overhead as a logo appears, featuring a green earth in a pyramid with hands around it. The music swells, then the scene fades to black.

"Are you selling cereal or something?" Jack said.

"It's our vision, Jack!" Pickle said. "Can't you feel it?"

"I feel ticked," Jack said. "I want my girl back."

"But she's there, you know."

"Where?" Jack said, rising to his feet.

Pickle laughed. "Close. You'll see her soon. Don't overclock yourself. There's plenty more to engage with here, as we haven't even scratched the surface on the exciting work we're doing. There's a place for you here, Jack, as a brand partner. Not to be too direct, but don't you want to heal the earth? She has a fever!"

Jack looked out the window at the gardens. A jacaranda was a few yards away outside, covered in brilliant purple-blue blooms. The gardens were amazing. He could not care less about volcanoes and sunsets. He didn't want anything to happen to the earth's plant life—that was the part he cared about.

"Picture yourself as a brand ambassador," Pickle said. "You could make a difference with your gardening, you know. You'll enjoy a competive salary and benefits with a dynamic role as part of a bleeding-edge content marketing team—and maybe even a place on the ark when the sea levels rise, provided you've navigated the mass die-offs due to our artisanally crafted fair trade plague viruses."

"Caused by you?" Jack said.

"Caused by everyone," Pickle said. "You and me. And all of the human race. Everyone knows the mass die-offs are an obvious eventuality, either from space viruses or war or violent video games or overpopulation or religion or CO_2 emissions and non-standard sea levels."

"I am not raising the sea level," Jack said.

"Oh Jack, of course you're in on the roll-out," Pickle chuckled. "Just by breathing."

"But aren't you guys doing more—like, melting the ice and that sort of thing?"

"In for a penny, in for a pound," Pickle said. "We are harnessing certain leverages to raise awareness."

"By raising the sea level?"

"The tipping point requires tangibles like flooded condos to drive home the point that we need to act," Pickle said. "We need to get the normies on board, which requires solid convexities. You're a smart guy, Jack. I would have expected you to know this."

Jack nodded. He knew all right. He knew he had to kill everyone involved in this madness. Not only was it the right thing to do, it was what Paul would have wanted.

"Where are you, Pickle?" Jack asked.

"San Fran, baby," Pickle replied. "Why?"

"No particular reason," Jack said.

"Jack?" came a voice from behind him.

"Penny!" Jack said, jumping to his feet. There she was, as beautiful as ever, dressed in a short aqua-green dress.

"Told you she was in your wheelhouse," Pickle said. "We can dialog more on sustainable native advertising at a future date. Think about the vision, Jack—it's a beautiful chance to be a thought leader." The screen went black. Hayworth still sat in his chair, eyes shut.

"Oh Jack!" Penny said, throwing herself into his arms. "Are you okay? What happened to your face?" she said in sudden concern.

"It's nothing," Jack said.

"I'll bet. I'd like to see the other guy!" Penny said.

"His head is in the bamboo," Jack said.

Penny laughed.

"It's not funny," Hayworth said, waking up suddenly and startling Jack.

EVERYTHING IS A WEAPON! Akras roared

Jack snatched up his chair and swung it, knocking off Hayworth II's head. It blasted through the window glass and bounced off into a stand of tree ferns. The remains of the robot squirted red fluid from the neck hole, spattering the ceiling.

"Oh my gosh!" Penny screamed. "You killed him!"

"He startled me," Jack said.

"And you decapitated him?" Penny yelled.

"He's a robot," Jack said. "Ignore the blood. It's fake. It's even patented."

"Oh my gosh," Penny repeated again, clapping her hands to her mouth. "Oh... my... gosh."

"It's okay," Jack said. "You'll get used to it. So—they didn't hurt you?"

"No," said Penny, catching her breath. "Uh, I'm fine, except that you literally just decapitated an old man. Are you sure he's a robot?"

"Sure," Jack said, kicking the body. "Ouch," he said, wincing. "Yep, he's a robot. All metal inside. If that was a real human body I could have kicked it without it hurting so much."

"How many people have you kicked, Jack?" Penny asked.

"Never mind that," Jack said. "Come over here and give Hayworth a good kick. You'll feel the metal inside."

"I don't want to," Penny said.

"Aw, come on. You wanted to know if he was a human. How else are you going to know? Just give the body a little kick."

"Fine," Penny said, then kicked the fallen man. "Ouch!" she said. "He *is* made of metal!"

"See? It hurts to kick a robot. When the first version of him kidnapped me I tried all kinds of moves. It was like fighting a suit of armor. The trick is to catch him off-guard."

"Wow," Penny said. "He kidnapped you? I can see why you'd be taken in... he just looks like an old man. I was kidnapped by a cartoon waiter bot."

"Yeah," Jack said. "I guess they thought they'd fool me. But tell me— are you really okay?"

"Yes," Penny replied. "I was scared for a bit. The woman, Elaine, the one you talked to on the phone—at first she explained to me that I wasn't really kidnapped. Just detained, so as to surprise you. She called you on the phone, then..."

"And then they tortured you?"

"The collar," Penny said, touching slim fingers to the band around her neck. "I'm sorry—it must have freaked you out!"

"Dirty weevils," Jack said. "Forget about me freaking out. They hurt you, of all people. For what?"

"I don't know," she said.

"For their brand," Jack said. He looked Penny up and down. "You look intact."

"You like the dress?" Penny said.

"Looks great," Jack said.

"They gave it to me," Penny said. "And Elaine apologized for shocking me. Said it was just business. The dress is supposed to be enviromentally responsible. The tag says it's made from 100% post-consumer grated parmesan cheese canister lids."

"Weird. They gave me a shirt and pants. I have no idea if they're environmentally sound or not, but they are uncomfortable enough to be. So far, they are keeping me clothed."

"You also have a collar," Penny said.

"Yeah, we're in this together," Jack said. "Only way to get to you was by giving in."

"You didn't have to," Penny said.

"Yes, I did. And now we need to make a plan to–"

"There's so much that can be heard out here," Penny interrupted. "Birds, waterfalls..."

"Right," Jack said, realizing she was alluding to hidden microphones. "Birds, and waterfalls... wonderful."

"Yes, sure is," Penny said. "Look, I know we were kidnapped and started out on the wrong foot, but we really should just go along with whatever they say. They're really trying their best to save the world."

"Maybe you're right," Jack said.

"Let's go see the waterfall," Penny said, taking his hand.

Jack let her lead the way to a towering waterfall pouring down a cliff covered in *Monstera* vines. They picked their way down a narrow path to the side of the waterfall and came to a group of rounded boulders moist with the cool spray from above.

"Jack," Penny said. "It's safe to talk here, I think."

"Good of you to think of it. I forgot they might be recording us," Jack said, reaching out and touching a ripening *Monstera* fruit. "Man, these gardens are something else."

"They are psycho," Penny said. "I hate that stupid robot that cleans my room. And Elaine is a psycho. And has an ugly haircut. Did you see her? It's short and gray, like a marine haircut or something. She wouldn't let me put butter on my toast."

"I hate her already," Jack said. "But I hate Hayworth more. I hope I killed the final version of him. Hey—look at those plants draped over the cliff here. Looks like a type of bromeliad."

"Is he human?" Penny said.

"No, he's a monocot," Jack said, examining the plant's bright red flowers.

"Hayworth, I mean!" Penny said. "Is there a human version of him somewhere?"

"No, I don't think so," said Jack. "I think he said his body was dead. Though he was unsure about a brain transplant or something."

"Does he have another head somewhere?" Penny said.

"I don't know. I've knocked off two so far."

"How horrible," Penny said. "That he used to be a man."

"I guess," Jack said. "Too bad I couldn't have knocked off the original's head."

"They didn't hurt you badly, did they?" Penny asked, running her fingertips over Jack's bruised face.

"I've had worse," Jack said. "This is nothing. But you—I came to find you—are you truly okay? Other than shocking you when I was on the phone, have they hurt you in any other way?"

"No," Penny said. "The fabric on this dress doesn't breathe, though."

"I imagine not," Jack replied. "Actually, my clothes feel like they're made of rubber. Maybe from the *Ficus elastica* here, come to think of it. Did you see the variegated one by the Japanese bench?"

"Did you read the tags?" Penny said.

"No," Jack said. "They have labels but there's no need. The variegation is obvious. It's a mutation in the genes that produce chlorophyll."

"I mean the tag on your shirt," Penny said.

"Right." Jack twisted to look at the tag on his shirt. "Dryclean only. 100% post-consumer LEGO tires."

"Wow," said Penny. "How would they even sort those?"

"Using AI-controlled robotic feet with touch sensors," came a voice.

They both jumped and turned to face the flickering form of an older man in a sweater. "How else?" the man continued. "You can't hand-sort those things from a landfill. But technology brings great possibility."

"Alright, I am getting really, really tired of people showing up randomly," Jack said, looking at the apparition. The man walked through a boulder, then hovered a little above their heads.

"Wait," Jack said. "You're a hologram!"

"Very perceptive," the man said. "How do you like my gardens?"

"I am quite impressed, though I'd like them more if I wasn't wearing a shock collar," Jack said.

"I'm sure," the man said. "Though we can't exactly trust you, now can we? No, we can't," he said quickly, answering himself.

"If you were drugged and kidnapped, would you have any reason to be trustworthy?" Jack said.

"It's a fair point," the hologram said with a shrug. "What do you think about Alan's offer?"

"I didn't even understand most of his offer," Jack said.

"Join or die is the offer," the hologram said. "Either by fire or plague or more direct means."

"That's what I thought," Jack said.

"You don't often get offers that good," the hologram said. "Usually there's a lot of negotiation, back and forth, stupid interviews, so on and so forth. But I am a direct man. I can't just let you go and have you spilling the beans on our project. Plus I could use a good gardener."

"You're Giles Batson, aren't you?" Jack said.

"Of course," Giles said. "Don't you watch television?"

"Not much," Jack said. "Unless it's a gardening show."

"Gardening is what we're doing better than anyone else," Giles said. "We have the largest private repository of plant genetics in the world. Right here at the North Pole."

Jack looked around and nodded. "It is impressive." Despite himself, he was fascinated. "What do you do for supplemental lighting? I imagine it gets really dark here during the winter."

"Great question," the hologram said. "We have high-powered fluorescent strips inside all the girders of the dome. We can also dim the smart glass during the super-long summer months, though we've found the plants don't really seem to need it. It's amazing how versatile plants can be. You should come out here and see the aurora borealis this evening—it's magical. You can lie on the floor of a tropical jungle and enjoy the northern lights above. Nothing like it in the world."

"That is amazing," Jack said, despite himself. The gardens were a thing of beauty.

"Jack," Penny said, seeing Jack's interest. "Don't let him get inside your head."

"I'm not, Penny," Jack said. "We just don't really have a choice. Either we die or we join. And at least they are saving plant varieties and hoping to save the earth. And they have a great collection of fig species."

"Jack!" Penny hissed at him under her breath. "You can't be serious."

"They even have a *Ficus opposita* over there." Jack pointed. "It's fruiting!"

"Jack!" Penny said. "Plants aren't the important thing!"

Jack looked at her as if she'd said, "no one actually needs lungs."

Jack turned to the hologram.

"Fine, Giles. If I can spend at least part of the day in these gardens, I'll join you."

Penny put her hand to her mouth with a small gasp. "Jack..."

"You'll be able to do much more than that," Giles said, ignoring her. "I knew you'd like the gardens. Welcome to WEEWEE."

✳ ✳ ✳

"I am so sorry we got off on the wrong foot," Hayworth III said. "You really have some anger issues."

"That's what they said at botany camp," Jack said, stepping into Hayworth's office.

"I'm the real Spence, by the way, so please don't knock my head off," the old man said, kicking a broken hockey stick out of the way so he could take a seat behind a battered wooden desk. A half-dozen other broken hockey sticks lay scattered around the room, but they weren't what caught Jack's attention. Instead, his attention was taken by a huge promotional poster on the wall. On it was a realistic rendering of the main garden dome, now floating in an ocean and surrounded by a veritable floating metropolis of apartments and other buildings of unknown use.

He turned from the image and looked closely at Hayworth. "I thought your old body was dead or something," Jack said.

"What nonsense," Hayworth said. "Did you hear that from Hayworth I or II?"

"Both, I think," Jack said. "I'm kind of losing track."

"No matter," Hayworth said. "I saw you looking at the poster. Alan's people put it together. You like our plans?"

"I suppose," Jack said. "I see the dome is floating, rather than sitting in ice. I didn't get a good look at the outside when I arrived, as I was drugged and unconscious."

"Yes, yes, I heard about that," Hayworth III said.

"You did it," Jack said.

"My autonomous robot body did it," Hayworth III corrected.

"You've got too many lives," Jack said. He looked closer at the illustration on the wall. "So there's nothing outside the dome right now—this is all a future plan?"

"It's in progress," Hayworth said. "We're securing some funding right now and working on the transportation lines. You know, we're technically an underwear manufacturer at this point, for some reason that only makes sense to the boss. Shipping up here is frightfully expensive but we get some of what we need through Norway, where the actual factory is located. Sometimes they accidentally send us pantyhose."

"I caught that," Jack said. "I haven't seen many people here at all. Where are they?"

"The limited staff we have right now is mostly technical. They keep the heat on, the electricity running, etc. Most live in the tunnels. The garden has subterranean heating, you know. Some of them manage that. And there are a score of gardeners, too, though they were told to stay out of the gardens until you got your bearings. It wouldn't do to have you knocking any heads off. It's expensive to get staff here, though we should get some dedicated drones soon. Most of them have been pressed into other work."

"Like trying to take people's heads off."

"You should talk!" Hayworth III said.

"Point taken," Jack said. "But it's like a prison here. If there's just the dome and some dorms and offices like this one, surrounded by the howling cold of the North Pole, you could do anything with your staff you wanted. Who are they going to call? There's no government overseeing this place. You could be burying them in the ice."

"Oh Jack," Hayworth said. "Jack, Jack, Jacky, Jack Jack. Jacky Jacky Jackity Jack Jack... you really don't understand anything. The UN has been here. We've had child activists here. We had the Tiara Club visit. It's not exactly a Siberian gulag. It's not a prison. It's an ark."

"An ark." Jack said. "For plants."

"And not only plants," Hayworth said. "Elaine is working on a process of gene storage that uses the essential salts of animals, allowing an ingenious scientist to raise any stored animal back to life."

"Sounds like something from a horror novel," Jack said.

"Nonsense. We're working to save endangered species. Mr. Batson wanted us to make raptors, too, but we're short on DNA."

"So what do you want from me?"

"We want you to be a gardener," Hayworth said. "I'm sure Mr. Batson shared that. We've built a nursery area alongside the main dome but the current manager isn't exactly innovative. He's mostly interested in ornamentals, yet the boss has said we should concentrate more on food production."

"You want veggie gardens?"

"Sure," Hayworth said. "And orchards. And living forests of food. We can get seeds for anything. And I do mean anything. The entire world is your seed bank, Jack. Any seed in the world, we can get it. That's what being a part of WEEWEE means."

"Any seed," Jack repeated. His mind raced. "Any seed in the world?"

"Yes," Hayworth said. "Any continent, any family—it doesn't matter. Our resources are functionally infinite."

"Can you get *Diospyros crassiflora* seeds?" Jack asked.

Hayworth shrugged. "I'm sure we could. I'm not sure what it is, but I can look." He flipped open the laptop on his desk and typed in a query.

"Ah yes, ebony. From West Africa. It says here we already have some seeds in the nursery bank. Just waiting for planting."

"Wow," Jack said, getting excited. He had been planning to go along with the bad guys for a while, then plan a prison break, rescuing Penny and hopefully killing everyone else—but he had to admit, this gig did look like a dream job. They actually wanted him to grow edible plants—and could get him any plant in the world? They may be psychotic extremists, but hey—a lot of employers were. Maybe this would work out after all. It was way better than going back to his stupid job propagating ligustrums.

Though Penny won't like it, he thought. She doesn't care about plants and just wants to go home.

Whatever. He'd worry about that later.

These people also want to drown most of the world and release plagues.

Sure, but they have honest-to-goodness ebony seeds in storage!

And you swore to take revenge.

Later! I can do that later!

Jack turned to Hayworth. "Can you show me the nursery?"

"Of course," Hayworth said.

* * *

The head of the nursery was a burly guy with a white handlebar mustache. He nodded to Jack and Hayworth as they walked in out of the dome into the moist and well-lit greenhouse area. The greenhouse extended for acres in every direction and was filled with benches of plants of all kinds. Mist systems hissed on and off above tables as robotic arms tended flats of seedlings.

"Hey there you fruit," the nursery manager said, punching Hayworth in the arm.

"Ouch!" Hayworth said.

"Oh, hurts does it then?" the nurseryman said. "Not the robot today, are we?"

"No," Hayworth said.

"So who'd you bring me here, Hayseed? A new android?"

"Human," Hayworth said. "He's a new recruit. He's going to help in the gardens."

"Broccoli," Jack said, extending his hand. The man took it and squeezed hard. Jack squeezed back and the man's face reddened as he pressed harder. "Jack Broccoli."

The guy finally gave up and stretching the fingers in his hand with a look of pain. "Well met. I'm Brink Jones. Good grip. Not a robot, though?"

"No," Jack said. "Though apparently the new ones do bleed red."

"Nuts," Brink said. "They keep messing around with stuff, don't they. One day they're gonna make robotic plants and put me outta business."

"I'll leave you two to talk," Hayworth said, turning to leave.

"You do that, you little nerdman," Brink said, waving. He turned back to Jack. "That guy is a stick in the mud."

Jack nodded. "I knocked his head off a couple of times."

"Good man," Brink said, slapping Jack on the arm. "So—you like gardening?"

"Of course," Jack said.

"What do you like to grow?" Brink asked. "I've got all kinds of stuff here." He pointed to some trays where a few seedlings were just popping above the soil. "There's some *Sterculia lanceifolia* right there. Hard to get those seeds, but they got 'em for me."

"I don't know that species," Jack admitted.

"Great genus," Brink said. "Malvaceae family. Amazing seed pods on some of them. Like artwork."

"Can you eat them?" Jack asked.

"No idea," Brink said. "I'm more of an ornamental guy. They want more edible stuff, you know, but I'm more of a chicken and potatoes type, not big on fruits and veggies."

"They mentioned wanting more food species," Jack said. "That's apparently part of the reason they wanted me here."

"Well, we got plenty of propagation space," Brink said. "And they can get you anything you want to grow. Name some weird berry in the Amazon and they'll have a guy get it, even if it has to be transported across miles of swamp on canoes dragged by crocodiles. They really take the plants seriously here. When all the animals die it's all we're gonna have. At least that's what Elaine says."

"Elaine?" Jack asked.

"Yeah, she's one of the bigwig scientists. Cold, nasty woman. Comes by now and again to poke around the orchid collection, though, so she can't be completely evil. So—you want to help move some potting soil?"

"Why not?" Jack said. "I need the exercise."

After a day of potting plants, sticking cuttings, talking Latin, and comparing knowledge, Jack had almost forgotten he was trapped at the North Pole.

* * *

After taking his leave of Brink, Jack found the cafeteria and was served by what he assumed was the same robot waiter—or same model—that had kidnapped Penny.

"Can you get me a hamburger?" he said to the robot.

"Oh no, sir, cow is not on the menu."

"What?" Jack said. "Why?"

"Cows cause global warming," the waiter replied.

"They do?" Jack said. "How?"

"There is no way to put delicately what it is cows do, dear sir, which cause said warming."

"Okay," Jack said. "But I thought you guys were speeding up global warming on purpose so you can fight it—or something like that."

"This servile unit is not equipped to share more, sir, as it is outside its functionality, but one may complain to management if one is not completely satisfied."

Jack ordered a plate of nachos instead.

Afterward, he headed to his apartment for a change of clothes. His room was fully stocked with clothing, shoes and toiletries, including multiple types of personal care products and creams he had never seen before and which he viewed with great suspicion. There was no way men needed skin creme or beard wax. Instead of showering in his room, he decided to take a pair of swim trunks to the locker room beside the huge swimming pool he'd discovered, take a shower there, then go for a swim. After his shower, he walked out to the pool—and found Penny swimming laps. They were alone. He watched her graceful form sliding through the water for a minute, then jumped in and swam over. She spotted him and stopped her laps.

"Hey," she said.

"Hey," he replied.

"I'm sorry," she said.

"For what?" Jack replied.

"I doubted you. You really seemed to be getting into the plant thing, and I..."

"Don't mention it," Jack said, wondering if he should tell her how psyched he was about the next day's plan to clone a series of rare *Ananas* species.

"Let's not talk now," Penny said. "Let's just swim. We can have dinner, then meet later—in the jungle."

"Great," Jack said, kicking away from her. "Beat you to the other side!"

After dinner Jack and Penny walked to the waterfall. As they walked, the sky above began to glow green. Penny looked up. "What are they doing—turning on a screensaver?"

Jack looked up as she said it, his mouth hanging open. Ribbons of light were appearing across the sky, mostly green but with quick hints of red and yellow as they flowed.

"Gotta be the northern lights," Jack whispered.

"You've seen them before?" Penny asked. "This is the auroras people talk about, then?"

"I think so," Jack said. "I've never seen them before."

"It's amazing," Penny said. For a few minutes they watched the slow dance of doomed particles before finally pulling their eyes from the sky and continuing on the path leading to the falls.

At the falls they chose a comfortable rock and lay back to watch the sky.

"Think they can hear us here?" Penny asked Jack after a few minutes of aurora watching.

"Probably," Jack said. "They can probably still read our lips if they can't hear due to the falls."

"Oh," Penny said.

"Here," Jack said, sitting up. She rose as well. "Let's see what they think of this." He kissed her and she held him tightly.

"I don't like this place," she whispered into his shoulder.

Jack said nothing.

"You're going to get us out, right?" she said quietly.

"Yeah," Jack said. "I will."

"Oh good," Penny sighed. "I thought you were going to let them seduce you with all their fancy plants and seeds and big nursery and gardens and..."

Jack stared off into space, thinking of all their fancy plants and seeds and the big nursery and the gardens. If she'd wanted to convince him to leave—which he had been planning on doing—talking about the gardens was precisely the wrong tack to take. Suddenly the girl pressed against him seemed very far away and very alien. Paul's death seemed remote and the promise of revenge just some rash words spoken in anger. Right here around him grew a verdant tropical paradise beneath the northern lights above. He had barely begun to explore the collection of plants. If he left, he'd also miss his chance to search the botanical treasure troves of the world for exciting species to propagate and grow. Penny could never understand the green heart that beat in Jack's chest. His true love and passion. His one and only true love and passi–

"I love you, Jack," Penny said, interrupting his reverie. She kissed him hard. "I know you'll get us out of here."

With the touch of her lips, Jack's reverie fell apart like a Chinese spading fork. In that moment he made his choice, though it tore something green and beautiful in his soul.

He would get them out. He had to. After all, they were going to kill millions. And he needed revenge. And of course, Penny wanted to leave.

"Can you get us out tonight?" Penny said softly.

"No way," Jack whispered into her hair.

"Why?" Penny said.

"This is the North Pole," Jack said.

"Oh, right," Penny said. "It's cold outside."

"Cold enough to kill us in a few minutes," Jack said. "Did you ever read that story by Jack London where the guy goes out in the Yukon and tries not to freeze to death?"

" 'To Build a Fire'," Penny said.

"Sounds right," Jack said. "I remember he spat and it froze before hitting the ground. It could be that cold outside."

"Spitting is gross."

Jack spat into the waterfall.

"Eww," Penny said.

Jack laughed, then leaned back on the rock to watch the sky. He would start on his plan tomorrow. For now, he had Penny and the Northern Lights.

Two weeks later, Jack was in the nursery laboratory again. The annanas were growing and they'd moved on to cloning orchids.

"Could we clone *Mutingia* the same way you're cloning these?" Jack asked, peering into a small glass jar with a speck of green inside.

"Dunno," Brink said. "What is that?"

"Jamaican cherry tree," Jack said. "Great fruit. Like cotton candy and popcorn. It's a pain to germinate, and the seedlings are variable. Seems like cloning would be a better bet."

"We could try," Brink said. "I'll bet we have one in the collection somewhere—or could bring a mature tree in."

"Great," Jack said, then remembered with a pang he wouldn't be around for the experiment. He reluctantly changed the topic to one more helpful to his plan of escape. "Do we have some *Pandanas utilis* around somewhere?"

"You bet your unfashionable socks," Brink said. "There's a patch of them at the edge of the Tahiti garden. You made it over there yet?"

"I didn't go through," Jack said. "Got torn up by some nasty briars on the way. Shorts were a poor choice."

"Problems in paradise," Brink said as he counted out spoonfuls of agar and tipped them into a beaker.

Since starting, Jack had been digging through the seed bank and planting every edible he could find while Brink watched in good-natured amusement in between tending his ornamentals. Brink had a knack for propagation techniques that went far beyond Jack's knowledge.

Though Jack liked Brink, his interactions with Hayworth were as irritating as they were common. He ran into the man/robot on a daily basis and Hayworth would natter on about him about the glorious future that would be revealed after everything was destroyed in poison and ash and flame. It was tiresome, especially since the man didn't care for plants. He considered knocking the man—or robot's—head off again, but he had to lay low and keep pretending they were on the same team. It was really annoying, expecially when Hayworth got going on his theories about plural marriages and psychedelic drugs.

That afternoon Jack took Penny to the Tahiti garden and was pleased to find some large Pandanus specimens growing beside a hideous stone idol.

"Help me strip off some nice leaves, Penny," Jack said. "We'll dry them and then I can do some weaving."

Penny shook her head. "I can't see how weaving will help us."

"Just wait," Jack said, hanging on a trunk and cutting leaves with a billhook he'd borrowed from a maintenance shed, then passing the fronds to Penny. "We need to dry these in the sun, but they can't get too crispy dry or they won't work as well."

"Whatever you say," Penny said with a shrug.

After a few minutes, Jack announced that he had enough.

"Okay," Penny said. "I still fail to see how this is helpful."

"Look," Jack said, taking the bundle of fronds from Penny and laying them on the ground, then taking her hands in his. "You need to trust me on this."

She searched his eyes, biting her lip slightly.

"If I were your cat, you'd trust me," Jack said. "I am not your cat, but I can still be trusted."

"Dinglebat," Penny said with a sharp intake of breath. "He's alone out there somewhere. I don't know what happened to him."

"He'll be fine," Jack said.

"I know," Penny said. "It's just that the last time I left him alone he got into the noodles and tried to cook himself a tuna casserole, then burned it. My apartment smelled like a burned-out fish market for three months."

"Oh," Jack said. There was really nothing else he could say, except for maybe, "I see," or perhaps, "right."

"Jack—you need to get us out of here fast," Penny whispered close to his ear. "There was a sale at the Oriental market. My pantry is literally stuffed with rice noodles right now, not to mention the Thai-flavored tuna I bought at the same time. If Dinglebat tries again..."

"Soon," Jack said, pressing a finger to her lips. "Right now I need to cut some sticks. There's a *Haematoxylum camphechianum* over there by the sandy patch that would work well."

"Speak English," Penny said.

"Bloodwood tree," Jack said. "It feels really hard—I think it will work well. After that, we need to get some bamboo. Wish we had jute, too, but we can't have everything. We can leave the pandanus fronds here—the tree is right over there."

They walked past the idol.

"Donated by UNESCO," Penny said, reading a small placard at its base.

"There it is," Jack said, pointing to a sprawling tree with smooth grey bark.

"Nice," Penny said, putting her hand on a branch, then pulling back quickly. "Ouch!"

"Thorny," Jack said, unfolding a small pruning saw. "Sorry—should have warned you."

"Is that why they call it bloodwood?" Penny asked.

"No," Jack replied. "This tree has a crazy history. Used to be super important for dyeing fabrics—really nice reds. Worth its weight in gold back in the colonial era. People died for this wood. Slaves and sailors. Ships full of the wood were sunk. Former loggers turned pirate and preyed on the vessels that had been sinking their shipments. Heck, they could have called it bloodwood just because of its history."

"People don't use it anymore?" Penny said.

"Not much," Jack said, laying a five foot section of branch on the ground, then beginning his cut on a second one. "At one point it fueled economic empires. Now it's just a curiosity, though it's still used as a staining agent for slides."

"*Sic transit gloria mundi,*" Penny murmured.

"Speak English," Jack said, poking her in the ribs.

She giggled and poked him back. "You know, if we get our timing just right we might get home just in time to have Dinglebat cook us dinner."

"I look forward to it," Jack said, finishing up the cuts on his second branch. He hefted it. "Heavy—maybe too heavy."

"For what?" Penny said.

Jack leaned forward and brushed aside a strand of her hair, then whispered directly into her ear. "Polar expedition."

Penny nodded, then hefted one of the sticks. "I can handle it."

"Good," Jack said. "Let's grab the pandanus fronds, then hit the Japanese garden for some bamboo."

Jack had carefully cut some of the older bamboo canes, then dragged them to the waterfall. There was a small cave he'd found there—in reality the entrance to a maintenance tunnel—and he had decided to use it for his preparations. So far as he could tell, no one was using this tunnel. Over the last couple of weeks he had discovered the main entrance to the dome and had actually helped Brink bring in a shipment of germplasm through what looked like an airlock.

The jungle ended at a terminal reminiscent of an airport, with high ceilings and polished terrazo floors. Beyond the terminal was a large warehouse area that was quite cold—and at the end of it were the doors. Inside were parked an array of construction vehicles, including bulldozers and tractors, all of which sported thick, climate-controlled cabs for their drivers. When Jack and Brink had been called about the arrival of Brink's shipment, the outside doors were already closed and the pallets from the most recent delivery were stacked neatly inside the doors.

"Is this the only entrance?" Jack asked.

"Naw," Brink replied, digging through boxes in search of his shipment. "There are some others, but they're mostly sealed off. The next round of funding and workers will come soon, then the outside party will really kick off."

"Can I help you guys?" one of the workers said. "Hey Brink," he said as he got closer. "I already pulled your package."

"Super," Brink said as he stopped strewing armfuls of packaging peanuts onto the floor.

"No problem," the guy said. "Who's the new guy?" the man asked, looking at Jack.

"Broccoli," Jack said. "Jack Broccoli."

"Nice to meet you, Mr. Broccoli. I'm Bob Celery."

Jack looked around, quickly identifying thirty-seven different objects he could use to cave in a human skull.

YOU RANG? Akras yelled inside Jack's head.

"Never mind," he murmured. "We don't have to kill this one."

"What's that?" the guy said.

"Thinking of something else, Bob," Jack said. "Nice to meet you."

"You too," the guy said, walking away.

"You know his name isn't really Celery," Brink said.

"I figured," Jack said.

"So," Brink said as Bob walked away. "I got something special for you."

"You did?" Jack said.

"Sure did. Hayworth mentioned a little something to me and I took it on myself to make a special purchase. Here," he said, tossing a small insulated box to Jack. "Open it."

Jack tore open the plastic and cardboard and looked inside to see multiple small bags of labelled seeds inside. He read their labels out loud. "*Diospyros tessellaria. Diospyros ebenum. Diospyros celebica...* whoa!"

"We can get everything," Brink grinned. "We already had *Diospyros crassiflora* in the seed bank, you know, but I got you a wider collection of ebonies. I also had them throw in some African blackwood. Different family, I know, but I wasn't sure if you liked just the *Diospyros* ebonies or were a fan of the whole spectrum."

"*Dalbergia melanoxylon,*" Jack said in awe. "This is amazing."

"Sky's the limit here," Brink laughed. "You can plant a garden just of ebony species. There's still a big clearing over towards where they're planning to put the tree fern exhibit. Lots of space."

"Thanks," Jack said, almost speechless at the gift. "I will treasure these."

"We could start them today if you like," Brink said.

"No, give me a few weeks. I need to plan some things out."

"Suits me," Brink said. "We can put them in the big fridge with the other rare stuff."

The big fridge was a treasure trove of plant species. It was a carefully controlled walk-in cold area with drawer after drawer of seed storage. Though Jack had harbored vague thoughts of catastropically sabotaging the facility, seeing all the seeds changed his mind. It would have been hard to destroy the main gardens, sure, but all those seeds, too? Sure, he could pull a Samson and bring the entire facility down on the heads of the rotten people that had kidnapped him and Penny and killed Paul—but he couldn't do that to these innocent sleeping embryonic plants. That would be pure evil.

Come to think of it, he couldn't kill Brink either. He wondered how the guy had gotten involved in this rotten mess. He also wondered if he could trust the man. His gut said yes, but if he made a mistake he had no doubt that he and Penny would be murdered. Batson had to die, that was for sure, and Pickle. And Elaine what's-her-name had to go. Too bad she had left, according to Penny.

Jack said goodbye to Penny, then started spreading out his pandanus fronds to dry on the floor of the maintenance cave. The air was dry despite the proximity to the waterfall. The floor was also warm with subterranean heat. It would probably be better than putting them up above where the artificial rain systems clicked on and off during the day. He wasn't sure, though, as he'd never worked with pandanus before. It's not like the stuff grew in Virginia. The perils of book knowledge were many. You could know about plants and how to use them without really knowing their uses in practice. Nothing beat experience.

Though good mechanical skills are a big help, Jack thought as he cut strips of bamboo and tested their flexibility. He would need a way to steam bend them. *It shouldn't be too hard to snag a heater of some sort and bring it out here*, he mused.

The next day he worked with Brink to plan out a small coffee orchard area. After some argument about coffee varieties and flavor, Jack convinced Brink to allow him to add *C. canephora*, *C. liberica*, and *C. stenophylla* to the orchard along with the *C. arabica* that were planned. Brink drew the line at adding *Psychotria nervosa*, however.

"That's just nutty," he complained. "Look, we're supposed to create the Colombian experience with this little spot. They even have a guy with a donkey coming eventually to do little tours. We don't need every weird coffee and/or coffee lookalike here."

Jack nodded, but did manage to slip a couple of *P. nervosa* seeds into one of the *C. arabica* trays when Brink wasn't looking.

After Brink left, he borrowed a small burner and an empty metal paint bucket and brought them to the cave. He knew he was being watched but hoped whoever was looking at the cameras wouldn't figure out what he was doing.

In the cave he was pleased to find his pandanas leaves had somewhat dried. He carefully did a few test twists and found the results satisfying. Within an hour he'd set up a little steaming station and was carefully bending bamboo into irregular hooped shapes. Once he had the outlines correct, he started twisting and tying the pandanus inside them. He was so engrossed in his work that he didn't immediately register the change in light inside the cave.

"What are you making, Mr. Broccoli?" came a nasal Yankee voice.

Jack almost dropped his project. He looked up to see the shimmering form of Giles Batson' hologram, then looked back at the shape in his hand.

"Dreamcatcher?" Giles offered.

"Yes," Jack sputtered. "Sorry, you surprised me."

Giles half smiled, walked through part of the wall, then attempted to sit next to Jack. It was a poor illusion, as most of his bottom ended up inside the floor. "So," Giles continued. "It's not all bad here, is it?"

"It's better than I thought it would be," Jack replied honestly.

"But your girlfriend is unhappy," Giles said.

Jack said nothing as he twisted pandanus fronds together.

"Your silence betrays you," the hologram continued. "If it were not for her, you would be happy here."

"Probably," Jack said. "She did say something about being a bird in a gilded garden or something like that. She doesn't really get plants."

"Women don't understand intelligent men," Giles said, continuing. "They cannot fathom the deep waters of a man's mind."

Jack shrugged. "Life is still better with a girl."

"You should see some of the androids we're coming out with now," Giles cackled. "They cook and clean and look better than any human woman. They also don't complain when you watch sports on the television."

"Do I look like I'd be tempted by a robot? Or sports? Or having someone cook for me?" Jack shook his head, then paused. "Actually, the last part sounds good."

Giles laughed, then broke into a coughing fit. "What if it were MMA matches? What if there were a beautiful android that would let you watch all the MMA you wanted?"

"Let me? I can watch whatever I like whoever the girl is," Jack scoffed.

"Oh, I'm sure," Giles said sarcastically. "You'd be in the doghouse. Women rule over men. My last ex took millions when she left me, that ungrateful golddigger. And she was a lousy cook. My android girls are great cooks. They never burn the noodles... unlike some girls you may know."

Jack looked up at the hologram with a frown. "Penny's cat burned the noodles, not her. If you're going to listen in on conversations you might as well get the details right. There's no excuse to be sloppy."

"I can be as sloppy as I like, Jacky." The hologram grinned a twisted smile and reclined partly through a boulder. Now it looked like Giles's head was emerging from the back of the rock. "I rule the world."

Jack shrugged as he wove fronds together. "Maybe you do, maybe you don't. The world is a strange place. Heck, I met a giant sentient mushroom once."

"I do rule the world, no maybe about it," Giles said. "I rule the world, and you are only here because I am keeping you safe."

"Why?" Jack said.

"Because I like you, Jack," Giles said, attempting to pat Jack on the arm but instead sending his hand through Jack's chest. "And I needed another gardener."

"I like me too," Jack said. "But I don't think you pulled off this eleborate kidnapping scheme just because you need another gardener here."

"You're the best gardener in the world," Giles said.

"That's true," Jack admitted. "But still, you're keeping me tied up here so you can do something out there."

Giles shrugged.

"Something big is about to happen and I'm being held here so I don't draw any attention to it," Jack pressed.

Giles shrugged again.

"Something within the month," Jack said.

A flicker of surprise jumped across the hologram's face.

"Something on the 17th of this month," Jack said, pressing his advantage.

"No," Giles said.

"19th," Jack said.

"No," Giles replied.

"You are lying," Jack said. "22nd."

"Stop it," Giles said. "This is ridiculous."

"23rd!" Jack said.

"No!" Giles sputtered. "It's definitely not the 23rd!"

"You have a terrible poker face," Jack said. "It is the 23rd. I saw a flicker of an expression."

"I'm a hologram. Of course my face flickers!" Giles said petulantly. "I'm done with this conversation."

The room dimmed as the hologram winked out of existence, leaving Jack alone with his weaving.

After an hour, he was done bending, weaving and tying. With a nod of satisfaction Jack held up a brand-new pair of snowshoes.

"How far do the shipments come before they reach us?" Jack asked Brink.

It was late morning the next day and the two of them were surveying a patch of ill-looking plants beside an unfinished fountain.

"Too much sun," Brink muttered. "What did you say?"

"Our plant shipments. And supplies. They're coming in from somewhere. Plane? Snowmobile? How far do they come in?"

"Maybe four miles," Brink said. "They got some snowcrawlers and AT-ATs. Snowmobiles too."

"That's it?" Jack said, incredulous. "What's there—a big town?"

"Naw, just a little base of sorts. Eventually we'll have a clear waterway right here," Brink said. "It's a massive plan they got going. As the ice recedes and clears, access will get a lot easier. The slush and cracking ice is a big problem now. Of course, this whole thing will be free-floating eventually, and they'll have special tugs ready to move us wherever we want to go."

"Can we go out there?" Jack asked. "See the pole? Maybe borrow a snowmobile or something?"

"Naw," Brink said. "No way. Too cold. Plus, we've got too much gardening to do."

He leaned in close and pretending to brush something off Jack's shoulder. "I know you're not 100% happy here. I'm not stupid. You could make the hike on a clear day—but there're other things out there that'll kill you. Best to stay here. I've gotten used to it myself."

"Definitely too much sun," Brink said loudly, straightening up and shaking his head. "Amateurs planted a half-shade plant in full sun. Typical. Gonna have to move 'em or just start over."

Jack's mind reeled. Brink was stuck here too. Unless his admission was simply a way to draw Jack into his confidence. Jack looked at the big red-faced man, weighing the possibility. No, probably not. Brink was too genuine, too open.

"I agree," Jack said. "We should just move them."

Snow goggles, warm clothing, two walking sticks, boots, food...

Jack paced his room, checking off a supply list inside his head. He had to stock up without raising suspicion. Though there were few workers inside the dome—and he'd seen no guards, which made him wonder what was outside—he knew he was being watched. He made a few crafts, such as baskets and carved wooden spoons, in between working on supplies. He wanted his work to look like some sort of a hobby, not an escape plan. As for food, he was able to secure a block of lard and a bottle of olive oil from the kitchen robot, telling him he wanted to finish some of his wood carvings. The fats would serve as long-burning energy that would also keep him and Penny warm, though as it might be repulsive to eat alone, he also collected some chocolate and crackers. And multiple bags of *Ocean Octaves!* Much to his joy, the robot waiter seemed to have an infinite supply of them behind the cafeteria.

He'd found some tinted goggles in a maintenance shed, as well as long-sleeved cover-alls and some over-sized plastic jumpsuits that looked like they were for protection from chemicals. He wondered if he could insulate them.

That was the big problem now. How to get clothing that would be warm enough.

A light bulb blinked on in his head the next morning when he helped Brink unpack a new hydroponic system. With it came boxes and boxes of rock wool.

Wool was an insulator. *Is rock wool an insulator?* Jack wasn't sure, so he asked Brink.

"Sure it is," was the reply. "They use it in construction all the time now. Actually, it's probably cheaper to buy it at Builder's Warehouse or something than get it from an ag supply like we do, but it ain't like money is in short supply round these parts."

So rock wool it was. Jack took a bunch of it, finding it surprisingly light, then decided to stitch it to some cloth cover-alls, then put a plastic containment suit over that. He snagged two sets of both and brought them to his room in the evening. At dinner he didn't see Penny, so he ate quickly and returned to his room to work on the suits.

As he stitched, Jack wondered about skis, then thought about what Brink had said. Maybe the snow wasn't deep enough for skis. Maybe even the snowshoes were unneccesary. The artificial environment of the dome was frustrating, as it provided little information on the world outside. He could see small drifts of snow now and again upon the top, but the automated systems cleaned them away rapidly—and the light above was more often grey-white and it was hard to tell where natural illumination gave way to artificial.

"What are you doing?" came Giles's voice. The hologram blinked into existence, standing awkwardly on the bed above where Jack worked on the floor, its legs half-way through the mattress.

"Making a suit," Jack said, his pulse jumping.

EVERYTHING IS A WEAPON! Akras yelled in his head as the adrenaline spiked in Jack's veins. Then a moment later, Akras said *WHERE IS THE ENEMY!?*

"A suit?" Giles said, his eyes narrowing.

THERE IS NO ONE HERE, yelled Akras.

"Right," Jack said, answering both of them at the same time. "I'm going to plant grass seed in the rock wool," he lied. "I'll be the world's first literal lawn guy. It'll be a suit made of grass."

Giles chuckled. "I am glad you're having fun, though I don't think the idea is original. I saw an article in some magazine years ago about some art event where a man had a jacket made of sod."

"Maybe I'll plant something else on it, then," Jack said. "Chia seeds, maybe."

"Fine, fine," Giles said. "You are quite the hobbyist, young Broccoli. I admit, I expected you to be different. Making dreamcatchers and weird outfits doesn't fit the picture I'd built of you in my head." He flickered out of existence and Jack realized he'd been holding his breath.

"Whew," he whispered to himself. "That was close."

TURNIP SEEDS, Akras yelled.

"What?" Jack replied.

PLANT YOUR SUIT WITH TURNIP SEEDS. IT WILL GIVE YOU GREAT POWER.

"Seriously?" Jack said. "I think they'll die without light. And in the cold."

THEY WOULD TAKE JOY IN THEIR SACRIFICE FOR THE CARETAKER.

"Any turnips?" Jack said. "You know I don't have Kiikala here."

THEY ARE SAFE ON YOUR LAND. RAIN HAS FALLEN.

"Good," Jack said, stunned to realize he hadn't even thought about his garden back home in... how long? Weeks? Months? Maybe Penny was right, and the bad guys were getting inside his head.

"I dunno, Akras," Jack said after a moment. "I think wetting the rock wool is not the best plan."

SUIT YOURSELF.

"That's what I'm trying to do," Jack said, going back to his stitching.

Jack caught Penny at dinner that evening. As they ate pita bread with hummus, goat cheese and olives—her suggestion—Jack realized he had no idea what she'd been doing with her time while he'd been working on their escape plan, so he asked her.

"Watching TV, mostly," Penny said. "And doing Pilates."

"Sounds really boring," Jack said.

"There's a ton to watch," Penny said defensively. "Haven't you turned on the TV in your room and seen all the channels?"

"Yeah," Jack said. "There was nothing on gardening or fist-fighting so I got bored."

"I've actually been bored since we got here," Penny whispered to him as she tried unsuccessfully to balance three olives and a piece of feta on a hunk of pita. "Once I got over the being terrified phase."

"You could wrap the stuff up like a burrito," Jack said, demonstrating.

"It's not done that way," Penny said.

"Or you could glue the loose stuff in place with hummus," Jack said, demonstrating again.

"This isn't a building project," Penny said, trying again. This time olives #2 and #3 rolled off the table onto the floor. Jack took a bite of his pita burrito and there was an audible crack.

"Ouch," he said, making a pained face. "These olives have pits!"

"That's the way they do it in Greece," Penny said.

Jack shook his head. "I like the ones with pimento in the middle."

"It's like a piece of fake red foam or something, isn't it?" Penny said.

"No, it's a slice of pepper," Jack said.

"Doesn't taste like pepper," Penny said, smooshing some olives into some feta and then picking up the mess with her pita.

"No, I suppose not," Jack said. "There you go, though—that's a good way to do it."

Penny nodded and chewed thoughtfully, carefully pitting the olives with her teeth, then spitting the pits onto her plate. "Sorry, not very ladylike of me," she said after swallowing.

"It's fine," Jack said. "I was just thinking about what you said."

"Which bit?"

"About being bored," he said. "I'm putting myself in your shoes right now. I know the gardens here aren't really your thing. And being kidnapped isn't really your thing either."

"I have a fulfilling life elsewhere," Penny said, taking a sip of her spiced chai.

"So do I. Almost too fulfilling, what with the robots, tornadoes, and eels."

"Eels?"

"Yeah, a whole tank of them," Jack said. "But they weren't robots. I don't think."

"Probably not," Penny said. "Though an eel shape would be easy."

"Like making snakes," Jack said.

"Exactly," Penny said, sipping her chai.

Jack looked up at her, studying her face. He'd just had a terrible thought. "Penny..."

"Yes?" she replied, seeing the strange look he was giving her. "What? What is it?"

"Are you a robot?" Jack asked.

"No!" Penny said. "Of course not."

"But if you were, you would deny it," Jack said.

"Sure, I guess so," Penny said, thoughtfully popping another olive in her mouth and chewing slowly, then spitting out the pit. "If I were a robot that was supposed to be someone I wouldn't just reveal that I was a robot."

"No," Jack said. "And I suppose robots don't get bored. Though you could fake that." A sudden image popped into Jack's mind of him knocking Penny's head off with a Ficus branch.

"Jack, if you're thinking of knocking my head off..." Penny said.

Jack said nothing.

Penny laughed. "I was just teasing," she said.

Jack decided to continue to say nothing, instead taking a swig of his Dr. Piper along with another bite of hummus and pita. He had to admit, it wasn't a bad meal. He also didn't really think Penny was a robot. He'd know if she was. They were too close. Unless they uploaded her mind into a robot, causing the robot version to truly believe it was her and act exactly like her.

"Do you remember when we first met?" he asked her.

"Of course," she said. "You were hiding behind a potted plant."

Jack took her hand and she smiled at him. He surreptitiously examined Penny's long delicate fingers, the little freckles on her arm, the pale blond hairs on her lightly tanned skin... no, it was her. There was no way they could fake the girl he loved down to that level of detail.

"Beep!" Penny said.

Jack almost jumped out of his seat.

"I saw you looking at me, Jack. You were thinking I was a robot."

"Not really," Jack said. "I mean, not that much." His heart thumped but he kept emotion off his face. She'd really scared him for a second. These people were making him go nuts.

Jack finished the last gulp of his soda. "Let's take a walk."

At the waterfall Jack held Penny close and whispered his plans into her ear, hoping that whoever might be watching would just think they were having some sort of cliched romantic moment—yet this was anything but a cliched moment. They were planning to head multiple miles across the frozen tundra of the North Pole, then to face down a group of potentially hostile dockworkers and to either hitch a ride or steal a boat back to civilization. That last part was fuzzy as Jack had no idea what he'd find at the end of their hike.

Though he knew he'd regret never planting a garden of ebony at the North Pole, as a red-blooded American, Jack knew instinctively that all the gardens in the world weren't worth sacrificing a single drop of freedom. At least that's what he kept telling himself. A large part of his heart wanted to go right back to the greenhouse in the morning and forget leaving the dome.

"Tomorrow?" Penny asked after hearing his plan.

"Tomorrow," Jack replied. "Meet me here at 7."

Early the next morning, Jack gathered his supplies from every place he'd cached them, then headed to the nursery to say goodbye to the seedlings.

"Grow in peace," he said quietly, setting down his bags and looking wistfully at the hundreds of trays of rare plants he'd started over the last month. Some of the *Coffea* were emerging already, as were the *P. nervosa*. He smiled, wondering how long it would take Brink to notice them. He lingered for a long moment, then turned to pick up his bags to go.

As he did, a movement off to one side caught Jack's eye. It was Brink.

"Jack," he said. "You're early."

"Just came to see the progress," Jack said quickly.

"Goodbye," Brink whispered, taking Jack's hand.

Jack blinked.

"I know, Jack. Be careful. It's clear today but there's still danger out there."

Jack nodded slightly and squeezed the man's hand, hard. Brink squeezed harder, then gave up. "I already know you'll beat me," he laughed. Then he spoke louder. "Catch you later, man—I'll see you at 8—we got a ton of willows to put in by the little pond."

"You bet," Jack said, slapping him on the back, then grabbing his bags. "Wouldn't miss it for all the tea seedlings in China."

"Later," Brink said with a wave.

Jack headed to the waterfall, finding Penny there already, wearing a long-sleeved shirt and a pair of jeans, along with the boots he'd told her to bring.

He hoped to God that both of them would make it through alive.

They got into the rock wool-reinforced suits inside the cave, then put on their boots and goggles. Jack gave one of his bags and the lighter backpack to Penny.

"Whoa, these are stuffed," Penny said.

"Stuff we need," Jack replied. "Hauling it all will keep us warm."

"You're the boss," Penny said, putting on her pack. "How do we get out of here?"

Jack smiled and pulled out a small jar of black liquid. He drank it in a gulp, then hefted a thick club he'd made from bloodwood.

"Like this," he said, moving towards the locked maintenance door.

"But wait," Penny said, grasping at her throat. "Our collars!"

"No worries. Let me get through the door, then I'll deal with those." He raised his club.

"Wait, isn't this a computer-controlled system?" Penny said, looking at the door. "We could just hack it. I wish Dinglebat were here—he's great at coding."

"No, I've got it under control," Jack said.

"So..." Penny said after a minute of him doing nothing. "What are you doing?"

"Waiting for help," Jack said. "Should be any second now..."

He stood still for another minute.

"Any second?" Penny said with a frown.

"Any second," Jack repeated.

EVERYTHING IS A WEAPON! Akras roared.

"Give me strength, O Great Protector of Turnips!" Jack yelled, then swung at the door. The club cleaved the steel like newspaper and the door broke loose on its hinges. Jack grinned and pushed it open.

"Whoa," Penny said. "What was in that jar you drank?"

"Espresso," Jack said.

"Whoa," Penny said.

"It's good stuff," Jack replied. "Akras—can you help me get these collars off?"

I SEE NO COLLARS.

"Ah, right," Jack said. "One sec."

He picked up some stray pandanas fronds and twined them around his collar.

"Can you see that thing around my neck now?" he asked.

YES.

"Can we break it without breaking my spine?" Jack said.

JUST GO NICE AND STEADY WITH A QUICK MOTION. LIKE SNAPPING A CARROT.

"You got it," Jack said, grasping the collar. With a quick motion, he broke it and tore the hatful thing from his neck.

"Wow," Penny said. "That really is good espresso."

"Let me do yours," Jack said, picking up another pandanas frond. In a moment, he had repeated the procedure and they were both free of their collars.

"You think they'll know we busted them?" Penny said.

"Undoubtedly," Jack replied. "Let's git."

The tunnel behind the smashed door stretched off ahead into deep gloom. Though there was a long line of light fixtures along the wall, there wasn't a switch that Jack could find. "Here," he said, handing Penny a small LED flashlight, then lighting one of his own.

"Are you sure this tunnel leads out?" Penny said.

"Pretty sure," Jack said. "I've spend some time studying the shape of the dome and the other places where doors emerge. This one is near the edge. I found a venting system by the edge of the dome that I assume is accessible via this tunnel. I think it's pulling in air from outside. Actually," Jack said, holding his hand up for a halt. "You can hear some humming from here."

"I hear it," Penny said. "Straight ahead."

In a few moments they reached the source of the sound. As suspected, it was a large air handler. The main tunnel teed directly into it. To their left and right, two tunnels curved away from them.

Suddenly, a shrieking alarm filled the tunnel.

"They know we're loose," Jack said. "Those two tunnels probably go around the edge of the dome," Jack said. "But through this air handler should be the outdoors."

"Through?" Penny said.

"Through," Jack said. "Stand back."

Penny did, and Jack swung his club, smashing through the enamelled front of the machine and into the coils inside. He rained blow after blow into it, throwing metal everywhere—and then he hit its motor, causing the machine to cease with a shriek and a crunch.

"Soon," Jack said, grunting as he rained down blows on the machine.

"Jack!" Penny yelled.

"What?" Jack said, spinning on his heel, expecting to face a threat. "What is it!?"

"There's a vent up there," Penny pointed, to where a large duct entered the ceiling. "It might be faster..."

"Right," Jack said, then swung at the duct, knocking it down the hall to his right. As he did, a shaft of light shone down from above and cold air flowed down over them.

"Come on, Penny," Jack said, helping her stand on top of the air handler then giving her a boost up to the square above. "Let's go for a hike."

A moment later, the two of them stood outside the dome, looking for the first time at the frozen wastes of the North Pole.

CHAPTER 14

As spiders fly from nests in spring is the aroma of dried meat in the pocket of a warrior.

—A State of Bean: Principles of Mung Fu

Jack spat into the icy air.

"Eww!" Penny said.

"Shh," Jack said. "We need to see if it freezes before it hits the ice. You messed me up. Gotta try again." He spat again. Then again. The results were inconclusive.

"Never mind," Jack said, giving up. "Now we head south, around the side of the dome and towards the harbor."

"Do we need to put on our snowshoes?" Penny asked.

Jack crunched his boot into the powdery snow. Underneath, the ice was hard. "No, the snow seems thin. We're safe for now. Let's go."

They walked around the edge of the dome. Jack checked regularly for pursuit but saw nothing. As they got farther from the exit the sound of sirens faded away.

As they rounded the dome, they saw a mess of vehicle tracks in the snow on what must have been the thoroughfare coming in from the harbor.

Then they saw something else.

"Jack," Penny said, her voice muffled by the cloth mask over her mouth. "Look over there!"

Jack spun his head in all directions, assuming the enemy was upon them.

"What?" he said, seeing nothing.

"The ice over there!" Penny said.

Jack looked in the direction she was pointing. The ice far in front of them and off to their left was black.

"Is it some sort of rock?" Penny asked. "Maybe volcanic glass?"

"I don't think there's any land or volcanos at the North Pole," Jack said. "I think it's all ice. That looks like black ice," Jack said. "Different from what drivers always complain about in Virginia, though."

"It's like it's flat black," Penny said. "Like someone painted it."

"It might be a mirage," Jack said, peering through his goggles. The small amount of exposed skin on his face already hurt.

They continued following the vehicle tracks. There was no one outside the dome except for them. He could see the greenery inside through the towering glass—an oasis in a sea of white—and a pang of regret struck him for a moment, then passed.

Freedom. That was the goal.

As they trudged forward, brittle snow crunching beneath their feet, Jack studied the black ice. It wasn't a mirage—it really did look like a slice of obsidian, though there was something strange about its edges. Back in Virginia, everyone loved to talk about black ice in the winter, sharing ominous warnings every time there was a freeze or a snow flurry. "Watch out for the black ice!" they'd warn as you got into your car. Black ice was apparently some sort of semi-mythical ice that would cause your car to skid without warning. A type of trickily camoflauged ice that took pleasure in ambushing unsuspecting motorists by blending into the asphalt. Despite looking, Jack had never really seen this terrifying form of ice, or if he had, he hadn't been able to distinguish it from run-of-the-mill ice. "Beware the black ice!" had to be said in a pirate voice, Jack decided.

"Thar be the BLAAAHK AYYYCE!" he said out loud to Penny, then realized she'd fallen behind. He slowed and allowed her to catch up. He'd been walking fast. Considering the temperature, it seemed like a good idea, but it must have been too fast for Penny.

"Man alive, Jack," Penny said. "This pack is way too heavy. What did you put in here?"

"Only what we absolutely need," Jack said. "I'll walk slower. We'll make it. Are you cold?"

"No," Penny said. "Not really. Except for my face. It's a bit cold." Jack leaned over and pulled up her mask a little. "Don't get frostbite," he said. "Dinglebat would be upset if I brought you back in less than pristine condition."

"So you don't care about me being in less than pristine condition?" Penny puffed.

"Is this one of those test questions that women like to run on men in order to determine their potential fitness as mates?" Jack said. "What do I need to say to not fail it?"

"You already failed it," Penny huffed.

"I figured. Did I mention those pants make you look fat?"

"We're getting closer to the black area," Penny said, ignoring him.

"Yes," Jack said. "It's definitely not a mirage. It's almost like... charcoal?"

"I don't know," Penny said. "If we keep on following the tracks, we'll be alongside it up there, where the little hills are coming up on the left."

"We'll find out soon enough," Jack said. He looked back to the silent dome. Still no sign of pursuit. He wondered what "other things" lived out here. Polar bears? At least they would see a bear coming a mile away. Polar bears were cold-blooded psycho killers when they weren't floating around on icebergs posing for photo ops. Jack was more worried about a vehicle approaching. It was possible they could be gunned down or run over on the tundra. There was no cover anywhere.

And no plant life, with the exception of the paradise behind them.

Jack thought of the ice beneath their feet and the uncanny feeling of there being no land beneath it. However deep it went, it was floating on top of a deep and merciless sea, likely populated by unseen eldritch horrors. One crack in the ice and they would plunge into the Stygian depths with no hope for rescue.

They were almost to the black area. Penny was huffing and puffing but gamely moving on. Jack was getting winded as well.

"Penny, let me take some of your load," he said. "We'll rest here for a moment, then press on."

"Great," Penny said, dropping her pack from her shoulders. "How cold is it out here?"

Jack spat on the ice and watched it freeze. "Definitely below freezing," he replied.

"Thanks, Captain Obvious," Penny said. Jack opened his pack, and moved aside the top of a towel he had stuffed in for insulation. He quickly opened her pack, pushed aside a second towel he'd put in hers, then started grabbing handfuls from her pack and stuffing them into his. As he did, something round and brown fell on the ice.

"You brought nuts?" Penny said.

"Seeds," Jack replied, scooping it up. "I hope this brief exposure isn't going to kill any of them."

"What?" Penny said. "You made me carry seeds?"

"Only some absolutely vital ones," Jack said. "Don't complain— I'm lightening your pack." He pulled out a bag of *Ocean Octaves!* and transferred them to his pack. "Look, there's another 12.8 ounces less for you to carry." Jack rooted deeper into her pack and found a pair of irregular bundles which he shifted into his own pack.

"What are those?" Penny asked.

"Nothing," Jack said.

"Yes they were something!" Penny said. "Those were cuttings, weren't they? Weren't they?"

"Shh," Jack said. "Save your energy for getting to safety."

"I can't believe you were making me hike across the north pole with a bag of sticks and seeds on my... Jack!"

"What?" Jack said, stuffing the towels back into the tops of the bags and zipping them up.

"Over there—on the black. Something is moving."

Jack turned and scanned the road ahead, then the blackness beyond.

Something was indeed moving on the black area. Something white. His heart caught in his throat. Maybe it was a polar bear. From this distance it was hard to tell—but the movement was strangely fluid, almost as if a ball of snow had been sent skidding across the mysterious surface.

"Let's keep moving," Jack said.

"Towards it?" Penny said, putting her now lighter pack onto her back, then stamping her feet and clapping her hands together.

"There's no other option," Jack said. "We don't know what it is, but we'll die of exposure if we don't get moving." His teeth were starting to chatter. Stopping even for a minute had taken its toll. They needed to move.

"At least my pack is lighter," Penny said. "Thanks, I guess."

"No problem," Jack said. The white object had disappeared behind a small hill. At their current rate of speed, he estimated they'd reach the anomaly in about ten minutes. They walked on without seeing the white thing reemerge.

Until they saw a second one, scooting in over the ice towards the position of the first. It was on the white ice this time, but where it moved it left a trail of black.

"It's a seal," Jack said, with some relief. "Not a polar bear."

"Oh my goodness," Penny said. "It is a seal! And look at that—it's leaving a trail!"

The seal paid them no mind but continued on its way. In a few more minutes, they had reached the black area. Jack stopped and crouched down to examine the ice. It appeared to be covered with some sort of paint? What type of paint would stick to ice? It seemed sticky, and smeared on his glove as he touched it. Like old motor oil. He shook his head. Something was very weird.

Then the strange words snapped back into his mind. "The sixth seal will blacken the ice..." he breathed.

They came around to the other side of the little hill where the first seal had disappeared. The hill was strangely symmetrical, almost like the top of a cylinder with drifts of old snow softening its sides. There was a series of slide marks coming from all directions around it. On the back, Jack saw what appeared to be an access hatch.

"It's like a little door into the ice," Penny said. "The seal must have gone inside somehow."

"I don't like it," Jack said. "We need to keep moving, though."

He rose, his legs complaining as he did. He was aching with cold and felt heavy and awkward inside his layers of clothing and rock wool. "We can't be too far from the harbor."

"If the entire North Pole is made from a big sheet of ice, how could they even build a harbor here?" Penny said. "Or that big dome behind us?"

"It's some sort of an ark," Jack answered. "That's what Brink said. And he said they had a little town. Maybe a temporary thing they keep rebuilding, I don't know."

"I hope he was right," Penny said.

"There are tracks in the snow," Jack said. "They have to be supplied somehow. We'll know in a minute. The ground is rising and it looks like we'll have a view once we get over the little ridge ahead."

Jack looked over at the black ice and could now see it stretching off for some miles. They must be painting it black to attract solar energy. When spring came and the sun really hit its peak, the black ice would start to melt! He wondered how much of the ice they planned on painting. Just enough to make a statement—or enough to raise sea levels and flood the entire world? It could send icebergs all through the Northwest Passage, too—maybe even down towards New York! Jack wasn't sure, but he was pretty sure that whatever was being done here was a very, very bad idea. They were lighting wildfires and melting the ice caps. He wondered what would happen with the next stage. What horrors were planned for the 23rd?

They reached the top of the ridge and looked down. It was only a short walk to the sea—and there was indeed a clear area of ocean out there, surrounded by some sort of floating barricade. A town of snow-dusted quonset huts lay below. Jack saw the tiny figures of men clad in bright orange loading up a snow crawler, presumably bound for the dome.

"Jack, there's another one!" Penny said, suddenly pointing backwards towards the patch of black ice.

Jack looked back and saw a small white seal approaching them. As he watched, the door in the squat cylinder opened, releasing another seal. Then another. And then a stream, one after the other. At first they circled around languorously, leaving trails of black along the edge of the previously painted area, interweaving their trails and erasing the white...

...and then something changed. The seals stopped, and one of them shot across the ice directly towards Jack and Penny, slowing about twenty feet away.

"It's adorable," Penny said, looking at the creature.

Jack had to agree. The creature was indeed adorable, with deep liquid black eyes and fluffy white fur.

"Hey little guy," Penny said, waving to the seal. "It's just a baby!" she said. "Maybe the bad guys enslaved them somehow," Penny said.

"Maybe," Jack said. Penny stepped nearer to the creature and it wagged its body, then scooted closer to her.

"Penny," Jack said. "That thing might be dangerous."

"Don't be ridiculous, Jack," Penny said. "Just because it isn't a plant doesn't mean it isn't worthy of love." She crounched down and beckoned to the seal. "Isn't that right, little buddy? Little cutie? Come here, baby—come here!"

The seal got closer slowly, finally allowing Penny to pet it. "See?" she said. "It likes me!"

The seal rolled over and let Penny scratch its belly.

"Okay, that is kind of cute," Jack said. He looked back and saw at least two dozen other seals dancing across the ice, slipping and sliding and leaving black trails. "I wonder how they're making the black ink or whatever it is?" he said, examining the seal's belly. He leaned closer and the seal flipped back over, raising his nose and sniffing the air.

"He smells something," Penny said.

"Yeah," Jack said. "I think he is smelling us. Anyhow, we need to keep moving."

Jack helped Penny up, but she was reluctant to say goodbye. "I know you can't understand it, Jack, but I love animals," Penny said. "I love nature... I mean, a moment like this is just magical for me. Being so close to something so beautiful, so– Omigosh, it's got crazy teeth!"

Jack's heart jumped into his throat. The seal had bared its teeth and they didn't look like any he'd seen in National Geographic photos.

"Get back!" Jack yelled to Penny, shoving her behind him. The seal growled low in its throat. Its mouth looked like it was filled with metal needles.

EVERYTHING IS A WEAPON! Akras yelled.

Jack brandished his club—and the seal attacked, so swiftly he barely had time to react.

He winged it in the ribs with his club, knocking it away from his legs. It was a blow that would have felled a Tyrannosaur, yet the seal skidded a dozen feet across the ice and snapped back around in a hairpin turn, then charged again—this time directly towards Penny. She swung at it and missed as the creature bit into the top of her boot. She cried out in pain as she fell to the ground. Jack smacked the thing in its side again, knocking it away from Penny.

These things are way too fast! Jack thought. Despite the power of his blows, the creature seemed unharmed. It spun around again, fangs bared, ready to make another run. Penny struggled to rise from the ground as Jack stood between her and the deadly baby seal.

"Are you okay?" Jack yelled, facing the seal.

"It got me in the calf," Penny said. "It's bleeding. Oh Jack—don't hurt it! It's just scared!"

"Are you kidding me?" Jack said. He didn't dare turn to help her up—he couldn't look away for a moment from the enemy, especially not with how fast he knew it to be. If he gave Penny an arm, they both might die.

And then a dozen new seals slid up behind the first one. Their eyes were calm and black and they looked as pretty as a picture in a fluffy row of white. For a moment, Jack hoped that only this one seal had gone mad and decided to attack them. *Maybe it's a rabid seal. Maybe a rabid mutant seal.* As he watched, the newcomers also bared their teeth.

No, Jack thought. *They aren't rabid. Or mutants. They're terminator seals.*

As he had the thought, the first charged again—and he swung, cracking it soundly on the skull as it raced towards Penny. There was an audible crunch and a burst of red fluid came from its mouth—and it slid to her feet, a motionless heap.

"You killed it!" Penny gasped.

"It was a monster," Jack said.

"Oh Jack, oh no, it was just a baby... you killed a baby seal. You literally just clubbed an adorable, sweet, baby seal!!!" Penny said.

The other seals moved into a half circle. Jack felt the tension in the air and knew they would strike at any moment.

"It bit you," Jack said. "It's a terminator seal."

"It was probably just scared!" Penny said.

"It was evil," Jack yelled at her. "Club them in the head! It's the only way!"

"Jack," Penny said. "I can't!" She looked at the seals around them, then at the dead one at her feet.

"Omigoodness," she said. "That poor thing!"

"Stay behind me!" Jack said. "Be ready—they're going to–"

And then they attacked, sliding forward in a wave of adorable fluffy white. Jack swung for their heads, spinning and jumping and trying not to lose his footing as they sent for his legs. He smashed the skulls of the first two that neared him, then almost fell backwards as a third skidded sideways against his legs.

"Fight, Penny!" Jack yelled.

Penny sobbed and swung her club, cracking one in the skull as tears ran down her cheeks.

A fourth seal shot towards Jack when he stumbled, latching its teeth into his boot and yanking at him. He brought the club down, crushing in its skull, then swung at a fifth as it pressed in from two o'clock, missing the head and smashing it in the ribs. It skidded sideways and Penny brought down her club on its head, damaging but not killing it. Another seal shot in, then another, as Penny and Jack whirled and wheeled and struck out with their clubs, smashing skulls... until finally, there was no more movement.

Penny wept freely, her shoulders shaking as she surveyed the carnage around them. "I can't believe it," she sobbed. "I'm a monster!"

"No," Jack said, stepping on one of the corpses. "Look," he said, dipping his finger in some of the red fluid spattered across the ice. "This isn't blood. It's oily."

Penny took a step and almost collapsed. "Oh, Jack," she said. "My leg hurts."

"The bite!" Jack said. He uncovered the wound for a moment and took a look. Exposure to the temperatures outside could be dangerous. The wound was bleeding slightly and the area around it was bruising purple, but it wasn't too serious.

"It's all right, Penny," he said, covering it up. "I'll help you to the harbor."

He took her pack and they headed down to the shore with him supporting her. The weight of two packs was hard to manage but there was no way he was going to lose their precious contents.

Jack looked back and saw hundreds of white streaks streaking across the ice. Down ahead of them he saw men in orange pointing up towards them. They'd been noticed. There were men ahead and terminator seals behind—and Penny was partially out of commission.

The seals would reach them in moments. Jack tried to run, half-dragging Penny. The icy air stabbed daggers into his lungs but he didn't dare stop—or even look back. He heard the hiss of bodies sliding in behind him and heard Penny yelp as she looked back.

Jack was nearing the edge of the small town. The seals sounded like they were right on his tail—had to go faster! With a yell of anguish, Jack threw down the packs and pulled Penny onto his back, taking great jumps through the ice towards the endge of the town. Still, the sound of the seals grew louder and Jack anticipated the fatal moment when teeth would sink into the back of his heels and drag him and Penny to the ground under a press of merciless and fluffy bodies.

A handful of men ran forward to meet them as they neared the harbor—and suddenly Jack realized the sliding sounds had stopped. He staggered forward and finally stopped and turned to see the seals had gone back towards the black ice. With horror, he saw a pair of them tearing open their abandoned packs, scattering priceless seeds and tender cuttings across the ice.

"Jack," Penny said as he set her down without a word. "Thank you."

Jack could say nothing. He just looked back with a feeling far beyond pain.

"NOOOOOOOOO!!!" He screamed across the ice towards the ravening seals. "NOOOOOOOO!!!"

Jack picked up his club and started back—only to be stopped by the hands of a couple of the men in orange.

"Älä ole hullu. Raja on olemassa syystä!" one of them said, pulling him back.

"Excuse me?" Jack said.

"The border is there for a reason," a second man translated. "They'll just keep coming until you're dead."

Jack knew the cuttings were already destroyed by the cold... but some of the seeds! Some of them could live through freezing! He pulled against the men—but they held him back. As he watched, more seals skidded up to an invisible line some yards away, then skidded away.

"It's electric," the second man said. "They won't come past it. You just made it, though. What the heck were you thinking?"

"We wanted to get home," Penny said, honestly. "They kidnapped us and put us in the dome. We escaped."

The two men looked at each other nervously, then back at Penny and Jack. "We don't know anything about kidnappings or all that, we're just working our jobs, yeah, don't want any trouble. Come on back to the office and you can talk to the boss, then, okay?"

Jack and Penny entered the office. It was a converted shipping container stuffed with layers of insulation, installed without the slightest care for the aesthetics of decent interior design. The fading maps taped to the wall helped somewhat, though the ugly sofa with a dingy green, black and red 70s afghan on it did not. Fortunately, it was warm.

A man sat at one end hunched over a battered metal desk, clicking around on an expensive-looking widescreen laptop.

"Well," he said, looking up. "You decided to tee up an alternative to our community, did you?"

It was Pickle.

"I thought you were in San Fran," Jack said.

"I usually telecommute, but I have to spend a week here every month. I'll be back in ol' San Fran tomorrow, buddy." Pickle said. "It's good to keep that synergy up, you know? Be in the thick of things, get some meatspace."

"So you can kill escapees from the Arctic Thunderdome?" Jack said.

Pickle shrugged. "Whoa, I'm getting a little cognitive dissonance here. We're definitely not monsters."

"Literally you are," Jack said. "Hayworth is an android. Giles is a hologram. You are a salesman."

"Giles's public appearances are simply unfettered from traditional standards, and we traffic in agile paradigms," Pickle shrugged.

"So you're not going to kill us?" Penny said.

"I'm not sensing an urgent need for enhanced conversion techniques right now."

"No need now?" Penny said. "Was there ever a need?"

"In order to facilitate the continued eco-relationships of our collective biosphere, everyone agreed that it was important not to have certain plans undone at certain times. We really just needed a few people to step outside their current activities, our Mr. Jack Broccoli included, and spend some down time, albeit under certain strictures. You, Penny, just got to go along for the ride. And of course, at this point, there's nothing you can do to stop what's going to happen."

"We could still go to the press!" Penny said.

Pickle laughed. "The media is our oyster. You can't possibly incentivize anyone to counter the number one philanthropist in the world, or the innovative organization actively working to save humanity from its own excesses. You aren't even on the playing field, dynamically speaking."

"There's social media!" Penny said. "We could share videos, talk to YouTubers, get the word out there..."

"Penny, are you trying to make him kill us?" Jack said, elbowing her.

"It's peachy babe, just let her emote," Pickle said, waving a dismissive hand. "At the end of the day, whatever you say now, Henny-Penny, isn't going to change our plans for you. We're going to let you go because we know that there's nothing at all you can do to stop the plan. It's practically turnkey at this juncture."

"Nothing?" Penny said angrily. "I won't be silent! I will speak out!"

"Super," Pickle said with a shrug. "Go for it. But your brand is tarnished, Penny. Who would listen to the ravings of a woman who literally clubs baby seals to death?"

"What?" Penny said.

"Like this," Pickle said, turning around his laptop and showing Penny bashing in the head of an adorable baby seal, over and over again. "Lookie this, got a sweet gif-maker. Already capped it."

"It was a monster!" Penny said.

"You two say that sort of thing a lot," Pickle said, watching the gif. "Man, gotta love this app. But back to your interjection. Some might call your tangent 'projection', seal-clubber." He turned the laptop back around and clicked through a few more images. "Oh my, what a brand you've crafted. We've got some great shots here of you beating baby seals to death, already in the cloud. Love the cloud. Great gun on you, gal. Look at you swing that club, cave-woman style. Perfect form for crushing the heads of defenseless and endangered animals. Good stuff, good stuff."

Penny made a gargled choking noise in her throat, too angry and upset to speak.

"Fine," Jack said. "So we won't speak out, then. You got us."

"Yes," Pickle said. "I do have you." He snapped his finger and the door opened. Four large men stepped inside. From the look on their faces, Jack guessed they were more androids like the ones that had killed Paul. Two of them grabbed him and two grabbed Penny. He struggled to escape but their grips were like iron.

"This model is significantly more robust than the previous release," Pickle said to Jack, then looked back at his computer screen. "I've love to continue this dialog but I'm reviewing some impressive listicles right now. '8 Ways to Reduce Your Carbon Footprint in Five Minutes or Less', '13 Companies Set to Profit From The Endless Summer,' oh yeah, wonderful stuff, team. Keep that awareness cranking. Good, good stuff. Gotta touch base with the image crafters, no more time for you kids." He guestured to the androids. "Take them away to be processed."

Jack and Penny were pulled out of the room and carried through the snow to a larger quonset hut, then stripped of their outer clothing and given jumpsuits to wear. Once clothed, the two of them were separated. Jack struggled to get out of the android's grip but even with the help of Akras, he couldn't get free.

"Stop struggling," one of the robots ordered.

"No," Jack grunted back, trying to break its grip.

"Fine," the robot said, extending a needle from its finger, then jabbing it into Jack's thigh. A burning pain spread through his body, then he knew no more.

When Jack awoke he was in a box. Light shone in around its corners. His head felt fuzzy, but he could hear the sound of engines and feel tremors of turbulence so he deduced he was in a plane. He kicked at the lid of the box, breaking apart the flimsy boards, then pulled himself to a sitting position and looked around to find he was in the cargo hold of a mid-sized plane. Other than a pile of pantyhose in one corner and a broken hockey stick, he seemed to be the only cargo.

A voice crackled over the intercom. "This is your captain speaking. We do trust you've enjoyed your nap and the flight so far."

It was Giles's voice.

"Where's Penny?" Jack yelled. "You said you were letting us go."

"No I didn't," Giles replied over the intercom. "Pickle said that."

"He promised not to kill us," Jack said.

"No, not technically," Giles said.

"You liar!" Jack spat, grabbing one of the boards from the crate he'd been stowed in and wrenching it free. If need be, he'd smash in the cabin and kill whoever was on board. "He said he wouldn't kill us, and he had pictures to keep us in line!"

"I am a precise man, Mr. Broccoli," Giles said calmly as he walked in through the wall. "Pickle only promised not to kill Penny. She is nothing to us and was only the bait to catch you. Though I've rather come to enjoy her spunk, so I think I'll have her sent to my place. I am not adverse to the lure of a beautiful woman, just as I am sure she is not adverse to the company of a billionaire. As for you..."

"As for me what?" Jack said, considering the chances of taking over the plane.

"You're going to experience the horrors of global warming up close and personal."

"What?" Jack said. "Are you going to flood the plane with CO_2?"

"Amateurish," Giles said.

"Give me a condo on Miami Beach so I can slowly watch the sea level rise and bite my nails about the future of my real estate investment?"

"Too costly," Giles said.

"Open a hole in the ozone and give me melanoma?" Jack pressed.

"Please," Giles said. "That's old, old news."

"Force me to listen to children lecturing me on my hamburger consumption?" Jack said.

"Enough," Giles said. "This is getting us nowhere."

"Force me to drive an electric vehicle with exploding batteries?" Jack continued.

"I said enough!" Giles said.

"Make me light my house with mercury-loaded fluorescent bulbs that emit light in headache-inducing wavelengths?"

"Stop it!" Giles said.

"Tell me that I need to eat nothing but soy-based snack products made from 100% recycled spilled chicken fe–"

"Grab him," Giles yelled, and four android guards entered the room and pinned Jack. "Goodbye, Mr. Broccoli. For the last days of your life you will experience the full horror of what a warming earth will bring to everyone—provided you don't get stepped on by an inconvenient hoof."

"Stepped on by what?" Jack said as a robot strapped a parachute on his back. Another tied his ankles and wrists together.

"Goodbye," Giles cackled as the cargo door opened. A robot kicked Jack out the entrance and sent him plummeting to earth.

The wind buffeting Jack as he spun in the air, attempting to find a pull cord on the parachute with his bound wrists. He found nothing. This was it.

"God!" he yelled as the ground came closer. "I have not always been a good man! I've sinned in a variety of ways, hopefully none of them being so offensive that I can't confess them now and–"

EVERYTHING IS A WEAPON! Akras yelled.

"Shh! I'm praying!" Jack yelled back.

YOU'RE GOING TO DIE! Akras yelled back. *WHY ARE YOU SO CARELESS!?*

"I was thrown from a plane," Jack said. "That's not carelessness, as it isn't something that accidentally happens. Let me finish praying before I die!"

THIS IS BAD, Akras yelled. *THE CARETAKER MUST NOT DIE BEFORE THE HARVEST!*

"Yeah, that is low on my list of things to think about right now," Jack said. He had figured out how to control the spinning with his arms and legs so he was gliding instead of toppling. The ground was still nearing, however. "There's not much I can do about my impending death except prepare to meet my Maker." Jack closed his eyes. "Our Father, who art in He–

YOU SHOULD HAVE COVERED YOURSELF IN TURNIP SEEDS.

"I said to be quiet! Are you really going to keep me from having a final word with God?" Jack yelled over the rushing wind.

I AM AKRAS, Akras said.

"I know," Jack replied. "But I need you to give me the last few seconds I have alive to make peace with–"

The chute popped open, stopping Jack's plummeting descent with a jerk. Now he was floating easily downward.

"Hallowed be Thy name!" Jack yelled in delight. "How the heck did that happen?"

I AM FILLED WITH JOY, Akras said. *NOW WE CAN HARVEST TOGETHER.*

Jack wrapped his wrists around one of the ropes coming from the pack and gripped it awkwardly. *The ejection must have been automated*, he thought. He looked down.

The ground beneath appeared to be a blasted wasteland. It felt hot even from high above.

Where am I? he wondered.

The answer came as he got close enough to recognize six species endemic to the Southwestern United States.

And then he landed amidst the rocks, cacti and thorns of a hot, dry desert.

CHAPTER 15

The Mung Fu warrior allows conflict to enter him as the honeycomb enters the mouth of a bear in a flurry of stings.

—A State of Bean: Principles of Mung Fu

The impact of landing jarred Jack's knees and spine. He tried to catch himself but his tied hands and legs caused him to crumple on the rocky ground, twisting his shoulder as he fell and gashing the side of his head. Shaken, he pushed himself up from the ground and looked around. From above, the region had looked like an uninhabited wasteland. It was worse from ground level. The air was hot and dry.

He looked up at the sun. It wasn't even noon and the rays were unbearable. If he couldn't find shelter, he would be simultaneously sunburned and desiccated.

Jack tried to cut the bonds on his wrists by rubbing them on the edge of a sharp rock protruding from the baked clay ground. The bonds appeared to be some sort of twisted multi-fiber metal. After a couple minutes of effort, he had only succeeded in wearing down the edge of the rock. The rope was untouched. Jack's mouth was already parched.

This wasn't good.

Jack looked around to see if there was a place to get out of the sun. The plain stretched out ahead of him, barren and rocky. Off in the distance there were a few scrubby plants, perhaps designating a place with underground water. It didn't look great, but it was better than laying in the sun. Jack started dragging himself in that direction. Despite his best efforts, he couldn't remove the parachute, so he was stuck dragging it behind him as he crawled. Sweat poured down his face as he inched along. The parachute lines repeatedly caught on the rocks as he crawled, requiring him to twist and jerk them free.

The oasis ahead didn't look like it was getting any closer.

"Akras," Jack croaked.

I AM HERE.

"Can you get me free of these bonds?"

I SEE NO BONDS.

Jack had figured as much, but had to try.

"Thanks. You're no help," he said.

YOU ARE A QUESTIONABLE CARETAKER.

"You are right," Jack said, wincing as a sharp rock dug into his elbow as he crawled. "But I'm not dead yet."

But his prospects didn't look good. He fumbled around in his jumpsuit pockets just in case there was anything useful there. All he found was his wallet and the small medallion he'd taken from Paul. He studied it for a moment, realizing there were tiny designs etched into the images. Like circuits, he thought.

"I need a deus ex machina," Jack muttered, rubbing it between his fingers. He felt the coin give slightly, making a click—but nothing else happened. No magic portal opened. No plasma knife shot out and cut his bonds.

Nothing.

Jack put the medallion back in his pocket and looked towards the far-off clump of green, then started dragging himself forward again. The sun was getting hotter. His tongue was thick and dry. Still he pressed on, painfully, slowly dragging himself across the baking hot clay.

"Okay, Giles," Jack wheezed. "I get it. This is the future of earth. Great. Glad for the illustration."

He thought about what the creepy entrepeneur had said about Penny. No, Penny wouldn't fall for a billionaire, especially one like Giles.

Would she?

In the hot sun, it almost seemed possible. He imagined her having anything in the world at her fingertips. She didn't seem like a material girl, but it would be a temptation. Or would it? Who could tell? He'd seen beautiful girls with really ugly men. Ugly men with money.

No. There was no way. Giles was just tormenting him. He hoped she was safe now.

The movement across the rocky soil became a torment. One awkward movement after another. He was cutting and bruising himself as he went. He barely felt it. All focus was on the small patch of green.

It looked a little closer now.

He heaved and twisted and dragged, movement by painful movement. The sun was high above in the cloudless sky. Jack's eyes burned and blurred under its intensity. His arms were covered in sweat. As he twisted, he suddenly felt a slight movement around his wrist. The bond—it was slipping slightly.

Perhaps if he couldn't cut the rope, he might be able to slip out of it.

How far towards being a skeleton would he have to go before it slipped off easily?

He didn't think on it. He just kept moving. He'd have no time to lose weight before he died of exposure. He felt ill and shaky.

And then he was there. As he suspected, the ground was slightly sunken and there was a small community of plants there. Some grasses, a few mesquites—and a prickly pear, still carrying the season's fruit. Jack's mouth watered, but getting close to the plant was not easy. It was a prickly mess. There was no way he could pick and eat any of the spine-covered fruit in his current condition.

Then he had an idea.

Jack found a fallen cactus pad and smashed his wrists against it, grinding it against the rocks. He gasped in pain as spines dug into his wrists, drawing blood, but he kept rubbing. The slick cactus juice and the blood mingled together around his wrists—and then, after much twisting and wrenching, he pulled his right hand free, then used it to work his left hand loose.

His bleeding hands and wrists burned and stung, but at least he could use them again. Jack quickly freed himself of the parachute, then reached up and picked a prickly pear fruit with his bleeding fingers. He scraped off the spines on a rock as best as he could and popped it into his mouth, letting the soothing juice run down his raw throat and over his rubbery tongue. It tasted like heaven, though he did manage to get a painful spine stuck in the roof of his mouth. He ate another fruit, then another. It was a good respite—but the fruit wouldn't hold out for long, and it still wouldn't be enough water. He looked around for any signs of surface water. None. Then he looked for a *Ferocactus wislizeni* that he could cut open to meet the need. No luck.

After eating a half-dozen fruit, Jack moved into the limited shade beneath a mesquite and went to work on the bonds holding his legs. He quickly realized there was no way he could free them without a cutting implement of some sort. The knots tied by the robots were pulled so tightly together as to be beyond his strength—and twisting his feet free would be impossible.

Jack had once read an article on a prepper website titled "The Top 17 Ways To NOT DIE In a Desert Survival Situation." He'd actually clicked on it by accident while looking up information about the wild fruits of arid climates, but he did skim it to see if it mentioned plants. One thing he hadn't realized about desert survival was that all deserts were not created equal. Apparently, outside of North America, some deserts didn't contain true edible cacti and were instead populated by toxic members of the *Euphorbiacea* family. He also remembered that the Very Top Way to NOT DIE In a Desert Survival Situation was to avoid sun exposure as much as possible. The author had recommended travelling at night, if possible. Jack looked up at the blinding sun peeking through the thin mesquite leaves and decided that would be a very good idea. There was still too much sun hitting him. Then he remembered the parachute and dragged himself back to it, then returned to the mesquite and threw it over the top of the tree to make a shelter.

He grabbed two more prickly pear fruit to help his renewed thirst, noting that there were only about a half-dozen ripe ones left. He would remember to pick them in the evening, then they could be rationed.

After eating the fruit, Jack shut his eyes and tried to think. His shoulder ached and his hands stung. The bleeding had scabbed over but the pain was intense. His arms and legs were spotted with brown and blue constellations of scratches and bruises.

Even if he was able to move during the night—how well would he be able to proceed? Hopping? Dragging his legs behind him? And what were his chances of finding another shelter?

Looking out at the horizon was not encouraging. There were ups and downs to the terrain, but picking the proper direction to find another space to rest the next day would be like picking a winning lottery ticket. He simply didn't have enough information.

Jack tried to remember what the terrain had looked like on the way down but couldn't think of any important details. Just a lot of brown and red rocks.

There were other perils in the desert as well. Snakes. Scorpions. Maybe wolves? Or hungry coyotes?

As he considered the many ways in which he might die, he drifted into an uneasy sleep.

Some hours later he awakened, parched and stiff. The sun was lower in the sky and a slight breeze had picked up, though it was still hot. Jack wondered if this were the same desert he'd been in when he came to resuce Hardin the year before. It looked similar, though it was hard to say since this time he wasn't tripping on accidentally ingested mushroom toxins. Considering his current shape, he almost wished he had consumed a few mushrooms. He felt like he could barely move and his throat burned. The skin on his arms and face were radiating heat and he realized that the time he'd spent in the late morning sun had given him a nasty sunburn to go along with everything else. He used the cooling day to gather himself together. He was able to remove the ropes from the parachute, then pack up the silk into a ball which he crammed back into the backpack. He wrapped the thin ropes up into a bundle and stuffed them in as well.

Eventually, the sun fell—and the sky lit up with a million stars. Jack pushed himself upright and scanned the horizon, seeing no sign of human lights. The moon hung a little above the horizon, waning and blue. Strange insects chittered in the night.

Jack decided to hike towards the moon.

Or hop towards the moon.

It was tough going. He could only hop for a short period of time before getting winded. His head was pounding with dehydration and a pronounced lack of *Ocean Octaves!* nutriments.

After about an hour of moving, he stopped to catch his breath, collapsing to the ground. The air was now getting cold and he actually felt chilly once he stopped moving. *How strange*, Jack thought, wondering what it would be like to try and garden in a climate like this. He wrapped himself in the parachute, intending to rest for a few minutes, then to press on.

Then he heard the cry of an animal. It was loud, and evil. The cry came again, a little closer. It sounded like... a tiger?

With a shock he realized there was one animal he hadn't considered yet. But did they live in Arizona? Jack wasn't sure, but as he heard the call again he thought he knew what it was.

A mountain lion. *Or more than one.*

In his weakened state and with his legs tied together, he was a sitting duck. It would tear him to pieces.

He heard the cry again, closer. His heart pounded and he expected Akras to show up—but nothing happened. Now Jack wished he had a fire. That would keep them off, right?

Then he heard a slight crunch of gravel off to his left, like a stealthy footstep. And another. He rose to his feet, casting off his improvised blanket and looking about for a rock he could use as a weapon. He found one that fit his palm, then picked up a few more for missiles.

The crunch came again—closer—and then the cry of a mountain lion—too close! Yet the cry was off to his right, and the sound of footsteps was in front of him. Did mountain lions have one lion howl to distract prey while another one came in and gutted the victim? Or more than one? Like the raptors in Jurassic Park? In that case, he should ignore the sound of the yowling lion and make sure he was ready to defend himself from the stealthy one creeping his way.

He raised his arm to throw a rock, then let it fly as he heard the sound again. He heard the rock skip across the ground out in the darkness, followed by silence. He had missed. But had he scared it? Or was it–

There was another cry from the mountain lion—now very close. Despite his theorizing about which direction death would approach from, Jack spun at the sound—and a shape zoomed past him from where he'd thrown the rock, almost knocking him over! There was a roar from the desert—then a sound of howling, followed by a crunching noise and a shriek of agony.

Then there was silence for a long, long moment. And then the sound of something approaching over the gravel. Jack peered into the darkness and saw nothing... and then the blurry outline of an animal shape. He winged a rock at it and was rewarded by the clank of metal.

Metal?

Then it appeared before him. It was a dog—just like the ones at Jonny's.

It eyed him and he eyed it back. Then it bared its teeth and Jack took a step backwards, forgetting his tied legs. He fell—and then it struck, jumping almost on top of Jack and tearing at his shins. There was a loud snap and Jack almost passed out—then realized the snap wasn't his leg. It was the rope binding them! He was free!

The dog learned forward and sniffed Jack, then backed off and let him rise.

"Thanks," Jack said. The dog said nothing. "I don't suppose you know where I can get some water?" Jack asked. The dog still said nothing.

There was another sound of gravel and a second dog shimmered into existence. Then a third. They all stared at Jack, who wasn't sure what to say to them. He felt the medallion in his pocket. He must have summoned them by pressing it earlier. Maybe the medallion emitted a radio signal of some sort that drew them in.

Or...

He looked at them as they looked back at him. Maybe they were here to kill him. Maybe–

Then there was a booming sound behind him that shook the desert and caused him to rock on his feet. It was followed by what sounded like the largest foghorn in the world, terrifying in the night.

Jack spun, wondering what could have made such a strange combination of sounds—then there was another boom that shook the ground, then the sound of the foghorn again.

He looked back at the dogs—they were gone!

There was another boom, then the foghorn sound again.

He peered into the darkness, trying to see if there was something out there he could identify. At first, he saw nothing—and then he realized that a portion of the stars looked strange. Almost as if they were rippling. The boom came again, almost making him lose his balance. Then the sound of the horn.

One patch of stars was definitely rippling. Jack wondered if he should move towards or away from the anomaly. Towards, he thought, making up his mind. He didn't know what it was, but he wasn't going to run, whether it was dangerous or not. It wasn't like his previous plan of walking towards the moon would be better.

Another boom, then the horn again.

And then he smelled something sulfuric. Like rotten eggs on the wind. It came from the direction of the foghorn.

He decided to follow his nose.

Dawn came after hours of moving closer to the strange anomaly. He couldn't see anything, but the sounds and stench continued until shortly before sunrise, then ceased. He saw no sign of the dogs, so if they had been sent to assassinate him, they must have called off the plan when the pounding and tooting began.

The early morning light revealed a long string of large pits in the ground. Very large. Perhaps four feet in diameter, they stretched off through the desert, then suddenly ceased near a patch of greenery. As he watched, some of the greenery rippled—then disappeared with a snapping and crunching sound. An entire tree disappeared.

What in the world?

Jack moved quickly in the dawn light towards the end of the pit where the tree had disappeared. As he reached the final four pits, he cracked his head into something invisible—and fell to the ground, pain shooting through him. He was at the edge of one of the pits. He put his hand out to the broken ground and found it interrupted by something invisible—like a column rising from the ground.

He moved his hand up and felt it. It felt like...

...like an animal hide of some sort?

Jack's brain tried to put together the sensations his fingers were sending him which were at odds with the images his eyes were sending him.

Another patch of greenery shook and then disappeared. Jack realized that the bushes were on the edge of a small stream and felt again his overwhelming need for a drink of water. Then another patch of bushes disappeared.

Jack shook his head, wondering if he was delusional from thirst, then got to his feet and staggered to the water, gulping it down. There was a sudden ear-splitting foghorn noise, then the air was filled with the sulphur stench.

And then the air shimmered around the trenches and a horror appeared.

Towering above Jack was a cow the size of the Great Pyramid, calmly chewing a clump of trees. It looked down at Jack and swallowed its mouthful, then lowered its head towards him.

Jack staggered backwards, tripping and falling to the ground as it came down, massive and bovine, with a look of incredible stupidity on its placid features.

It looked into his eyes. The head was as large as a city bus. And then Jack saw what was in its eyes. Its right eye, to be specific. There was a dim shape inside the pupil—an outline of someone, inside the cow!

"Hi Jack," came a hugely amplified voice. "Did you know America's obsession with beef consumption is a primary driver of anthropogenic climate change?"

"What?" Jack said—that voice—it was familiar. There was another massive foghorn sound, then a laugh.

"Hayworth!" Jack yelled at the silhouette. "Why are you inside a giant cow?"

"I'm saving the earth, Jack," came Hayworth's voice in return, amplified and overblown. There was another blast of the foghorn. Jack's eyes were watering as the stench settled around him. In horror, Jack realized the sound was coming from the back of the cow.

"You're filling the air with methane!" Jack yelled. "You're deliberately creating greenhouse gasses!"

"Someone has to do it before it's too late," Hayworth replied.

The cow's head rose to the skies, followed by another blast of methane. Then it lifted a giant foreleg, raising it far above Jack's head.

An inconvenient hoof, Jack suddenly realized, as the leg started downwards towards him. He turned and ran from the stream. It came down fast, slamming the ground a mere ten feet behind him and sending him sprawling as it shook the entire earth. Something shimmered off to Jack's left and Jack realized it was one of the dogs.

"I don't suppose you could get me a flamethrower?" Jack yelled, but it was already gone. Apparently, even deadly robot dogs didn't want to stick around robot cows the size of skyscrapers.

"Jack, people simply don't pay attention to anything beyond today," Hayworth said, voice echoing like a sports announcer. The cow had a great PA. "They don't plan ahead. They'll use a straw once, then throw it in the sea for turtles to stick up their noses."

"Why do they stick straws in their noses?" Jack panted.

"That's not the question we need to be asking," Hayworth replied. "We shouldn't be tempting them with straws to begin with."

"Maybe the answer is better education," Jack said. "Knowledge is power."

Jack was back on his feet, but the hooves were fast. The other leg came down a few yards to his right, knocking him down on the ground again. He dropped his pack and started running.

"We need bans," Hayworth said. "Consider that the average plastic grocery bag is only used for a few seconds, then thrown into the trash. How many millions and billions of them are made only to be thrown away after an infintesimal lifespan?"

Another hoof came down, this time only six feet from Jack. He wasn't going to make it by running. The cow was too fast.

"I thought enviromentalists got us to switch from paper to plastic?" Jack yelled back. "They didn't want to cut down trees, right?"

Hayworth pressed on, ignoring him "...so you use your plastic bags, maybe a half-dozen per shopping trip, then throw them in the trash. Where does all the trash go? It goes to landfills, Jack. And people just keep going to the store and using more and more bags, day after day. And don't say going out to restaurants would solve the problem."

"I didn't," Jack yelled.

"You know what happens when you eat a steak, Jack?" Hayworth said. "It makes global warming!"

BOOM! Another hoof came down. Jack dodged to the right on that one, jumping when it hit and managing to keep his feet, then got a few more yards ahead of the monster.

"You're making global warming!" Jack yelled back.

"Yes, but in a scientific and guided way. Like laser surgery. The system needs a reset. Humanity needs a dose of hormesis, Jack. Poison to fight the cancer. A radical operation. A partial climatectomy so men and women will wake up and start to fight!"

The cow reared up suddenly and stomped the ground so hard that Jack was thrown ten feet onto the rocky ground. He felt something crack in his back when he fell. He struggled to rise but fought his way back up. He wasn't going to die that easy.

"Giles is a genius, Jack. You little petty fool! You should love him as I do. He made me live forever inside a new body."

"Wait—I thought I met the human version of you at the North Pole?" Jack said.

"There is no human version of me," Hayworth replied. "You met the final and ultimate android version. I just told you I was human so you would stop knocking my head off. I thought it would make me seem more vulnerable and build camaraderie, but no, you had to go run away. I should have killed you back then but Giles was sentimental. I am grateful he has given me a final chance to redeem myself by crushing you into jelly."

The cow brought another hoof down, causing Jack to stumble. It had been inches from severing his right foot.

"If you had only seen the light, you could have joined us," Hayworth chided. "See, people like you want to destroy all the children of the future. You may not think that's what you want but that's functionally what you're doing while you grow your beets and turnips, oblivious to the long-term. No future thinking, Jack! And turnips... what an awful thing to grow. Shame on you."

HE DOESN'T LIKE TURNIPS?! Akras roared from inside Jack's head. *WE MUST DESTROY HIM!*

"I'm open to suggestions," Jack panted, staggering out of the way of another hoof coming down. He didn't see anything organic he could use to fight the monster.

I AM LIMITED ON MY OPTIONS, Akras admitted

"When I was young I read *Silent Spring*," Hayworth lectured. "Have you read *Silent Spring*? I'm going to assume you haven't. It's a book about the enviroment and what happens when man doesn't respect the little things. Like mosquitoes."

"Forget mosquitoes!" Jack yelled. "You're literally sending death egrets to kill people!"

"Robots are cleaner than man," Hayworth said. There was a huge foghorn noise and the air filled with fumes. "You must realize that."

Two more hooves came down on either side of Jack, knocking him over. He looked up at the belly of the cow and its massive dangling udder. There was something overwhelming and majestic in its gargantuan pink convexity. The back legs kicked up and the udder soared above him. Jack rolled to one side, scrambling as the legs came down again—a near miss that sent him flying to smash his arm painfully on the ground.

He wasn't going to live through this unless he changed tactics. He remembered the rope. His pack was about a hundred feet behind him. He turned and ran towards it, tearing it open and pulling out the coil of rope as a hoof impacted behind him, knocking him face-first into the ground. He spit out a mouthful of dirt and staggered back to his feet.

"Mankind lives like lice on the emaciated corpse of his once-beautiful mother," Hayworth said. "The lice need to awaken and become the butterflies they were meant to be. And if that means we need to pick some nits, then we will. And we will make robots—climate-saving robots that free man to paint and draw pictures of beautiful women, live without money, enjoy communal marriages with a variety of interesting and exotic–"

Not this again, Jack thought, running to the closest leg. He hooked a loop of rope around it and around his waist, then started to climb.

To his surprise, it was easier than he had thought. The cow had long, thick hairs like yarn fibers which were easy to grasp and climb. He made his way up the side of the android cow, eventually just re-coiling the rope when he realized it wasn't necessary.

"I don't see you," Hayworth said. "Where did you go? Did I smoosh him?" he said. "Maybe I did?" He moved the cow's head down and turned up the animal's hooves one by one to search for smooshed Jack. By the time he was done, Jack was on the creature's back. The view from the top was glorious. The heat of the morning sun was already intense but Jack was too happy to be out from under the hooves to mind the temperature. He lay back and caught his breath.

"Where did he go?" Hayworth muttered, still over the intercom.

IT'S RAINING ON THE GARDEN, Akras said to Jack. *I THOUGHT YOU WOULD LIKE TO KNOW.*

"Gee, thanks," Jack said. He wasn't sure how to proceed from here. The best plan was probably "wait and see." The hairs were so long on the animal's back that he could tie himself here if need be. Though as the sun started to really warm him, he realized he wouldn't last that long in the heat.

As he had the thought, he saw something on the horizon. It looked like a road—yes, it was—and there was a truck moving along it. He wasn't super far from civilization, then. Maybe twenty miles. Though twenty miles in the desert heat was a death sentence.

The cow started moving around in a spiral, moving outwards, head pointed towards the ground below. "Where did he go?" Hayworth muttered. "He's gotta be here somewhere."

"No more playing," came another voice. A woman's. "Turn the shield on. If he's out here, we'll spot him. If not, the plague will get him in a few weeks anyhow."

A moment later the cow beneath Jack shimmered, then dissappeared, giving him a view almost 500 feet down. He gripped the hairs—they were still there!—but could see nothing of the cow but a slight shimmer. The effect was nauseating. It felt like he was laying on his belly above thin air.

"I really wanted to smoosh him," Hayworth complained.

"If you'd let me drive we would have," Piknik said.

"You can't drive this thing," Hayworth replied.

Piknik snorted. "Typical male."

"I am not!" Hayworth said. "I'm very sensitive. I hate it when you say things like that. It's really not fair."

"He's not going to live in the desert very long anyhow," Piknik said. "Even if we don't squish him."

"I wanted to really smoosh him, though," Hayworth said. "Really flat and mashed, like a possum. But even if I can't, I think I told him pretty much everything he needed to know about his own hypocrisy."

"More than he deserved," Piknik said. "How are the tanks?"

"We could use more," Hayworth said. "Ah, look at that—PA is still on. No use disappearing when everyone can still hear what we're–"

The PA clicked off and Jack was left alone, floating high above the desert. The cow moved steadily back towards the river, then languidly consumed a large clump of trees, then drank what must have been thousands of gallons of river water.

There's got to be a huge methane digester inside this thing, Jack mused. Mimicking animal digestion, perhaps, but it wouldn't need to be near that complicated. It likely was not powered by the trees and water directly—they would just feed a big anaerobic tank that would create methane. A robot this size probably ran on nuclear power.

The sun got hotter. The robot finished consuming its meal, then started east.

The sun was burning the back of his neck so he pulled his shirt up slightly. A few minutes later, he could feel the sun burning his lower back. His mouth was dry and parched, his head pounding. He was starting to get light-headed and realized he was in danger of passing out and losing his grip. He'd only gotten a little water this morning—and it had been before he'd played chicken with a giant cow.

The river lay behind him now, far behind. It might make sense to just climb down and head for it.

No. If he did that, he would still be stuck in the desert. Surely Hayworth and Piknik didn't live inside the cow full time. They had to park it and get out somewhere. That somewhere would be air conditioned. It might even have a Coke machine.

The cow moved along deliberately, leaving craters in the desert as it went. Jack could see another set of craters leading towards them, meaning the cow had either passed this way outwards to where he first met it, or there was a second one.

It was now unbearably hot on top of the cow. Jack shut his eyes and hung on, feeling the massive beast rolling beneath him. After a time, he fell into an uneasy slumber.

He began to dream. He was standing on the ice of the North Pole again, cool, cool ice. Penny was next to him. They held hands and watched the Northern Lights until the sky suddenly went black with smoke and a giant egret came down and snatched Penny away from him. As she was swept away, she threw him a bag of *Ocean Octaves!*. He caught it, his eyes burning, jaw set in anger, then opened the bag. After the first few crisps, he started to make a plan to save her—then the egret came back and snatched the bag away from him. He ran after it, but it leapt into the sky, squawking... and as it squawked, its squawks became barks, like the bark of a dog, over and over again...

He snapped awake. There was still barking.

He looked down through the cow and saw a silvery dog running behind the beast with something in its jaws. Something long and tubular. Another two ran beside it, barking for his attention. When he saw them, they went silent but continued their run, keeping up with the cow. Jack peered at the tubular thing, then laughed.

A flamethrower. They brought him a flamethrower.

He scrambled down the side of the cow as carefully as he could, shutting his eyes and feeling his way down. He reached the bottom of a leg and yelled to the middle dog.

"Hey—Fido—get up here! Get me that thing!"

Each step rose up and down fifty feet, which made for a terrifying reach, but the dog ran faster and timed his approach, leaping towards Jack at the leg's lowest point. He snatched the flamethrower with one hand, almost losing his grip on the leg. He panted and dragged the flamethrower all the way up to his previous resting point on the back of the cow. The dogs turned and disappeared as he watched.

I should get a dog, Jack thought to himself, wondering if normal dogs could be taught to fetch heavy weaponry. Though it would be nice if they had also brought bottled water.

He carefully tied the flamethrower into the hairs behind the head of the cow and looked forwards into the desert, shading his burning eyes with his hand. They were nearing a large ridge. In a few minutes, they reached it—and then the side of the ridge rolled open, revealing a massive cavern down into the ground. Jack was boggled by the size of it as the cow entered—the ceiling was still over his head as they descended. Once it was inside, the cavern doors closed behind the cow, shutting out the light of the desert. The air inside was cool and dry. There was the sound of clanking as large switches were thrown by some unseen means and lights came on inside the tunnel.

Jack looked at the flamethrower and wondered if it would have any effect at all on the massive cow if he simply pointed it at the head and fired it up.

Probably not before he was discovered and crushed.

They passed through a second set of doors. Jack looked down and realized there was a concrete channel running through the floor filled with water. It must be some sort of drainage—or perhaps it was a watering channel for the cow—or cows?

No, this was probably just a prototype. Or perhaps just a showpiece. Maybe they had smaller ones already out in the fields. He imagined a group of ranchhands butchering a cow and finding out it was an android.

"Whelp, Cody, dangedest thing you ever saw."

"What's that, Tex?"

"We done butchered one of those steer last week, you know, the newer batch, figuring we'd put some meat in the fridge."

"Yep, good time of year for it, nice sleek ones there."

"Yeah but tweren't like you'd think, you know. Weren't no meat inside."

"No meat? Bony, then?"

"Naw, Cody, not even bony. Was fulla wires and tubes. Big tank in its gut fulla rotten stuff."

"What the heck—you joshin' me, dude?"

"Nope, that cow was 100% certified Angus Android."

"A robot cow? You serious?"

"Serious as mad cow, boss. Sarah couldn't believe it either. Worst-tasting stock she ever made."

Jack's thoughts were interrupted as another gigantic door clanked shut behind them. They were now in a smaller chamber. Maybe this was where they'd get out and he could sneak off and find a Coke machine. A red light came on and lasers ran over the surface of the cow—and then stopped on him. Alarm bells rang, then shut off abruptly.

"Well, what do we have here?" Hayworth cackled, the PA crackling on, almost deafening in the enclosed space. "We found Jack, now, didn't we?" The cow's head turned enough that one large eye was angled back towards where Jack clung to the android's thick pelt.

"Wait a minute—he's on our back?" Piknik said. "Wow, that's actually pretty athletic of him. You know, it's a shame to kill such a handsome man. Maybe we should lobotomize him and keep him as a slave."

"He is a lice," Hayworth sniffed. "He needs to be picked."

"A louse," Piknik corrected.

"Whatever," Hayworth said. "Let's smash him."

"We could just let the drones get him," Piknik said.

"That would take the fun out of it," Hayworth said testily.

Jack looked into the liquid eye of the cow. "So long as this stupid thing doesn't pass any more gas."

"Gas," Hayworth laughed. "Oh, how delightful. What fun." There was a large rattling sound and something engaged inside the cow, then a massive foghorn noise almost blew out Jack's ears. The sound was following by an eye-watering stench. And then it happened again, and again.

"You global-warming deniers disgust me," Hayworth said. "You suck the oxygen out of the room."

The foghorn was almost continous now.

"I didn't deny anything," Jack yelled.

"You opposed the only organization really working for integrated community oriented carbon neutral climate resiliency solutions, Jack."

The room was filled with choking fumes. Jack wondered how long it would take to asphixiate. If he didn't time this properly, it wouldn't be enough... but get it wrong and he'd pass out. He was rapidly moving towards the second outcome. He untied the flamethrower and dragged it beneath him, keeping it out of the line of sight of the cow's giant eye. Hayworth was still rattling on about hypocrisy and lice as Jack climbed down the cow's back leg, gripping the flamethrower.

"Oh, you think you'll escape?" Piknik yelled shrilly over the foghorn noise. "You can't escape by going down to get below the gas! Eventually the whole room will be filled—the vents are only bleeding out right now, no fresh air is coming in!"

Jack tumbled onto the ground, gasping for air, but it just made it worse. The sulphur stench was sickening. The air was absolutely loaded with methane now. He set the flamethrower down on the concrete floor and slipped down into the drainage canal. The water was icy cold but felt strangely invigorating to his sunburned skin.

"You want global warming?" he hissed. "I'll give you warming."

He picked up the flamethrower and pointed it towards the backside of the massive cow, ducked beneath the water, then pulled the trigger.

It wasn't the kind of explosion you could experience with all your senses. It was beyond that. It was a concussion and a rush of fire that rattled through a man's bones, jarring his soul sideways into a place where angels watched in surprise, wondering if they would be required to take him into heaven or hell. Then the soul snapped back into a body still jiggling like jello, with bleeding ears and vibrating bones.

Jack surfaced and found the doors and vents of the room had been blown out, allowing in a rush of fresh air that he gulped greedily as he surveyed the flaming cow towering above, now charred and nakedly burning like a bag of plastic trash thrown onto a barbeque, great flaming drips of fire falling to the concrete beneath it. As he watched, the joints of the head burned through and the cockpit fell to the ground. Jack pulled himself out of the canal, numb, soaked and almost deaf and staggered towards the head. As he did, the mouth opened wide and a man came out.

What was left of a man.

It was Hayworth, shaking and bubbling, half-melted and leaking fluids.

"You killed Piknik," he slurred, pointing back into the burning cow's head. "You killed her!" The android's legs suddenly locked up, making it fall to the ground. Hayworth clawed at the concrete, pulling himself towards Jack. "But more evilly, you killed Giles's cow!" he shrieked. "Do you know how long it took me to convince him I could drive it? It had its own AI. I didn't even need to volunteer. But I did, because I believe in our mission!"

His speech was getting more garbled.

"I was waking people up, you stupid turnip-lover! I drove the cow because I believed in the mission, not to mention its awesome fun to consume entire forests and smash holes in the ground while passing massive amounts of gas! You took the cow from me! And I'm the last Hayworth. Did you know that? I'm the real, final, Hayworth, with the brain of a brilliant man inside this perfect body! You are a murderer and an awful person. How dare you! HOW DARE YOU!" Hayworth shook a bony metal finger at him from the floor. "Come on, Jack— what do you have to say for yourself?" Hayworth demanded.

"Goodbye," Jack said, pointing the flamethrower at Hayworth and pulling the trigger.

As he watched the android shriek and burn and melt into the floor under the relentless gush of flame, he could almost feel the warmth of Paul's smile from somewhere above up among the clouds.

* * *

It turns out, there was a Coke machine. And a candy bar machine. Unfortunately, Jack had to smash both of them open because he didn't have any change. This was getting to be a pattern with him.

The staff at the facility were too busy fighting fires and fleeing to pay any attention to him stealing food and drink, let alone the Polaris ATV he found in the empty garage. There were a half-dozen off-road vehicles as well, but they were locked and keyless, unlike the Polaris.

Jack hummed to himself as he drove through the desert, down a long rocky road away from the facility and onto a state highway. He could barely hear himself humming through his damaged ears, but he hummed anyway, quite satisfied with his day so far.

He reached a service station before the batteries gave out on the Polaris, hit the ATM and withdrew money on his credit card, bought some water and snacks—there were no *Ocean Octaves!*, which didn't surprise him but still hurt—and a road map, then sat down at a little picnic table outside and made a plan. Giles might track his ATM usage but it couldn't be helped.

San Francisco was a long way away. Might as well start now.

CHAPTER 16

Boldness does not lead inexorably to victory, even if accompanied by creeping vine, stubborn headless worm and dried meat.

—*A State of Bean: Principles of Mung Fu*

"I don't normally pick up strange men," the driver said, batting her eyelashes at him. Her name was Heather or Heidi or something. Jack had forgotten already. He guessed her age as about 55. She was lean, with bleached blonde hair, big sunglasses and a large floppy hat. They were riding in her car—a white 1970s convertible Cadillac El Dorado. "But you just looked like such a nice guy," she continued. "I just had to. I hope you won't take advantage of a woman's kindness," she said.

"Of course not," Jack said. "Never crossed my mind."

"Oh," she said. "Are you sure?"

Jack ignored her.

She laughed. "I love the country out here," she said. "You know, my first husband owned a ranch. He had great muscles, tall and lean. He was a cowboy."

"I've heard that America's obsession with beef consumption is a primary driver of anthropogenic climate change," Jack said.

"What?" she replied.

"Never mind," Jack said.

"My second husband was an airline pilot," the woman said. "He had a great uniform."

"Mmph," Jack said.

"Of course I left him for an oil sheik," she laughed. "I still feel bad sometimes, but you can't help these things."

"I guess not," Jack said.

"It's all so romantic, you know."

"Yes," Jack said.

"Why are you all beat up—are you a fighter?"

"Sometimes," Jack admitted.

"So what else do you do?" she said huskily. "Are you an athlete?"

"No," Jack said.

"A billionaire?" she pressed.

"Not yet," Jack said.

"A spy?" she said.

"I'm the chosen one," Jack said.

"Ooo!" she squealed. "I knew it!"

Jack sighed. Next time he was going to get a ride with a trucker.

Two days later Jack stood outside of a red brick building with brushed stainless letters on the front reading "ERI". There was a green pyramid on the door. This was it. He looked in the shiny plate glass of the front window and fixed his hair, then wiped a lipstick mark off his cheek with the back of his hand. Turns out that some truckers had girlfriends that rode along with them. They had dropped him off at a motel but he'd just checked in and not bothered going up to his room. But now he knew where Alan's office was—he just had to get in. He turned away from the building and walked on down the street to find a clothing store. He wore cheap S-mart jeans and a T-shirt from the clearance bin with a picture of a pink dinosaur on it. The getup wouldn't do. Not for a place like this. He needed to dress the part.

Two hours later he'd managed to borrow a hundred bucks from a nice lady, find some new clothes, eat a bag of *Ocean Octaves!* and drink a surprisingly good and surprisingly inexpensive espresso at a place called "Sherri's." He stood again in front of the glass, checking out his duds. Now he wore a T-shirt with a picture of the earth on it surrounded by smiling people of all races holding hands. It looked like a kid drew it. Cynically, he imagined a graphic designer stealing his daughter's crayons and scratching out the design until he got it right. It looked like a kindergartener had drawn the image but had the stink of professional design all over it, especially since he doubted any child could draw a continent that didn't look like the blob that ate Chicago. These continents looked too perfect. His jeans were black skinny jeans and he wore sandals that looked like Birkenstocks but cost quite a few bills less. It would have to do. Confidence would get him through.

He pushed the entry button and smiled at the camera. The door buzzed and he opened it and walked in. The air inside was ice-cold. A man sat at the front reception desk. Shoot. This was not his day.

"Yes?" the man said, looking up from his computer terminal.

"Morris," Jack said, grinning. "Good to see you." He handed the guy a wrapped pastry. "You gotta be as bored as a bird watcher at a dog show here, man."

"Thanks," the guy said, taking the pastry. "You brought me a pastry?"

"We're all brothers, man. I appreciate all the hard work you do. Alan mentioned you, Franklin," Jack grinned, reading the name on the business cards by the desk.

"Oh," the guy said with a sigh. "Franklin is out. He's in Bali at the seminar. I'm Jase."

"The Jase?" Jack said. "Heh. Surprised you aren't running the place yet."

"I just started a month ago," Jase said, taking a bite of the pastry and spilling crumbs over a brochure showing sad African children standing around a dry well. "You know me?"

"He told me about you," Jack said. "Said you were doing great, kid."

"Wow," Jase said. "He did?"

Enough lying, Jack thought. That wasn't his style. Sure, it would work—but he was here to kill people, not do something that would damage his conscience. "Actually, he never mentioned you."

"I knew it," Jase said.

"Is he here—still in the old office?"

"Yep," Jase said. "Stairway on the left, third flood, second door. Why do you need to see him?"

"I need to help stop the end of the world," Jack said.

"Awesome," Jase said. "Good luck."

And just like that, he was in.

He walked up the stairs, smiling at a girl with thick black glasses who was walking down, completely absorbed in her phone.

He reached the third floor. Then the second door. It was slightly open. He peeked in and saw a desk with no one at it. But there was a laptop on it—and it was the same model he'd seen Pickle using at the North Pole.

This was it. He steeled himself, his heart racing. He had decided that the best way to kill Alan was to let Alan make the first move, then to kill him in self-defense. Technically, that wouldn't count as murder. He was sure Alan would freak out when he arrived, then he could quickly kill him with whatever organic thing he found in the office, then leave. Actually, now that he was here, the whole thing started to seem a little iffy. He pushed the door open before he changed his mind. *This is for you, Paul.*

The office was large and filled with marketing posters and various framed awards. It was also completely empty.

Maybe Alan had stepped out to get something to drink or talk with a colleague. Jack could hear voices down the hallway. He looked around the office for a good place to hide. He could jump out, scaring Alan, causing Alan to attack him, then throw... throw something like...

He looked around for something to throw and his eye rested on a miniature baseball bat. It was made of compressed and laminated strips of bamboo. "Greening the Game Award, 2017" read a placard behind it. The bat was signed by about thirty people. That would do. Akras would arrive, give him superstrength, and he could smash Alan's skull with a tiny autographed bamboo bat.

Okay, this was getting stupid. Maybe it was time to leave. Suddenly, this whole revenge killing thing was seeming not only immoral but verging on ridiculous. He'd let Alan go, just walk out, take a deep breath, then go kill Giles.

But you promised Paul. And Alan may have killed Penny like he tried to kill you. And he's going to kill millions of people.

Okay, good enough.

Jack heard approaching footsteps in the hall and ducked behind a bookshelf filled with more tropies and awards.

Alan came into the room, followed by a photographer with a large camera and a woman with aggressive cheekbones.

Jack peeked through a crack in the back of the shelf as Alan sat at his desk and clicked his laptop out of sleep mode, dissolving a repeating slideshow of poached giraffes.

"...it's a scheduling thing. I'm the roll-out guy on the new program, you know, and it's happening in just a few days, boys."

"We know all about the next phase," the woman said. "We're ready for it."

"And there's gonna be a lot of collateral damage, you know, which they won't know was us, you know, the hoi polloi and the outsider demographic, meaning the mooks at home, to borrow a New York colloquialism, but it'll blow the brand sky-high for us, provided we get the timing just right..."

"Should we really talk about this now?" the woman said, inclining her eyes towards the camera guy, who was looking down out of the plate-glass window.

"Fozzie is all over it, Cheryl," Alan said. "Aren't you Fozzie?"

The cameraman nodded. "No question, Alan. You know I eat and breathe the mission."

"Remember, he's my brother's kid," Alan said. "Berkeley brat, great talent. Top shelf. If I told him jumping out that window would save a spotted parrot, he'd jump."

"Man is a virus," the cameraman said, looking out the window again.

"Good boy," Alan said. "When the plan rolls out you'll get a spot the bunker, buddy."

"Great," Cheryl said. "So what should I tell the girls?"

"Ah, right, right. The girls. I love the concept, really, high art. The body-painted continents on pretty girls. Great idea. My idea, so of course it's great. Total breakout stuff. Viral campaign all the way. Body-positive, earth-positive. They're here now?"

"Down by the pool," Cheryl said, looking at Fozzie who was still looking out the window. "Right, Fozzie?" she said.

"Totally," he said.

"You got me a fat one for Europe?" Alan asked. "Remember, most carbon emissions are–"

"Yes," Cheryl said. "Fat is a crude word, though. And another... curvy... one for North America."

"Great, great. I love it. So punchy. People will make the connection."

"It might not be the right connection," Cheryl said. "Should be a fat man for North America. In a cowboy hat, beating a woman painted as the earth."

"A fat man?" Alan said. "And violence? No subtlety. Lookie here, it's going to run in women's mags, it just makes sense. I've got a vibe we're going for. I mean, I validate your idea, yes, for sure, because you are a unique part of our synergy and you know I always listen to all of us–"

"You're right, of course, you're the marketing whiz," Cheryl said. "I'm sorry. They're down there by the pool. When you're done, make sure you catch me about the rollout. We don't time this right and we go down too. The penguins are–"

"I know, babe, I know. And the cattle stampede. And the icebergs— all in hand, all in hand."

"It's gotta all happen together."

"Hey, Cheri, you know me. I run a tight ship. Integrated management. We'll interface. Gotta go see our girls, though, get that shoot going, then we can hash out the details. Plenty of room. And hey, since you're here, would you see if you can get my copy machine to reset—I think I jammed it again."

"I'll look at it," Cheryl sighed. "It's just if we don't get the timing..."

"Great, great," Alan said with a big grin. "Good team effort. Let's go, Fozzie."

They walked out, leaving Cheryl by the copy machine. *What plan?* Jack wondered. *What were they going to do?*

Cheryl pulled out a paper tray and peered inside, then tugged on a half-printed sheet of crinkled 8.5 x 11. She shook her head, and was about to give it another yank—then gasped as Jack held a tiny autographed bamboo bat to her throat.

"Don't move," he whispered. "If you cooperate, I might not strangle you and throw you out the window."

Jack wondered if Penny would approve of him throwing a woman out a window on top of a group of painted girls, a camera man and an evil marketing guru. Paul would certainly approve. He'd probably compost the whole group of them and grow sewage tomatoes on top of them. Paul would be ruthless.

"What do you want?" Cheryl gasped.

"Tell me the plan," Jack said.

"The plan?" Cheryl replied.

"Don't play innocent with me," Jack said. "I know you are planning something horrible. I just don't know what."

"I don't know what you're–"

Jack pulled the bat tighter against her throat. "You get one chance, global-warming-creating scum!"

"Don't kill me with a tiny autographed bamboo baseball bat!" Cheryl sobbed. "Oh sweet Gaia, I don't want to die by being killed with a tiny autographed bamboo baseball bat!"

EVERYTHING IS A WEAPON! Akras roared. *WAIT... ARE YOU GOING TO KILL THIS WOMAN WITH A TINY AUTO-GRAPHED BAMBOO BASEBALL BAT?*

"Maybe," Jack whispered.

"Maybe? Maybe I want to die!?" Cheryl said.

"Tell. Me. The. Plan." Jack said, wondering if he really had the stomach for this and hoping she would just tell him.

"Okay, okay!" she gasped, turning slightly to see his face. "Wait!" she said in sudden recognition. "You're the hunky guy they sent up to the North Pole! I was so hoping you were going to be there after we released the entire herd. Why are you here? Where's your girlfriend? Do you need a new girlfriend?"

"The herd?" Jack said.

"They're everywhere. Tunnels have been built all over North America. And of course, the robot locusts for Africa. And the dragonflies are gonna manage California and Australia. And the icebergs are coming, too, but that's after the penguins get out of beta. The seals are too slow and expensive. The fluffiness, you know. Smart fiber isn't cheap," she babbled. "And the new killer whales are running late, which is a real issue right now. Alan just has to make one call and everything goes down, we're just hoping everything rolls out okay. All about timing. Of course, we'll still have a few million dead, which might be enough, because just flooding the coastlines with the Terror Tectonicus will be awesome, you know. It's so epic. I pick on Alan sometimes, but he really is a genius at coordinating stuff. He's heck on a copy machine though. I'm sorry... I'm just running at the mouth... so are you still going to kill me with that tiny bat or..." she paused, swallowing hard.

SO YOU ARE TORTURING THIS WOMAN?

"No," Jack said. "Not really."

"No?" Cheryl said. "It's not enough? What else do you want?"

"Just be quiet or I will have to kill you. I'm here for Alan."

"To kill him?" Cheryl said. "Oh Gaia, oh no!"

DO YOU WANT TO THROW HER OUT THE WINDOW? Akras asked. *WE COULD MAKE HER GO REALLY FAR.*

"No," Jack said.

"So you don't want to kill him?" Cheryl said.

"Sorry," Jack said. "Wasn't talking to you. I have voices in my head."

"Oh snap!" Cheryl said, her face going white. "Of course you do!"

"Just be quiet," Jack said. "I am going to take the bat away from your throat. If you make any noise I will throw it at you so hard it goes through your body and out the window."

"Is that even...?"

"Promise me you will be quiet," Jack said.

"Yes," Cheryl said.

YOU SHOULD KILL HER, Akras said. *SHE IS EVIL TOO.*

"She's a woman," Jack said.

"What?" Cheryl said. "Who is?"

"Wasn't talking to you," Jack said. "The voice in my head said I should kill you."

Cheryl gasped and fainted, crumpling into Jack's arms. He laid her on the floor.

SHE IS STILL ALIVE, Akras observed.

"Yeah," Jack said, stepping over her and looking out the window. Three stories below was an Edenic vista. Ferns and palms and scrampling ivys flowed down to a swooping swimming pool. Multiple painted models sat at the edge of the pool on a natural wood bench, smiling for the camera. Jack saw the camera guy but not Alan. Then he saw Fozzie look back towards the building as if receiving directions from someone. Jack moved beside the copy machine and looked down, spotting Alan almost directly beneath the window.

He wondered if he should wait for Alan to come back up. Then he looked at Cheryl passed out on the floor and the tiny bat in his hand. If she woke up...

Time was against him. And against the entire earth. If he failed, millions would die. It needed to happen now. It wasn't just about Paul. It was about saving the earth.

He looked at the copy machine. He looked at the plate glass window. He looked at the tiny bat in his hand. He looked down and saw Alan standing perfectly beneath the window.

"Akras?" he said.

YES, CARETAKER.

"Give me strength," Jack said, then took a deep breath, cranked back his arm and threw the tiny commemorative bat through the plate glass, exloding the window outwards with the power of a missle strike. Below, Alan looked up—just in time to recieve an expensive and still jammed copy machine to the skull.

Jack saw Fozzie drop his camera and all the continents scatter, then stepped back over Cheryl and walked quietly down the stairs, passing the same girl in dark glasses who was now running up towards the sound of shattering glass, no longer absorbed in her phone. He walked casually out into the lobby.

"Hey, Mr. Morris—everything okay up there?" Jase said.

"Yes," Jack replied, then stepped outside and walked away.

* * *

The air was crisp and cold, the sky above grey with clouds.

The Batson house was considered a marvel of Smart Technology. A house like no other. As Jack walked up, he knew his eyes were being scanned and his height measured, his face checked against databases and his personal information sent directly to the house's owner. He knew he was being scanned for weapons, and also knew the scans would find nothing.

He didn't care about the scans. He knew the man would let him in, just for curiousity's sake. And knowing Jack was weaponless, he knew the man would also try to kill him.

The landscaping was perfect. The walkway was made from polished concrete, inlaid with Geiger-esque robotic patterns, none of which seemed to repeat. The guards were androids, Jack already knew. He'd simply knocked at the gate, then a few moments later, the gate had opened to admit him.

Now he stood in front of a beautifully carved pair of mahogany doors, inset with cameras and scanners cleverly hidden inside a ribbon of turqoise and obsidian inlay. He would go inside and either he or Giles Batson would die. Quite possibly both of them, Jack thought.

Now the plan was in motion. If he was wrong about any part of it, he would die. But he would die avenging Paul—and quite possibly Penny—so it would be a good death.

The large doors swung open and admitted him to a shiny black, white and stainless living area with tasteful wood accents and a large, angular, plate glass chandelier that emitted a slowly flowing spectrum of colored light.

It reminded him of the Aurora.

"If you're here to repent, I'm not in a forgiving mood," came a familiar nasal voice from the hall at the end of the room. "I know what you did to Alan. I know it was you. And Spencer and Elaine! But I am better protected than any of them. And you can't stop my plan by killing my minions."

Giles stepped into the room, older than Jack had seen him before. The hologram must have been programmed when the man was younger. Giles frowned at Jack. "I could kill you in a hundred ways right now, just by lifting my hand."

"I know," Jack said.

"So why are you here?"

"To stop you."

Giles laughed. "You can't stop me. You see, I've already beaten you, Jack."

"No," Jack said. "You ha–"

And then Jack froze, because behind Giles a woman stepped into the room, wearing a bikini and dripping water on the floor as she towelled off. "We have company?" she asked, then gasped when she saw their visitor. "Jack?" she said.

It was Penny.

"See," Giles said. "You've lost more than you know."

Jack looked at Penny. She looked back at him, a sheepish look on her face.

"He's really a good guy," she said. "I mean..."

"So?" Giles said, smiling wickedly at Jack. "You were going to say something?"

"I have nothing to say," Jack said. "I am just here to make a delivery."

He reached in his pocket, then tossed something across the room to Giles. The old man caught it from the air and examined it.

"What is this?" he said, eyeing the small medallion.

"It's a gift from Jonny," Jack said.

"From Jonny? Jonny Lay–"

Giles froze as three massive robotic dogs shimmered into existence, sparks flying from their bodies as they tore forwards.

Jack turned and sprinted towards the door, ducking as the android guards opened fire on the dogs and the sound of terrified screams filled the air. As he rushed towards the gate, the other guards were heading indoors, apparently called to defend their doomed master. The sounds of fighting grew louder, then the screams suddenly ceased.

At the gate, Jack stopped running, straightened his collar and stepped onto the sidewalk.

As he did, a single snowflake fell onto the shoulder of his jacket. He smiled. It might be a pleasant winter after all.

EPILOGUE

"So you KNEW she wasn't me?" Penny laughed, stirring her malted milk with a paper straw.

"Sure," Jack said. "She was with Giles."

"Maybe I would fall for a billionaire," Penny said, taking a sip of her malted milk. "After all, you looked at my apartment and I was gone. When you saw me in his place, you couldn't have known for sure I was an android. A girl could do a lot with a billion dollars. Were you 100% sure it wasn't me in the bathing suit?"

Jack shrugged and took a swig of his stout. "You were with Giles. In the off chance it was you, you would've deserved it anyhow."

"Wow," Penny said, choking on her malt and coughing. "Wow. You're something else. You're not like other guys, you know."

Jack said nothing, waiting for her to continue.

"You're really manly," she said. "Like, I know that no matter what, even if things get totally bad, even if you make a mistake or accidentally get distracted by a seed display—you're going to press on. You promised to avenge Paul and you did it. You went all the way to the North Pole and went through the ice to save me. You... you're just..." she blushed, then took another sip of her malted milk.

"Marriage material?" Jack said. He grinned and reached into his pocket. Penny's eyes went wide.

"You don't have another one of those death medallions, do you?" she gasped.

"Naw," Jack said, removing a small box and handing it to her. "I've got something better."

Penny gasped as she opened it and saw the ring inside. She picked it up and looked at the woven gold band, wrapping up and around a diamond.

"Are these little vines on it some sort of ivy?" she said.

"No. A pair of entertwined carrots. See the pattern?"

"Wow," Penny said. "So it's a full two carrots?"

"Yes," Jack replied.

"I don't know what to say!" Penny said.

"Say you'll marry me." Jack said.

Penny nodded her head up and down, then hugged him tight.

Jack hugged her back, tight, then kissed her forehead and smelled the *Cocos nucifera* scent of her long hair.

"Yes," she murmured over and over. "Yes, yes, yes, I'll marry you. Yes!"

"Thank you," Jack said, turning her chin up with his thumb and kissing her on the lips. "Just one thing, though, if we're going to make this work."

"Anything!" Penny said.

"Great," Jack said, letting her go and taking a final swig of his stout. "Let me take you in for a quick Xray before we set the wedding date."

Made in United States
North Haven, CT
09 December 2021

12339287R00145